The Chidham Creek Murders

THE
CHIDHAM CREEK
MURDERS

PAULINE ROWSON

The Solent Murder Mysteries Book 18

Joffe Books, London
www.joffebooks.com

First published in Great Britain in 2024

Cover art by Dee Dee Book Covers

ISBN: 978-1-83526-637-3

CHAPTER ONE

Wednesday 13 September

The house smelled of death. Not rotting flesh, but a mustiness that wrapped itself around Horton as he entered. There was also that special kind of coldness that was hard to describe. It was as though the walls, carpets, curtains and contents had been frozen in time, holding their breath in anticipation of something.

He stepped into the lounge and rapidly took in the scene. A woman, late sixties perhaps, was lying on her back on an orange velvet sofa that had no arms to it. It was pushed up against the wall. Her right arm was crooked over her blue and yellow striped T-shirt, palm down, nails manicured and immaculately varnished in pale blue. Her left arm hung rigidly over the side of the sofa. On the third finger was a diamond ring and, on her wrist, a jewel-encrusted watch that looked expensive. She was slender, neatly dressed in navy-blue trousers, and slippers. Her stylish, short-bobbed, white-blonde hair framed a heart-shaped, lined face. Her eyes were closed. On the low coffee table beside her, in a neat row, were a champagne bottle, a glass and a tablet bottle, all empty.

'Are those exactly as you found them?' Horton addressed the uniformed officer beside him.

'Yes, sir.'

She looked peaceful, and, even though there was nothing to indicate that she'd suffered, Horton still felt that stab in his gut at such a sorrowful sight. He was conscious of Cantelli behind him chewing his gum more rapidly than usual.

'Who reported it?' he asked.

'Mark Lindley. He's a funeral director.'

Horton knew him well. They'd called Mark out on many occasions. 'Why was Lindley here?' There had been no sign of him outside.

'The deceased was a celebrant, and was scheduled to officiate at a funeral today organized by Mr Lindley. When she didn't show, and didn't answer her phone, he came here, tried to get an answer and, when unsuccessful, called the emergency services. That was at 15.10.'

Horton glanced at the quirky metal clock on the wall above the mantelpiece. It was almost four thirty.

'He confirmed ID, sir. Her name is Juliette Croft. I ran a basic check on her. She's the owner-occupier of this house and there's nothing previous on her. There's also nothing to indicate she was at risk of taking her own life. Mr Lindley had to leave for a prior engagement and said he was happy to give a full statement tomorrow, and that his firm would be on hand to transport the body to the mortuary when required.'

Horton knew Mark would have put that suggestion diplomatically.

'How did you get in?' Cantelli asked. 'The front door's not been forced.'

'The garage door was unlocked, Sarge, as was the door from it into the conservatory. That door into here was also unlocked.'

'Careless.'

'I let PC Gregory and Mr Lindley in.'

'Any sign of an intruder using the same route?' Cantelli again.

'Not that I could see. There's no evidence of a burglary, nothing has been disturbed here or upstairs.'

2

'Was the radio, TV or music centre on?' asked Horton.

'No. All was quiet.'

Horton wondered if Woodley had been about to add 'as the grave' and quickly changed his mind.

'Were the curtains drawn or pulled back?'

'Drawn down here, pulled back in the deceased's bedroom. Mr Lindley told us that he'd seen Juliette Croft last Thursday at a funeral where she was the celebrant, and his firm corresponded with her by email on Monday to check all was OK for today's ceremony. She had assured him it was. There was no answer from the neighbour on the right, but Mrs Rogers, on the left, last saw Mrs Croft go out yesterday in her car at about eleven o'clock. She didn't know her that well. She doesn't know if there are any family members, nor does Mr Lindley. We haven't found anything to give us those details but we haven't searched the premises, sir.'

'No suicide note?'

'No, which is one of the things that made me query if it was suicide, although I know not everyone leaves a note,' he hastily added. 'I wondered if it might be on her phone or computer, except I haven't found either. I've seen a few suicides, sir, but this one doesn't look right to me, which is why I called it in.'

And it was why Sergeant Wells had asked CID to attend. Horton shared PC Woodley's view, but Cantelli interjected before he could speak.

'For starters, how did she manage to put everything so neatly in a line when she was desperate, depressed and under the influence of alcohol and drugs?'

Precisely, thought Horton.

Cantelli leaned down and sniffed over the scene like a springer spaniel. 'There's no smell of alcohol on her clothes, or on the sofa or floor. And no drink stains. If she was under the influence of drink and drugs, surely she'd have spilled drink over and around her. No odour of alcohol in the bottle or glass either, unless my nose is on the blink.'

Horton knew it wasn't.

Cantelli cricked his neck to read the champagne label. 'Veuve Clicquot Ponsardin. Good quality. There's nothing written on the tablet bottle.'

'So how do we know if there were any tablets left in it?' Horton asked.

'That's what I wondered, sir,' Woodley answered. 'If she'd knocked back some tablets and drunk champagne, I'd have said she would have passed out long before she finished them all.'

Horton agreed. This clearly wasn't right. Nevertheless, he tried to think of plausible reasons for what they were seeing. 'She could have swallowed the tablets quickly. They didn't immediately render her unconscious. She then drank the bottle of bubbly before collapsing on the sofa. Yes, I agree it sounds unlikely,' he quickly added at Cantelli's sceptical look. 'Aside from the neatness of the items, her body's not positioned as though she collapsed in a heap. Was it the police doctor who came out, Woodley?'

'No, it was Dr Lancaster from her local practice. I thought she might have been undergoing medical treatment for depression. He confirmed life extinct and said he couldn't issue a medical certificate of cause of death because he didn't know of any underlying health issues. She hadn't been to the surgery since October last year and that was only for her flu jab.'

Horton knew as well as Cantelli that not everyone in that wretched state sought medical help. Many suffered alone and in silence.

'Did he give an estimated time of death?'

'No. He said rigor was fully established.'

Horton could see that, and that lividity was also complete, indicating she had been dead for some hours, but there was, thankfully, no sign of maggots or flies.

'How closely did he examine her?'

Woodley pulled a face. *Not very, then*, thought Horton.

'He felt for a pulse in her neck, opened her eyes, peered at them and that was it, sir.'

'And he saw what we're seeing. There are no visible marks of an assault, no signs of a ligature or bruising round the throat, no contusions and no blood, but she could have been poisoned or asphyxiated and someone made it look like suicide.'

'They made a clumsy attempt at it,' Cantelli said. 'Anything in the pockets of her trousers?'

'Haven't checked, Sarge.'

Horton did the honours and found only a tissue, which he handed to Cantelli. 'Bag it up, just in case. Woodley, ask PC Gregory to continue with her enquiries along the street for last sightings of Juliette. Make sure no unauthorized personnel cross the driveway.' To Cantelli, he said, 'There's not enough to treat it as a full-blown crime scene but it does need further investigation. I'll get Taylor over here. I'll also call Lindleys, and take a look around upstairs.'

Cantelli said he would do downstairs.

Horton rang Taylor, relayed what they had, and asked him to take pictures of the body instead of requesting the official police photographer's presence. He then called Lindleys. Angie Lindley answered. Horton knew her well.

'Mark's out. Isn't it awful about Juliette?'

Horton agreed it was and told her that they were treating her death as unexplained for the time being. 'Do you know who her next of kin is?'

'There isn't anyone. Mark is Juliette's executor.'

'Then he knew her well?'

'No. She asked him if he would mind as she didn't have any relatives and she didn't wish to burden her friends, and anyway they might very well go before her. Mark, being younger, made more sense. She said there wasn't much to leave, but we don't know that for certain.'

'Why not ask her solicitor to be executor?'

'I don't know. Perhaps she didn't know him, or her, that well.'

'You don't know who it is?'

'No, nor does Mark. We haven't seen the will. In fact, she might have changed her mind, or not even made one

5

since she spoke to him about it two months ago. She also said she didn't want a funeral, just a walk-through.'

Horton thought this fitted with her having taken her own life, which meant there was an explanation for the neatness of the items and the lack of alcohol odour, although what that was he couldn't see at the moment.

'Did you or Mark have any inkling that she might have a drink or drug problem? Or any financial or personal difficulties?'

'None. She told us she'd been widowed for many years and had no children. She always seemed happy, very bright and cheerful, and was very empathetic with the clients.'

'Does she have a website, or was she on social media?' They could check, but he thought it worth asking.

'Neither, as far as I'm aware. And I don't think you'll find her listed on the UK Society of Celebrants website because she told us that she didn't work for any other funeral directors, only us. She said she wasn't in it for the money, just for something to do alongside her other passion, singing. She used to sing at nursing and retirement homes, that's how Mark met her. He was at the same one helping with the funeral of a resident. Juliette was a very good celebrant. We had no hesitation in putting her name forward, particularly when it came to the death of an elderly person, or rather, I should say, anyone from about sixty onwards, which isn't that old these days. It's terrible what's happened. Such a shock. Do you wish for us to collect the body?'

'If you would.' He rang off and entered the bathroom at the back of the house, mulling over what Angie had told him. Had Juliette been lonely? Angie had said she hadn't wished to burden her friends; had that been a lie? Perhaps she didn't have any.

He shelved that sad thought and made a quick search of the bathroom cabinet, aware of Cantelli moving about downstairs. The cabinet contained some over-the-counter medicines for indigestion and coughs, some antihistamine tablets, paracetamol and ibuprofen. There were no prescription medicines.

Cantelli called up the stairs. 'I've found her car keys. I'll check it out.'

Horton crossed the landing into Juliette's bedroom. The first thing that struck him was the bed. He had never seen one like it before, with its curved heart-shaped black velvet headboard and deep-red velvet cushions. It was lower than a typical double bed and was perched on small brass feet. The duvet was white with bright poppies. Beside the bed was a white-painted wooden table on which was a lamp and a medium-sized brown leather handbag. In it Horton found a set of keys, a small make-up bag — containing cosmetics — a couple of tissues, a small tube of antibacterial hand gel and a purse. He opened it to find her credit and debit cards, a bus pass, a supermarket loyalty card, another from a coffee shop chain store and a plastic driver's licence. Juliette Croft had been seventy.

He replaced the items in the bag and took another look around the room. Opposite the bed on the wall was a large round gilt-framed mirror, and above the bed a colourful abstract painting, like the ones he'd noticed in the lounge. The only other furniture was a curved, ruby-coloured velvet bucket-style chair on curved brass legs. Her taste here was similar to what he'd seen downstairs — very contemporary, and with more of a Continental flavour than traditionally British.

He crossed to the window. Cantelli was in the front passenger seat of Juliette's Renault on the driveway, his old Ford parked beside it. PC Woodley was in conversation with an elderly couple, and the police activity was drawing curious looks from those at the bus stop bordering the common opposite, where two dog walkers had also stopped to observe the goings on.

To his right, Horton could see the sun glimmering off the water in Langstone Harbour and the masts of the yachts on the moorings. His yacht, where he lived on board, was farther round, in the marina. He'd been desperately trying to find a flat or house to rent so that his young daughter, Emma, could stay with him more often — a condition laid down by his ex-wife, Catherine, for reasons of greater access — but that had been before Catherine had dropped the bombshell that Emma was to become a full boarder at her school. And she'd waited until last weekend to tell him, when Emma had already returned to school.

He suppressed his anger. There seemed little point in it. Emma, he had learned, was ecstatic with the decision as it meant more time with her friends, and she loved the school. She was happy and that was all that mattered. And on the up side, he could abandon his search for somewhere else to live. Every place he'd viewed had been depressing and unsuitable. He'd got used to living on his boat, despite it being cold in the winter. He enjoyed the freedom it gave him to sail when he wanted, work permitting.

He turned back to survey the room, and wondered where all of Juliette's clothes and shoes were. That question was answered when he entered the small box room next to the main bedroom. Juliette had turned it into a dressing room, equipped with stylish portable wardrobes, drawers and shoe racks on both of the side walls. The sheer number of clothes and shoes took his breath away. No wonder she had needed another room for them all. Skirts, blouses, dresses, trousers and jackets were all neatly hung. He didn't even begin to count the shoes, many of them sandals but some with high heels, and a few pairs of modern trainers. With latex-covered fingers he rifled through the clothes, mentally noting the labels, then opened the drawers. In a deep one he found several handbags. He heard a car pull up, then voices. The adenoidal tone of one indicated that it was Taylor talking to Cantelli.

There was nothing of any significance in the handbags, but again he noted the labels inside them. They, like the clothes labels, were mainly in Spanish or Portuguese. He turned to the other drawers, where he found cardigans and T-shirts. Also, in one, an engraved wooden box containing jewellery, much of which to him looked valuable. There was still no mobile phone or computer.

8

As voices came to him from below, he crossed to the rear of the house and into a small double room. It was empty save for a large cardboard box. From the window he saw Cantelli in the alleyway that backed on to the house.

He crouched down and pulled open the flaps of the box, and delved inside. There were six photo albums, with labels on the spines starting in 1972 and ending in 1993. Why none after or before that? Maybe she'd had the pictures digitized and had uploaded them onto her computer. If so, why not do these years too? Perhaps she hadn't got round to it. And where *was* her computer? Surely she must have had one for her work as a celebrant. And still no sign of a mobile phone.

He opened the first album and saw a very young woman he assumed to be Juliette Croft, although there was little resemblance to the poor woman on the sofa, save for the shape of her face. She had a microphone in her hand and a small band behind her — three men with long hair and moustaches. Juliette, with her long brown curly hair, heavy make-up and tight-fitting, sparkly halter-neck dress that emphasized her shapely figure, was very attractive. He flicked over the page and saw pictures of her on the deck of a ship. There were also some of her on the Continent. Nothing was written underneath them, but he removed one from under the plastic film and read on the reverse: *In action, 23 December 1972.*

Horton replaced it and withdrew a cardboard folder containing various documents. Her will could be one of them. It wasn't. There were the deeds to the house, her birth certificate, two marriage certificates and four death certificates, those of her husbands and her parents. There was also her passport. Opening it, he saw that it explained the furnishings and the labels on her clothes, because according to the stamps she had lived in Portugal until March last year, with a couple of trips to the UK in the December of the preceding year and February last year. After replacing everything else, he took the folder, handbag and jewellery box downstairs.

As he reached the bottom there was a knock at the door, and he let in the undertakers. He led the way into the lounge, where Taylor nodded to indicate he'd got the photographs. Horton watched in silence as they lifted Juliette on to the body bag on the trolley. Cantelli slipped in and stood beside him. Horton could see that there was nothing amiss with the back of her head, no signs of blood or cuts.

'Anything?' he asked Cantelli when they had left.

'No discarded tablet bottles or packets. And no bottles of booze anywhere in this house or in the bins outside. The kitchen door was unlocked and the back gate unbolted. She was very lax about security.'

'Or thought it didn't matter because she'd no longer be around.'

'Nothing of any note in her car either. I ran a vehicle check. She's got a full clean licence, the car is taxed, insured and has a current MOT. It also has an almost full tank of petrol. What have you got there?'

Horton told him, and relayed what Angie had said. 'Any sign of a mobile phone or computer?'

Cantelli shook his head.

'I'll call Angie again.' She confirmed that Juliette had both, her computer being a laptop. She gave him Juliette's mobile number. Horton tried it.

Cantelli cupped his ear. 'Can't hear it. Maybe she ditched it and the laptop before taking her own life, not wanting anyone to pry into her affairs.'

Horton addressed Taylor. 'Any prints?'

'Several around the doors and mantelpiece, and in the kitchen, probably the deceased's. There are some on the rear kitchen door handle and under the rim of the coffee table, but not clear enough to be identified. No trace of alcohol down the cloakroom toilet, or the sink, but I've taken samples around the bowl and plug just to be sure, although someone could have flushed the loo and run the tap. Nothing in the kitchen sink either. There are no prints on the bottle, champagne flute or tablet bottle.'

Cantelli looked mystified. 'She couldn't have wiped them clean while drugged.'

Horton answered. 'Maybe she put the items there and wiped them of her prints before swallowing some other tablets.'

'Then where are they? I can't see her swallowing them, then calmly going out into the yard and putting the bottle in the dustbin. And before you ask, I haven't been through the domestic rubbish bins.'

'And I won't ask you to. I think you're right, Barney. In fact, I know you are. This whole setup is wrong. PC Woodley was right to query it. Taylor, get the items over to Joliffe at the forensic lab to examine. After that he can send them to Dr Pooley at the university in case he can lift any prints by using his magic machines.' Horton knew from a previous investigation that Pooley had some ground-breaking technology that could obtain traces of prints invisible to the naked eye and basic examination.

Horton locked up. Woodley and Gregory had nothing new to report. He thanked them and requested that they let them know if they picked up any intelligence on Juliette Croft. In the car heading back to the station, he said, 'Inform the coroner, Barney, and request a forensic autopsy.'

'It's a pity Gaye's not around to do it. Have you heard from her?'

'Only that she'd arrived safely at the Perhentian Islands and was looking forward to exploring them by sea and land.'

'You didn't think of joining her?'

'Malaysia's too hot for me, and holidaying with three other pathologists is not my idea of relaxing conversation.'

Cantelli smiled.

'Gaye said they have a golden rule not to talk shop,' Horton added. 'I don't believe that for a moment. But if true, me butting in with a corpse wouldn't be welcomed.' Nevertheless, he would like to have discussed this with her, but she deserved a break. 'Contact Juliette's medical practice. They might have a next of kin on file.' His phone rang. 'It's Mark Lindley.' He put it on loudspeaker.

'It's about Juliette,' Lindley said. 'I wondered if you had a moment. Could we meet? The Thatched House pub at Milton Locks in, say, half an hour?'

'I'll be there.'

Horton rang off. 'Drop me back at the station, Barney. I'll take the Harley. Log those things in and let me know how you get on at the doctor's. I'll see what Lindley has to say.'

CHAPTER TWO

Lindley looked tired. There was a strain around his broad mouth and a hint of regret in his light-brown eyes. Perhaps the undertaker had cultivated that sorrowful look over the years, thought Horton as he stretched out his hand in greeting. Lindley had discarded his black tie and jacket but still sported a white shirt and immaculate dark trousers, indicating that he had come straight from work. Horton ordered a Coke for himself and a non-alcoholic beer for Lindley.

'I could do with something stronger,' Lindley said, 'but I'll wait until I get home. It's been quite a day, what with Juliette not showing up, a grieving family to pacify and then finding her like that. Inside or out?'

'Out, it's quieter.'

'Glad you said that. I'm not sure I can handle screaming kids.' The pub was busy with young families eating.

They took their drinks to one of the wooden tables on a strip of grass overlooking Milton Lake, which fed into Langstone Harbour on its eastern side. 'It must have been a shock for you finding Juliette like that,' Horton said, sipping his drink. There was a slight chill in the September air, which he welcomed after the blistering heat of the summer.

'I still can't believe it. She was one of our best celebrants. A lovely woman. It's not that I haven't seen death before, I've witnessed some dreadful sights, but finding her dead was the last thing I expected. I was worried when she didn't show for the funeral and, I have to admit, very angry. Then finding her like that, I felt awful.' He ran a hand over his balding head.

Horton remained silent, letting him continue to get it off his chest.

'You see, not only did we have the Nichols family this afternoon extremely upset, as you can imagine when the person they had confided in didn't show, but Juliette's other clients are also understandably distressed. They're suffering their own grief and to have this additional stress is hard for them. They'd got used to her, and it's additionally painful for them to have to start the process again with a new celebrant or come to terms with someone stepping into Juliette's shoes. Rachel, my deputy, oversaw the Nichols funeral today. She's highly competent, but it was still like having a stranger stand up and recount your loved one's life. Oh, I know a celebrant is a stranger, but they get very close to their clients. And Juliette was exceptional, she made them feel that she was part of the family. She was like a bereavement counsellor.'

'Angie said you met her at a nursing home where she was singing to the residents.'

'Yes. We got talking when she'd finished her act. I was waiting for the nursing home manager to do the formalities regarding the death of one of their residents. Juliette told me she'd sung on the cruise ships years ago.'

That confirmed it was her in that photograph. 'Did she have a backing band?' He wondered if they might help them locate a next of kin, but Lindley dashed that idea.

'No. She performed solo. Sometimes she did private parties — wedding anniversaries, birthdays — mainly for the over-sixties, her generation, she said, and her type of music. Lovely voice, mezzo-soprano with grit, bit like Dusty Springfield. I asked her if she'd ever thought about becoming a celebrant. She hadn't but she said she'd look

14

into it. That was July before last. You can train online. They offer fast-track intensive courses.' He paused to drink. 'She walked into our office last October, fully trained, and asked if we would recommend her where we felt suitable. We give our clients a list of two or three people to choose from. Sometimes the family will ask specifically for a man, other times a woman. Occasionally they specify they want someone older or younger. It's down to them. Often we refer them to the online directory so they can go through the profiles and choose, but some people are too upset or too busy to do that, and they leave it to us.'

'Why did she only work with you?'

'She said she preferred it that way. She conducted a few funerals a month, and the rest of her time she devoted to her singing engagements. Because she was an entertainer she had no qualms about speaking in front of people. She knew how to use her personality and voice to suit the occasion and audience. She was good at advising on the right songs and poems, and how to put the service together. We shall miss her.'

Horton drank some Coke. The dead woman was coming a little more alive for him. 'Would seeing death, and having so much to do with the bereaved, have depressed her?'

'I'd have said not. After all, she sang in the nursing homes, plenty of death there. But who knows? It might have got to her.' Lindley's eyes flicked to a noisy family leaving the pub who were shouting as they climbed into their car and slammed the doors.

'Do you know much about her background?' Horton asked. 'We're having difficulty finding her next of kin.'

'Only that she was widowed, twice.'

As the death certificates he'd found testified. Maybe there were stepchildren.

'She was a very private person, she never gave out anything about herself. She was very skilled at getting information from people though, putting them at ease. She was totally unselfish, always interested in anyone and everyone.'

'She didn't speak about living in Portugal?'

15

'No. Did she?' he asked, surprised.

'It seems so from her passport. We can't find a copy of her will. Do you know who drew it up?'

'No.'

Lindley played with his glass. Horton could see he had more to say, and that he was slightly uneasy about it. The real reason for his request for a meeting, perhaps. Maybe he thought it would sound foolish, or it was of a sensitive nature. He'd help him out. 'What's bothering you, Mark? Anything you have to say could help us, no matter what,' he encouraged.

Lindley looked up. 'I've seen lots of deaths, Andy — suicides, accidents, homicide. I know a thing or two about it, and although Juliette's affected me personally there was still that element of professionalism when I saw her.'

'Go on.'

'Well, for a start it struck me as odd that the bottle of champagne, pills and glass were all neatly lined up on the table. In my experience it's never like that.'

'Our thoughts too. And there was no smell of booze in that room.'

'Which doesn't surprise me because that's the other thing that puzzled me. Juliette said she didn't drink. Yes, she could have lied to me, but she told me once that drinking wasn't her scene. She said she'd had her fill of alcohol as a young woman. Not sure what she meant by that. Maybe wild parties that got a bit out of hand.' He shrugged. 'I guess she could have changed her mind and, not being used to alcohol, knocked it back and it affected her dramatically. Or she took it to speed up the end of her life, but surely the champagne bottle would have been rolling about on that table or on the floor. And, as you say, the room would have stunk of it, so too would she, and I can tell you that there wasn't a whiff of booze about her.' He took a swig at his drink. 'There's also this man.'

'Man?'

'The one in the yellow shirt. I know it sounds peculiar,' Lindley hastily added, 'but he's appeared at three of Juliette's

16

funerals recently, each time wearing a yellow shirt, whereas most male mourners are in white, purple or dark shirts, or even Pompey football shirts, but not this one. And he's only appeared at the funerals where Juliette was the celebrant. And I'm not making this up or going mad.'

'I didn't say you were.'

'No, but you looked it.'

'Us coppers are trained not to look anything. Must be losing my grip,' Horton teased. Then more seriously, 'Is there a connection between the families, or friends, of the bereaved at those funerals?'

'Not to my knowledge. The first was a lady in her late eighties, three weeks ago. The second a week later at the funeral of a man in his mid-sixties from a big Portsmouth family. Then up popped Mr Yellow Shirt last Thursday.'

'Did he go into the funerals?'

'The first one, yes. After that I'm not sure. I wasn't really looking.'

'Did Juliette acknowledge him in any way?'

'Not that I noticed. Before coming here I asked the pall-bearers if they knew him or had noticed him. Kevin Pace had, twice, but he didn't see Juliette talk to him or acknowledge him. She might have done though, and we missed it.'

'Was Yellow Shirt at today's funeral?'

'I don't know. I wasn't there, neither was Kevin. I can ask Rachel and the pall-bearers if they noticed him.'

'Please. When is Juliette's next funeral scheduled?'

'This Friday.'

Horton thought it might be worth attending.

'But what can it mean, Andy?'

'Perhaps he was training to be a celebrant and came to hear how she conducted the services.'

Lindley looked doubtful. Horton didn't blame him. He thought it was a bit off-beam himself. He'd try another idea, perhaps even weirder. 'Or he was considering nominating her to do his own funeral when he passed away, or that of a close relative with a terminal illness. Yes, all right, I do have a vivid imagination,' he joked. 'Describe him, aside from the yellow shirt.'

'About mid-fifties, light-brown hair flecked with grey, clean-shaven, five feet eleven or thereabouts, slender, distinguished looking. He held himself well and his suit fitted and looked to be of good quality. He also had an air about him. It's hard to describe. He was detached, cold even.' He rubbed a hand across his tired eyes, then gave a weary sigh. 'I'm probably imagining things. The chap probably has nothing whatsoever to do with Juliette.'

Nevertheless, Horton would take it seriously. Mark wasn't one for flights of fancy. 'How would he have known that Juliette was officiating at those funerals? Has anyone been making enquiries about her?'

'Angie said she hasn't taken any calls like that. She's going to ask Joanne tomorrow, she also answers the phone.'

This man had got the information from somewhere. Could Juliette have told him? Had she arranged for him to be there, perhaps to see how things were done, as Lindley had suggested? If they'd had her phone and computer they might have been able to find him. He could be a close friend with no idea of her death. A past boyfriend maybe, who had come across her recently. But Mark had said the man was in his fifties, so that was unlikely, albeit not impossible.

'When was the last time you saw Juliette?'

'At Thursday's funeral.'

'And the last time you spoke to her on the phone?'

'I haven't for some time. Most of the correspondence is conducted over email or text unless there's a problem. You'll be able to see that from her computer if you can get into it.'

'We would if it wasn't missing, as is her mobile.'

Lindley looked bewildered. 'But that doesn't make sense. Surely they would be at her house.'

'She could have ditched both before taking her own life to prevent anyone from seeing personal information.'

'Maybe.' He rubbed his nose.

18

'Would the service for today's funeral and this coming Friday's be on her computer?'

'Yes. Celebrants send us a copy, in case of emergencies, although we've never had one until today. Often the bereaved have a copy too, but that's entirely up to them.'

'So what happened this morning when Juliette didn't show?'

'Rachel had already given the crematorium staff the video and music, as is usual. When it was obvious that Juliette wasn't going to show, Angie sent the service over to Rachel's mobile and she delivered it. She read out the eulogy that Juliette had written. Rachel asked Lee Nichols if he wished to deliver it — he's the deceased's son — but he chose not to. Public speaking isn't everyone's cup of tea, and he was naturally upset, not only at the death of his father but also the disruption to the service.'

'I'd like the contact details of the next of kin of those funerals where the man in the yellow shirt showed up, plus the Nichols one. And those of the forthcoming funeral.' Horton wanted to know if Yellow Shirt had put in an appearance at today's service, and if he would show on Friday. Lindley's staff might be able to answer the first question, but if they couldn't then he might have to ask Lee Nichols if anyone in his family had seen the yellow-shirted man. Of course the man could have changed his shirt, but, as he seemed to fancy the colour, Horton suspected not.

'I'll send them over to you when I get home.'

'Leave it until the morning, Mark. You look exhausted.'

'I am a bit whacked.' He drained his glass.

Horton's phone sounded. He quickly checked it. 'I need to take this.'

'I'm off anyway, unless there's anything else?'

'No. Hold on, Barney,' Horton said into his phone. 'Thanks for your help, Mark. Let me know if anything new occurs to you. I'll take the glasses back.' Lindley nodded wearily. Into his phone Horton said, 'What did you get?'

'Precious little and I had a while waiting for that. Not their fault, they're rushed off their feet, with two nurses off

19

sick and a doctor short. I spoke to Dr Lancaster, who was very curt — said it wasn't his job to provide a comprehensive examination, he wasn't paid or retained as a police doctor. No next of kin on her records. She registered with the practice seventeen months ago. They did a blood pressure and cholesterol check, everything was fine. And, as PC Woodley told us, she hadn't visited the doctors since, save for her flu vaccination last October. If we need more we'll have to apply to see her medical records. The coroner has approved the forensic autopsy request. Dr Simon Hobbs will be conducting it.'

Horton didn't know him. He hoped he'd be as competent as Gaye.

'I've spoken to him and he's scheduled it for Friday. What did Mark have to say?'

Horton told him.

'Something definitely fishy about this, Andy.'

Horton agreed. He took the empty glasses back to the bar. The families were leaving. There would be a lull before the evening crowd arrived. He could take advantage of the gap and order something to eat but he didn't fancy sitting alone.

He walked across to the old canal lock. From here the footpath to the north bordered Milton Common to the west and Langstone Harbour to the east. It was a short walk to Juliette's house around the southern edge of the common. Lindley's new information made him even more suspicious about her death. Who was this man in the yellow shirt? How significant was he? Had seeing this man at the funerals prompted her to take her life? He didn't like to think of her so afraid that she couldn't see any way out other than to end it all. Surely there must have been someone she could have talked to? Had she been that alone?

His heart felt heavy at the thought. From his experience in the job, and personally when his marriage had ended, he knew what it was to feel utterly desperate. He'd taken himself off in his small boat with the intention of never returning.

But his instinct for survival had been stronger, along with a determination to pick up the pieces of his shattered life after that false rape allegation had wrecked it. But not everyone could do so. And even if you had friends and family, when you were that despairing you often didn't wish to burden them.

He returned to his Harley still wondering if she could have taken her own life. Taylor hadn't found any evidence of someone being with her, although they still had to check out the prints he'd lifted. Perhaps someone had drugged her without her knowing. But with what? Gaye could probably have given him several possibilities. He hoped Dr Hobbs would.

CHAPTER THREE

Thursday 7.30 a.m.

'Maybe this Yellow Shirt just likes going to funerals,' Walters said, biting into his bacon sandwich after Horton had updated him and Cantelli the next morning.

'Only Juliette's.'

'But we don't know that for certain, guv. He could have a thing about them, you know how weird some people are. He could visit every crematorium in the area — I count four if you throw in Southampton and Chichester. Or the poor woman might have been depressed at having to do all those funerals. It's enough to make anyone sad.'

'No one forced her to become a celebrant.'

'Maybe she needed the money.'

'I'd have thought she'd have been better off singing at more nursing and retirement homes.'

'That might have got her down too, all those dribbling old people and their ailments.' Walters wiped his sauce-smeared mouth with a paper napkin. 'And she was no spring chicken herself. Maybe she thought, *My God, I'll end up here. Better to go now and do it my own way.*'

'So check if she put a call through to the Samaritans.'

'They won't give that information out over the phone.'

'Then call at their Portsmouth office later.' Horton had been giving a great deal of thought to the case overnight, and on his run along the promenade that morning. 'We'll follow up the Yellow Shirt angle when Mark or Angie send us the details of those funerals. For now, Walters, you start looking for her next of kin.' Horton spread out the documents on the desk between the constable and Cantelli. 'Her birth certificate — born Portsmouth, parents Cedric and Mary Inglis, both deceased.' He indicated the relevant death certificates. 'Cedric in 1968 and Mary in 1971, both died in the local hospital. Her first marriage to Howard Gleeson in 1973 and his death certificate of 1978. He died of cardiac arrest, aged forty-nine, address Maidenhead. She remarried Nathaniel Croft five years later in 1983. He died ten years after, aged fifty-three, pulmonary aneurism.'

'She didn't have much luck,' Walters said.

'Nor did they. Check to see if Juliette had any brothers or sisters. Also if there were any children by either or both of her marriages, although she told Mark Lindley she had none.'

'There might be stepchildren.'

'Concentrate on direct relatives for now. It's a pity there were no old family photos in the house. We might have got more on any siblings. The photo albums start at 1972 and end at 1993.'

'The year her second husband died,' Cantelli said thoughtfully.

'There could be more albums in the loft,' Walters suggested.

'We didn't look up there.'

'I'll get the keys and check it out,' Cantelli volunteered.

'We'll both do that later. I want to interview the families from the three recent funerals Juliette officiated at, not only to ask them about Yellow Shirt but whether Juliette revealed anything about herself.'

'Not sure that's a good idea,' Cantelli ventured. 'It's a vulnerable time for them.'

'I know, but they're the best chance we've got at the moment of getting to know her and finding a possible friend or relative.'

'We could put out a public appeal,' Walters suggested.

'I'd rather hold back on that until we've exhausted these possibilities. Cantelli, check with the Department for Work and Pensions. Juliette, being state pension age, must have been in receipt of one. They should have her address in Portugal, if she claimed it there. Then we can get in touch with the local police to find out if there are any living relatives there. Also Walters, start ringing round the solicitors to find out who drew up Juliette's will.'

'I thought I was trying to find siblings on the Register of Births, Deaths and Marriages.'

'You can do more than one thing, can't you?'

'Yeah, but not at the same time.'

'Tackle the solicitors first then.' Horton pulled himself up. 'I'd better report in to Superintendent Reine.'

DCI Bliss was on holiday with her friend Eunice Swallows, who ran a private investigation agency in Portsmouth. Reine sniffed and grunted while he listened to Horton's report. Then, peering over the rim of his steel-framed spectacles, he pronounced that it sounded very much like suicide and that Juliette, for reasons only known to her, had laid out those items in that manner. The man in the yellow shirt Reine dismissed as a fancy of Mark Lindley's. Aside from making an effort to find the next of kin, he didn't feel anything further was required, not unless the autopsy said otherwise. It was no more than Horton had expected.

Dismissed, he returned to CID, where Cantelli greeted him with the news that Juliette Croft hadn't been in receipt of a state pension. 'The DWP have no record of her, which means she didn't pay enough contributions to warrant a pension. And she couldn't have contributed to a pension abroad, otherwise she would have transferred it here when she moved back.'

'So what has she been doing all these years?'

'Living off her husbands?' Walters suggested. 'Maybe they were wealthy enough for her not to bother about working. She thought she'd be well provided for on their deaths and in her old age, so she didn't need to worry about a government pension — which, let's face it, is peanuts anyway. And by the time I get to the qualifying age they'll probably have put it up to ninety and I ain't going to live that long.'

'Not with the amount of junk food you eat,' Horton rejoined. 'She worked on the cruise ships judging by the photographs and from what Lindley said.'

'Yeah, but that was yonks back. If she paid into the system then, the contributions were probably discounted because they keep shifting the rules, or she didn't pay in enough, as the sarge says.'

'You seem to know a lot about it.'

'My mum constantly moans about her pension.'

'Would Juliette have earned enough to live on as a celebrant and singer?'

Cantelli answered, 'Funeral celebrants can get anything between two and three hundred pounds per funeral.'

'Think I might change career,' Walters grunted, with his ear to the phone. 'Hello, it's Detective Constable Walters, Portsmouth CID,' he said into the mouthpiece.

Horton moved to the other side of Cantelli's desk. 'She'd already conducted three this month with Lindleys, with two more booked. Mark said she only worked for them, but maybe we should check that out. I wonder how many singing engagements she did a month and what she charged.'

'Probably a similar fee,' Cantelli replied. 'If she did one singing engagement per month and two funerals, that would give her about eight hundred pounds, so she'd still be under the tax threshold. She's not registered as a taxpayer either. Which could be the reason why she only did funerals for Lindley. It's not a lot to live on though, especially if she had a mortgage. Then there's all the household bills and a car to run. It might be on finance, although I didn't see any documents indicating that, either in the car or in the drawers and cupboards. She could have a private pension, or savings she dipped into. As Walters said, her husbands could have left her money.'

'Well, she's certainly got a lot of clothes and shoes, and of good quality, as is her furniture. It didn't look to me to be the usual department store stuff.'

'Her clothes might be old. She might have bought them when she was in the money.'

'Yes, and in Portugal. Then there's her jewellery. I'd say it's good stuff.'

Replacing the receiver, Walters piped up, 'That's the first law firm going to ring me back. I bet I get the same with the others. Maybe Juliette was fiddling the taxman, both here and in Portugal. Perhaps that's why she left.'

Cantelli popped a fresh piece of gum in his mouth. 'They've caught up with her, and she saw the only way out was to take her life. Or she might have borrowed money and was under pressure to pay it back. She could have been heavily overdrawn, or behind with the mortgage and car payments. I didn't find any accounts or bank statements in her house. She could have destroyed them beforehand.'

'It might explain why she ditched her mobile and computer too — both could contain evidence of this, and the exchanges between her and a possible moneylender.'

Walters said, 'Would she have cared about getting rid of them though, when she knew she'd be long gone?'

Horton replied, 'She might if she was proud.' He didn't like to think of the emotional turmoil the poor woman would have gone through. She could have talked to someone — the bank, mortgage people, Citizens Advice. 'As well as the Samaritans, Walters, check if she put a call through to Citizens Advice.'

Walters nodded. 'We could put out a notice to the jewellers and pawnbrokers with her description to see if she hocked anything.'

'I don't think that's necessary. If she bought that house in Dunlin Way last year then the estate agents will have a previous address. Do a search on the internet for the property and the agents who sold it .Some linger on there long after they've changed hands.'

Horton's phoned pinged. 'Lindley's sent over details of the funeral Juliette was due to officiate at tomorrow. His deputy, Rachel, says she didn't see Yellow Shirt at the Nichols funeral, nor did the pall-bearers.'

'Was that because he knew Juliette was dead?' Cantelli mused.

'Mark's receptionist says she hasn't taken any calls from people enquiring specifically about Juliette's funerals.'

'Could the crematorium staff have told this man?'

'We'll ask them tomorrow when we attend the funeral Juliette was scheduled to give. Well I never.' Horton's eyes rounded in wonder. 'Mark's also given me the details of the three funerals where Yellow Shirt was present — one of them was that of Norman Cranley.'

It took a nanosecond for Cantelli to register the name. Walters followed suit a little later.

'I didn't know Cranley was out,' Cantelli said.

'Me neither,' rejoined Horton.

Walters was keying into his computer. 'He must have died in prison because if he was out on licence we'd have been told.'

'We could have been and the email is buried somewhere deep in my inbox,' Horton replied.

'No, guv, it's not. He died in St Mary's Hospital on the Isle of Wight having suffered a stroke in Parkhurst. You're not going to ask his widow about this geezer in the yellow shirt, are you?' Walters looked shocked.

'Why not? He could be a friend, relation or former prisoner.'

'You're mad. She'll chew you up and spit you out. You know how much she loves us.'

'She might have softened over the years.'

Walters gave a hollow laugh. 'I'd better check the Cranley boys are still banged up. If they're not, you'll need the riot squad.'

Cantelli said, 'I could go alone and use my charm. I'm not planning on having any more kids.'

'We'll both go. That way at least one of us will survive.'

'What about the other two funerals?'

Horton consulted his phone. 'The first was Georgina Barlow, three weeks ago, then Cranley's, and the last one, a week ago, was a Roy Whiteman. We'll get the nasty medicine out of the way first and start with Sheila Cranley.'

Walters looked up. 'Well, you're safe as far as Norman's sons, Frankie and Isaac Cranley, are concerned. Both safely tucked up at His Majesty's pleasure.'

'He's welcome to them.'

Cantelli reached for his phone.

'Who are you calling?' asked Horton.

'Backup, and I don't mean uniform, I mean the SAS.'

Horton smiled.

* * *

Horton wasn't smiling forty minutes later after Sheila Cranley, a large woman with more tattoos and colourful vocabulary than a navy and more piercings than a pincushion, had displayed her usual flair for the English language by omitting all the words that didn't begin with F, B and C as she told them just how much she loved the police, what she thought of them and what they could do with themselves.

'At least we're still in one piece,' Cantelli said, as they walked down the stairs from the run-down flat in the Portsea area. 'And she did blink when you said Juliette was dead. In fact, for half a moment I thought she was going to say something nice, but then I am inclined to be optimistic. It was when you mentioned a man in a yellow shirt that I thought she was going to poke your eyes out. How was she supposed to see what colour shirts men were wearing when she was too busy saying goodbye to dear Norman?'

'She didn't put it quite as civilly as that. But she has a point. And she must have been upset. It was rather naive of me. Still, it was worth a try.'

'And then for you to use the S word.'

'Suspicious?'

'That was like waving the green flag at a Grand Prix with Sheila in the Ferrari. There you were accusing her dear Norman of murder when he'd been dead a month. Not that she'd put it past us framing him for it, being the "Bs" that we are. I particularly liked the bit about him rising from his ashes; at least I think that was what she said when I filtered out all the F bombs.' Cantelli waggled a finger in his ear.

They stepped onto the concourse just as a lanky youth appeared almost on top of them. He froze, his protruding eyes darted upwards, then he did a quick about-turn and scuttled off as fast as he could without actually breaking into a run.

'We have that effect on people,' Horton said. 'Do we look like coppers? Don't answer that. Who is he?'

'No idea. He's not known to me.'

They crossed to Cantelli's car. 'He fits the description of one of our betting shop bandits,' Horton mused. They'd had three robberies recently, two in the town centre and one not far from here. 'A tall streak with a bullet-shaped head and pop-eyes. I'll ask Wells to put out a notice to the community coppers around here, one of them might know him.'

Cantelli paused before unlocking the car and looked up. 'Just checking Sheila's not about to hurl anything at us. No, we're safe. Maybe she really does miss Norman. After all, they'd not been married long.'

'Forty years.'

'And for thirty-five of those either he or she has been inside. It's a marvel they managed to have any children.'

'I suppose Frankie and Isaac were let out for their father's funeral.'

'Why? Are you thinking of going to Wormwood and Dartmoor to ask if *they* remember seeing the man in the yellow shirt?' Cantelli looked horrified.

'I think we'll pass on that,' Horton said with a smile, strapping the seat belt across him. His phone pinged. 'It's

Walters, he hasn't found Juliette's property listed for sale on the internet. Ask around the neighbours when we get there, Barney; one of them might know who the estate agents were.'

'How on earth did Juliette deliver a eulogy that didn't read like a charge sheet?' Cantelli said, heading in that direction. 'She'd have been hard-pressed to find memories that didn't involve GBH, robbery with assault, common assault and burglary.'

'And the list of places Cranley served time in would read like a roll-call of HM Prisons by a government minister.'

'Maybe she cited "The Ballad of Reading Gaol".'

'Could have done, although I think that was one prison Cranley didn't serve time in. I've a good mind to ask Angie to send over the service. It would make fascinating reading. In fact, I'll ask for them all.' He sent her a text. 'Mark said Cranley's funeral was a big affair. If we'd known about it we might have managed to make some arrests — after the service, of course. There were bound to have been some wanted criminals among the mourners.'

'How did they afford it? Funerals don't come cheap.'

Horton threw Cantelli a pitying look.

'Yeah, all right — proceeds of crime, no doubt. But not Cranley's own, he must have had a criminal benefactor. Maybe you were right. Yellow Shirt could be a fellow crook.'

'But surely not known to the other bereaved. Still, just to make sure, I'll run their names through the database.' Horton did so while Cantelli led them through a maze of streets heading east across the city. 'Both Georgina Barlow and Roy Whiteman are clean, as expected. So too is Gideon Nichols, and Joshua Fells, the funeral Juliette was due to give tomorrow.' His phone rang. It was Walters. Horton put it on loudspeaker.

'Just wanted to make sure you and the sarge were still in one piece,' Walters said.

'We are, thank you, and Mrs Cranley was her usual pleasant self. She has no idea who Yellow Shirt is and can't tell us anything about Juliette and wouldn't even if we used

30

thumbscrews on her. Wouldn't even give us an opinion in case we use it as evidence against her. Sergeant Cantelli thought he caught a glimmer of sorrow when we told her Juliette was dead, but that was probably wind. I hope you're ringing with some positive results.'

'Sorry, guv, nothing doing. There are no siblings, and neither the Citizens Advice people nor the Samaritans will discuss their clients over the telephone, as I suspected. But they will if I call in person and show them my ID. I could go there now.'

'And get off phoning round the local lawyers?'

'Done that. Two have never heard of her and the others say they'll call me back; either they have to look it up, or the partner dealing with wills and probate is with a client, on holiday or sick. I stressed urgency but I don't think that word exists in a lawyer's diary. I'm amazed they didn't quote me a fee.'

'They might do yet.'

'Got to go — the phone's ringing, that might be one of them.'

Cantelli pulled up in front of Juliette's house. While the sergeant went to question the neighbours about the estate agent, Horton took the loft. There was nothing in it except cobwebs, spiders and dust. He collected the box of albums from the spare bedroom and returned to the living room. The coldness he'd felt on first entering the house had gone. Now it felt empty, anonymous and pointless. All this expensive modern furniture and artwork, all the clothes and personal effects . . . they meant nothing. Not unless they could find someone they had meaning for. There was nothing left of her personality, which made him more determined than ever to try to define it. He was glad to lock up behind him.

Cantelli had returned to the car. 'Mr Melbourne, three doors down, said the house was rented for fifteen years and it was all I could do to stop him giving me a litany of each tenant and all their faults. But the interesting piece of information is that Juliette owned it during that time. She didn't purchase it recently.'

Horton put the box of albums in the boot.

'She gave the last tenants two months' notice a year ago,' Cantelli continued, 'had the place redecorated and moved in last March, which ties in with her passport. She never made any attempt at neighbourliness. Mr Melbourne certainly didn't witness any will, and as far as he's aware no one else did, but that's just his view. According to him, Juliette had airs she wasn't entitled to give herself, but that's probably because she thought him a moaner and ignored him. The house was let by Delamore's. They have a branch on Copnor Bridge.'

'That's on our way to Mr Barlow's place. We'll drop in there first.'

CHAPTER FOUR

'She was a very good landlady as far as we were concerned,' said the estate agent, whose name badge declared she was Nadia. 'She never quibbled about anything, and let us get on with managing the property without moaning or questioning us every five minutes, like some do. I'm sorry to hear of her death.'

She didn't look it. It seemed an effort for her to pull her flitting, heavily made-up eyes away from her computer screen and the mobile on her desk. Perhaps she was overworked — she was the only one in the office — or maybe she was awaiting confirmation on a big property deal.

'We understand she lived overseas before moving back to Portsmouth,' Horton said.

'Yes. Portugal, just outside Lisbon, in Cascais. It's along the coast.'

'You have the address?'

She tapped at her computer with the tips of her sparkly mauve fingernails and relayed it to Cantelli, who jotted it down. 'She told us she'd sold the villa and wanted to take possession of her house.'

'Did she say why she was moving back?'

'Her husband had died.'

'Mr Croft?' Cantelli said, without throwing a curious glance at Horton.

'It was quite sudden, I believe.' Again her eyes dropped to her phone and she frowned.

'How long did she rent out the property?'

'Twelve years.'

And Horton knew, as did Cantelli, that Mr Croft had died a lot earlier than that. In fact, several years before.

'Did she mention any children or relatives?' Cantelli again.

'Not to me, but then I only met her once when I did the formal handover of the property at the end of our agreement. It was strictly business, aside from her telling me her husband had died. We corresponded by email and the occasional text. She might have said more to my previous colleagues. I don't know where they're currently working. I've only got their names on the file. Or she could have said more to the boss, Clive — he owns the agency. He's on holiday in St Kitts. I can give you his email and mobile.'

'Please.'

That done, she was clearly eager to get shot of them, especially as her mobile was ringing.

Outside, Cantelli glanced at Horton. 'Juliette lied.'

'Perhaps it was easier to tell Nadia that than go into lengthy explanations. Juliette might have been living with someone in Portugal who died. Or they'd split up and she didn't care to broadcast her personal background. See if you can speak to Clive when we get back and I'll contact the Lisbon police and ask for their cooperation in finding out what happened, and if there's anyone who can tell us more about any relatives.'

'It could involve a trip to Portugal,' Cantelli joked, unlocking the car. 'Especially as Bliss isn't here to stop you. I'd have thought she'd have sent us a postcard by now: *Having a lovely time in sunny Sweden, the police are extremely efficient, which is more than I can say for you. Hope you've solved all our outstanding cases. I expect a full report on my return.*'

Horton laughed. 'I pity the Swedes.'

Cantelli made for Mr Barlow's residence. The curtains were drawn. He could still be in bed, or he might not have felt like opening them. Alternatively he might be away. Cantelli received no answer to his knocks. He peered through the letter box.

'Can I help you?' a woman hailed them from the neighbouring property.

Cantelli straightened up. Horton quickly showed his warrant card. 'We were hoping to talk to Mr Barlow.'

Her expression softened. 'He's gone to stay with his son and daughter-in-law in Gosport for a few days. Poor man is distraught over Georgina's death, and who can blame him? She was a lovely lady and they were a devoted couple. They'd been married for over sixty years. There's nothing wrong, is there?'

'No, just some formalities that need to be gone through,' Horton bluffed. He could see she didn't believe him. 'We'll contact him at his son's.' He didn't ask for the address. Mark Lindley could give them that.

In the car, Horton said, 'Let's try Mrs Whiteman.'

Cantelli headed out of the city to an impressive modern detached house set back off the road on the upper slopes of Portsdown Hill. It gave panoramic views of the crowded city to the south, and the town of Ryde across the Solent on the Isle of Wight. Several yachts were sailing in the brisk breeze, with the ferry and hovercraft travelling between them. Down in the harbour, Horton could see the Condor *Commodore* ferry making its way out of the port, heading for the Channel Islands.

A woman in her late thirties answered the door. By her age Horton knew she wasn't Mrs Whiteman, but from her drained expression he surmised she was a close relative. He made the introductions and apologized for disturbing them at such a difficult time. 'We'd like to ask Mrs Whiteman a couple of questions about a mourner who she might have seen at Mr Whiteman's funeral. It's nothing for you to worry about,' he quickly added when the woman's hazel eyes flashed anxiety. Maybe Cantelli was right and this was an unnecessary intrusion.

'I'm not sure my mother will be able to help you.'

'Then perhaps you can, Miss . . . ?'

'Mrs Rails, Alice. You'd better come in.' She stepped aside, closing the door behind them, and gestured them into the spacious living room overlooking Portsmouth and the Solent. The room was festooned with bereavement cards. Clearly Roy Whiteman had been a popular, much-loved man. They hadn't got a glimpse of any cards in Sheila Cranley's flat because she hadn't asked them in. From Horton's quick glance at the many photographs on display, he could see Mr Whiteman had also been a good-looking guy even in his later years.

'Mum, these police officers want to ask about Dad's funeral.'

The petite woman with short white-grey hair and red-rimmed eyes looked at them with a bemused expression on her lined face, as though trying to recollect who police officers were rather than why they were there to ask questions.

'It's all right, there's nothing for you to worry about, Mrs Whiteman,' Horton gently reassured. He felt a heel for disturbing her. 'We won't take up too much of your time. We wondered if you know, or recognized, a man who was at your late husband's funeral, about five feet eleven inches, between fifty and fifty-five, short dark hair going grey, held himself well, wearing a black suit with a tie and a yellow shirt.'

Mrs Whiteman shook her head. Her hands trembled in her lap. 'I don't remember him, but then I don't properly recall much. I didn't see him at the wake either. Did you, Alice?'

'No, but I did see him at the funeral.'

This was more than Horton had expected. Lindley had been right then. 'Can you tell us about him?'

'There's not much to tell. Please sit down.' She gestured them into two comfortable armchairs and sat beside her mother.

Cantelli removed his notebook. 'Is it OK if I make some notes?'

'Of course, but there might not be much for you to write down.' She gave a tired smile. 'Why do you want to know?'

'It could help us regarding an investigation. I'm sorry to have to tell you that the celebrant at Mr Whiteman's funeral, Juliette Croft, has been found dead.'

'Oh my God, how awful.' Alice reached for her mother's hand and squeezed it. Mrs Whiteman looked confused, as though she couldn't quite take in what they had said. And Horton thought she probably couldn't. She looked like a woman in shock.

'How did she die? I mean, you being here . . .' Alice asked.

'We don't know for certain yet, we have to look into the circumstances. It's been brought to our attention that the man I described at your late father's funeral was also at another funeral conducted by Juliette, and we would very much like to trace him. He could be a friend or a relative. When did you first notice him, Mrs Rails?'

'It was after the service, when we were all outside the chapel. People were coming out, stopping to talk to me and Mum. He was standing some way back.'

'As though he'd been at the service?' Cantelli asked.

'I don't know. I assumed so. I'm not familiar with all of Dad's former colleagues, customers and friends, and there were a lot of them. My father was very well-liked and respected, wasn't he, Mum?' She smiled and again squeezed her hand. Mrs Whiteman returned the smile but it was just an echo.

'Dad ran a very successful electrical contracting business until he sold it and retired fifteen years ago,' Alice continued, proudly. 'He was also a very talented musician.' Tears welled up as she looked at one of the photographs on the mantelpiece. Horton saw a lively, grey-haired man playing the keyboard. 'He had a lovely voice too,' she said, clearing her throat. 'He was in a small band. They did weddings, private parties and some care homes, which was where he met Juliette. Did you know she was a singer?'

'We did.'

'Because she had known Dad, she was our natural choice to be the celebrant.' Again she looked at her mother, who gave no response. Alice continued. 'Mum was busy talking to people outside the chapel. When I looked again for the man you described, he'd gone. I didn't want him to think I had ignored him. He could have come from one of the care homes that Dad played at. I made a point to speak to him if he was at the wake but he wasn't there.'

'Did you ask anyone about him?' Horton said.

'No. I was busy trying to talk to everyone and making sure everything was all right.'

And, Horton thought, looking out for her mother, who seemed to be elsewhere. 'What made you particularly note him?' he asked, wondering if he'd get anything new about the stranger.

She looked thoughtful. 'He was standing apart from everyone. He was very smartly dressed, as were others, but I noticed his yellow shirt. I thought how nice it looked and how striking against the black tie and suit jacket. His suit looked good too, expensive, and it fitted him well.' She withdrew her hand from her mother's and pushed back her curly hair. 'Now, thinking about him, there was another thing that I noticed. He was standing on his own, which was why I thought I ought to make an effort to speak to him, but I couldn't catch his eye, he was looking away from us.'

This was interesting. 'Where away?'

'Mum and I were on the right-hand side as you come out of the chapel, with people milling all around. He was looking beyond us, farther up the aisle towards the end of it. It comes out by the fountain and the gardens that lead to the car park.'

And who was there, I wonder? 'Was Juliette with you?'

'Yes, she was.'

OK, so I was wrong there.

'But I don't know when she joined us. She left the service after all the mourners had filed out. She might have gone out of the front door, where the funeral directors were, and then around the aisles to join us.'

So it was possible that Yellow Shirt had been waiting for her, and saw her approach.

'People were complimenting her on the service. Mum was on my left, weren't you?'

This time Mrs Whiteman nodded, although judging by her bemused expression she had no idea what she was agreeing with.

'Did Juliette stay until you left for the wake?'

'Yes. We thanked her, asked her to come back to the wake but she politely declined.'

'And did you see this man when you left in the funeral car?'

'No.'

'Did you see Juliette get into her car and leave?'

'No. I'm sorry I can't tell you more.'

'You've been very helpful.' Horton rose. Cantelli put away his notebook. 'I'm so sorry to have troubled you both, and please accept our condolences.'

'I'll show you out.' Alice jumped up.

At the door, Horton quietly said, 'I didn't like to ask in front of your mother, who I can see is in deep mourning, but can you tell us anything about Juliette?'

'About her personally? Not really, aside from the fact she was a good singer. Dad mentioned her a few times. He said she was really talented and that she had missed her chance of being big some years ago.'

'How?' asked Cantelli.

'I don't know. It happens, doesn't it? In another life Dad would have been playing for a well-known rock group, but he went into the dockyard, as his father had done, and became an electrician. Then he met Mum. Marriage, a mortgage, business followed. And kids — me and my brother; he died in a road accident when he was eighteen. There weren't the opportunities then like now. But even now it's not easy to break through, is it?'

Cantelli admitted it wasn't.

'Juliette helped us to put the service together. She advised on the poems and hymns. And I put together a video that Juliette said was perfect. I gave an address and Juliette did the rest.'

'Did she stumble in her words, or lose her place or leave a long gap?'

'No, she was perfect, hardly looked at her notes. It was as though she had rehearsed and memorized the eulogy, but then she knew Dad. She was lovely, very patient and understanding, especially with Mum. As you might also have gathered, Mum has dementia. The shock of my dad's death has made it worse. Dad was as bright as a button and wanted to look after her. His death came very suddenly, heart attack. I explained this to Juliette but I needn't have done because she could see right away how Mum was. She went through all their old photo albums, which helped Mum a lot. She picked up on Dad's personality and key qualities, but she knew them from having performed with him at the retirement and care homes.'

'How many times was this?'

'A few, I think.'

'Do you have the names of the care homes?'

'Not offhand but I can get them if it would help.'

'No, don't trouble yourself. If you could give us the names of the other band members, we'll ask them.'

Cantelli again retrieved his notebook.

'Dennis Sperryman, he's the drummer, 61 Bolton Way, Milton; and Greg Harrison, the guitarist, 20 Cresta View, Southsea.'

Cantelli handed over his card. 'If you think of anything else, just call me.'

'I will.'

'Nice woman,' Cantelli said, climbing into the car. 'The other end of the human spectrum from Sheila Cranley.

Interesting what Alice said about the stranger. It seems as though he was looking at Juliette.'

'Yes. And just because he was at the end of the queue of mourners doesn't mean to say he joined them from the chapel. He might not have gone inside for the service. He could have hung about outside and joined them from the garden of remembrance behind the chapel.'

'Do you think Juliette clocked him?'

Horton shrugged. 'Difficult to say. But we could talk to the other band members. They might have seen him. They might also tell us more about Juliette. She could have spoken to one of them about her personal life, friends, relatives. Make for Greg Harrison's place.'

CHAPTER FIVE

Cantelli's knock brought to the door a sturdily built man in his late sixties with fleshy lips, a ruddy countenance and brown hair that Horton thought must be dyed, because his eyebrows were grey. His yellowing eyes widened as Cantelli went through the introductions and explanations. He showed them into a lounge that smelled of food and cigarette smoke. The remains of lunch were on a table against the wall. A robust woman in her mid-sixties was sitting on a sofa covered with colourful crochet blankets with a West Highland Terrier beside her. It barked at them. She petted it instead of telling it to be quiet, and flicked down the sound on the TV.

'They're from the police. My wife, Christine. *Quiet*,' Harrison snapped at the dog. 'It's something to do with Roy's funeral, love? *Shut up*. Take a pew.'

They did, on two armchairs, while Greg Harrison settled his large frame the other side of the dog, who had now decided to obey his master. He reached across to the small table and picked up a packet of cigarettes. His wife gave him a black look. He put them back.

'Can I get you a tea or coffee?' Christine asked.

Horton declined. She looked relieved as it meant she didn't have to haul herself up.

'We won't keep you long. It's regarding the celebrant who oversaw Mr Whiteman's service, Mrs Juliette Croft. I'm sorry to say she's died and we're investigating the circumstances surrounding her death.'

Christine's mouth gaped, while her husband spoke for them both. 'I'll be blowed! You don't say.'

'Mrs Alice Rails gave us your details. We've spoken to her and Mrs Whiteman.'

Cantelli took out his notebook and removed his pencil from behind his ear.

Christine quickly recovered her composure, and from the gleam in her eyes Horton didn't think she had cared that much for Juliette. 'She seemed so full of life on the two occasions I met her. The first was at a gig Greg was doing at a nursing home over Southampton way and the second at Roy's funeral. How did she die?'

'We've yet to have confirmation but we're treating it as unexplained at present.' Horton had used *unexplained* rather than *suspicious*, not wishing to cause speculation, but he could see he wasn't fooling Christine. 'When did you last see her, Mr Harrison?'

'At Roy's funeral. She seemed fine to me.'

'She did a splendid job,' Christine chipped in, not wanting to be left out.

Her husband quickly broke in. 'Alice has to take credit for putting the service together, with Juliette's help. She compiled an amazing video of Roy's life including the three of us playing together. She set it to one of Roy's favourite artists, Bob Dylan, and his song, "When the Ship Comes In".'

'That choked me up,' Christine sniffed. Horton got the feeling she'd like to have reached for a handkerchief and dabbed at her eyes for effect. 'I love that song, especially the bit about the breeze ceasing to breathe and the stillness in the wind. It makes you think, doesn't it?'

'Roy used to play the harmonica as well as the keyboard.' Harrison patted his wife's hand, although her distress still looked phoney to Horton. 'He could really make the harmonica sing, if you get my meaning, and he had a good voice. The Blue Boys, we were called, after Pompey football club colours. Me, Roy and Dennis. We played a bit of Dylan, bit of rhythm and blues, pop and jazz, it was very much determined by the age group and type of audience. With Roy gone, we might have to chuck it in. No one could take his place, not really. It just seems so unfair that he was taken like that, although some say it's better to go quick — heart attack, no warning, right out of the blue — than suffer and linger on. He was intending to look after his wife; she's got dementia. He thought she'd go first, but you never know, do you?' He looked wistful, then drew himself up. 'We first met Juliette at a care home last summer and ran across her a couple of times after that. Our acts complemented one another. Roy was in charge of bookings and I think he recommended her to a few of our regular clients. I can't believe she's gone.'

Horton interrupted, as Christine looked about to pronounce. 'Did she speak about her past?'

'She'd been a professional singer in her youth — clubs, cruise ships, that sort of thing. I think she'd have liked to have been famous, not in a big celebrity kind of way, but maybe a few records in the top twenty. Still, that's the way it goes. I'd liked to have had a chance on the music scene myself, but that takes guts, money and no matrimonial ties. Not that I'm complaining,' he hastily added, seeing another dark look from his wife.

Cantelli diplomatically interjected. 'Did she speak of any relatives or friends? We're very keen to trace her next of kin.'

'She said she'd been married twice, and widowed. Never spoke about any kids. We didn't get the chance to talk much, too busy performing.'

'You also knew she was a celebrant?'

'Yes, she told Roy — oh, must have been last autumn. Poor man didn't know then she'd stand up and deliver his funeral less than a year later. Juliette was as shocked as we all were when Roy died.'

'You've spoken to her since then, excluding at the funeral?'

'Yes, when she was putting together the eulogy. She came round to see me and Dennis. Roy and I go right back to the seventies, when we were apprentices in the dockyard. We used to play together even then, thought we were the bee's knees.' He grinned. The dog yawned as though he'd heard this all before. 'Roy left soon after his indentures to work with an electrical contractor before branching out on his own, while I stayed with the dockyard. We lost contact. Then, by accident, we met up at a music festival fifteen years ago and took up where we'd left off, only this time we thought we'd do it for some pin money on our retirement. Dennis had come across Roy many times during the course of their work. Dennis worked for a builders' merchants. He wasn't at Roy's funeral, he's on holiday, couldn't call it off because his wife would have been furious. I think he tried to see if he could return for it but he's over in Ireland. Back next week. He had a link from the funeral directors so that he could watch it. He texted me to say he'd managed to see it.'

Horton said, 'We're trying to trace a man who was at Mr Whiteman's funeral. Neither Mrs Whiteman nor Mrs Rails recognized him, but I wondered if either of you saw him.' He gave the description.

Christine said, 'It sounds a bit like Harold Findley.'

'He's gone grey.'

'Could have dyed it and had highlights put in.' She glanced at her husband knowingly and he scowled at her. His hand went up to his hair but he resisted the temptation to smooth it.

'Findley wasn't wearing a yellow shirt.'

'So this man doesn't ring any bells?' Horton said. 'You didn't see him in the aisles behind the chapel after the service?'

They both shook their heads.

'Nor in the car park or at the wake?'

'I don't think so,' Harrison answered. Christine again shook her head. 'I don't recall him, but then I can't remember everyone who was there. It was a big funeral and you only speak to the people you know.'

'Do you have a list of the care homes you performed at where Juliette was on the same bill?'

'There was one at Fareham, another at Gosport and one the other side of Emsworth, but I don't remember their names. They all sort of blend into one. We've done a fair few in Southsea too but not with Juliette. Roy kept all that.'

Which meant they'd have to trouble Alice Rails again, and Horton was reluctant to do that. He couldn't really see how it would help them anyway. Not unless the care home managers knew more about Juliette's personal life, and he was beginning to doubt if anyone did. Lindley, it seemed, had been right when he'd said she hadn't spoken about herself.

As they returned to the car, Cantelli voiced the same view. 'Doesn't seem much point following this line of inquiry.'

'We'll see if Walters has got anything from the solicitors before we disturb Mr Barlow and Mrs Nichols.'

Walters greeted them with the news that three law firms had now confirmed they didn't hold a will for Juliette Croft and she hadn't consulted them. He was still waiting on two.

'Leanne Payne's also been on, guv. She wants to run something in the local paper. Are we treating the death as suspicious? I said you'd call her back. There's some stuff on social media about it, pictures of the patrol car, PC Woodley looking serious, and a good one of you, Sarge, poking around in her car, although your rear end might not win any awards.'

'Ha ha.' Cantelli put the box of Juliette's photo albums on one of the vacant desks.

'No mention of her name, just speculation: "What were the police doing opposite Milton Common last night?" That type of thing. If we don't put out something soon all the loonies and conspiracy theorists will be saying there's a homicidal maniac or aliens on the loose. Leanne's probably already sniffing around the neighbours.'

'And as we've spoken to a few people about Juliette, it's bound to be leaked.' Horton thought particularly of

Christine Harrison, who had probably already been on the phone to her friends and chatting to her neighbours. 'I'll give her a statement and get the communications team to put something on the website.'

'How did it go with Mr Barlow and Mrs Whiteman?'

'Didn't see the former.' Horton gave Walters an update on their conversations with Alice and Mrs Whiteman and with Greg and Christine Harrison.

The constable scratched his nose. 'I've been thinking, guv. Yeah, I do sometimes. How do we know that Yellow Shirt really exists? You've only got Lindley's word for it—'

'And Alice Rails, as I've just said.'

'Yeah, but maybe she told you that because you suggested it.'

Horton knew that could sometimes happen. 'She seems a reliable witness. And there's Kevin Pace, the pall-bearer.'

'He could be in league with Lindley.'

'But why would Lindley lie about Yellow Shirt?'

'To throw suspicion off himself.'

'You're saying that Mark Lindley killed Juliette?' Horton said incredulously.

'Could have done, he did report finding her. Maybe she was blackmailing him. She'd found out something about Lindley and the business, and threatened to reveal it.'

No, Horton couldn't believe that. He'd known Mark for years. He couldn't see him involved in such a heinous crime — but sometimes a dispute, a grudge, a festering wound, or a secret that could ruin a reputation or lifestyle could lead to murder, as it had done with his own mother. And as Walters had said, Lindley had been first on the scene. And it was Lindley who had called the police.

'I can't see Mark staging a suicide in such an amateurish way,' he said. 'He's seen enough death to know how to do it without making it look wrong. And he pointed that out to me.'

'Maybe that was why he did it, another thing designed to divert suspicion.'

Horton was liking this less. He perched on the corner of one of the spare desks. 'Go on, seeing as you're building up a head of steam.'

'Maybe Juliette was going to report something damaging about Lindleys to the National Association of Funeral Directors that would ruin their business.'

'Have you anything specific in mind?'

'You hear about people having sex in mortuaries and funeral parlours. Juliette could have caught Lindley in the act, and not with his wife, maybe with this Rachel, his deputy. Or Angie could have been having it away with one of the pall-bearers — Kevin Pace, for instance.'

Horton shifted uncomfortably. Cantelli too was looking disturbed.

'Then there's the sale of body parts, not to mention theft of belongings,' Walters persisted. 'There are some serious weirdos out there, as we well know.'

'I just can't see the Lindleys being involved in anything like that.'

'Me neither,' added Cantelli firmly.

'Ah, but why did they handle Cranley's funeral?' Walters said pointedly. 'Sheila Cranley lives in Portsea, the other side of the city; there are undertakers closer to her home. And I'd have thought the Co-op would have been her first choice.'

'You're saying Lindley did it gratis because he's involved in criminal activity with the Cranleys?' Horton said disbelievingly.

'Or one of their mates. Funerals don't come cheap and I can't see Sheila having that sort of money.'

He'd already said as much to Cantelli. It seemed too incredible, but then sometimes they had to believe the unbelievable. 'I think you're wrong, Walters, but we'll keep it in mind. And we'll see what Dr Hobbs finds from the post-mortem. Now, get me some sandwiches or a roll from the vending machine, anything will do — and a coffee. And I'm sure Sergeant Cantelli would like a tea to go with his home-made sandwiches.'

Walters waddled out muttering something about slaves and dying. Horton took no notice, knowing that Walters would use the opportunity to get something for himself, even though he'd probably already eaten.

'I'll contact Leanne Payne and send a request to the Lisbon police; you try Clive Delamore, Barney.'

Leanne answered promptly. Horton gave her the deceased's name and explained that any sudden and unexpected death was always investigated, and that they were trying to trace Juliette Croft's next of kin. Leanne pressed for more information, as Horton knew she would. He released Juliette's maiden name, age, and the fact that she had come from the area. He also said she'd been a singer, mainly around the nursing and retirement homes. He wondered if that might prompt a response from any of them. It was possible she had some forthcoming bookings and they would be wondering why she didn't show. He made no mention of her being a celebrant, as he didn't want the recently bereaved bothered. He sent a statement to the communications team and an email to the Lisbon police, then joined Cantelli.

'I've left a message for Clive Delamore to call me back. I'm not sure what time it is in St Kitts.'

Horton consulted his watch. 'They're about four hours behind us. Must be about 10 a.m. Perhaps he's having a lie-in.'

'Or he's in the pool.'

'Let's take a look at those albums.'

Cantelli delved into the cardboard box and placed the six albums on his desk. 'The dates are a bit haphazard. They start at 1972, but there's nothing for 1977, 1979 or 1982. Then there's a six-year gap from 1984 until 1990 and a few from 1991.'

'I'll take the first three, you the last. There are a lot of her on the cruise ships with various men.' Horton flicked through the first of his batch.

'No women?'

'No. Some with the band behind her.'

'Not the Blue Boys, is it?' Cantelli joked.

'Doesn't look like it, but who can tell all these years later? Harrison didn't mention playing on the cruise ships, and, from what he said about him and Roy working in the dockyard, I'd say they didn't. Dennis Sperryman might have done. Ah, this man has his arm round her and there's another of them on the deck, looking very pleased with themselves. It must be Howard Gleeson because here they are on their wedding day, Juliette looking radiant and glamorous in a very revealing wedding dress.'

Cantelli cricked his neck to look. 'She's got the figure for it. He looks happy. Seems she picked herself a sugar daddy. He must be twenty years older than her.'

'He might not have had much money. He could have been working on that cruise ship.'

'Any of him in uniform?'

'Not that I can see. But not all staff wear uniforms. What occupation did his death certificate give?'

'Hang on.' Cantelli reached for the document folder on Walters' desk. 'Financial director.'

Of what? Horton wondered. Not that it was significant. It was a long time ago. 'No children in the pictures at the wedding, which looks low-key, a handful of people outside a registry office, throwing confetti. Could be some of Juliette's relatives.'

'Might be gone by now. Hold on, here's another wedding picture, this one with her second husband, Nathaniel Croft, and there are a few adults and children in it. Could be stepchildren.'

'Or nieces or nephews.'

'Those two little girls look positively mutinous, and that boy doesn't seem too happy at being stuffed into a suit and tie.'

It was Horton's turn to swivel round to where Cantelli was pointing. The girls, in their best dresses with wrinkled white socks, looked as though they'd be much happier on a climbing frame, and the boy looked sullen and resentful.

Once again, Juliette was glamorous, happy and heavily made up, with perfectly styled blonde hair and a tight-fitting dress that made her look as though she was about to appear on stage rather than at a wedding. Her new husband, at least ten or twelve years older, dark-haired and brown-eyed, beamed.

'Nothing written on the back,' Cantelli said, after extracting the picture and flicking it over.

'What did Nathaniel Croft do for a living?'

Cantelli rifled among the papers. 'Manager.'

'Of what?'

'Doesn't say.'

Walters entered and placed Horton's coffee and sandwiches in front of him. He peered over his shoulder. 'Quite a looker in her day. Can't believe everyone had such big hair — and that's just the men.'

Horton continued with the photo albums. Some of the pictures were of the happy couple outside a substantial property that he took to be their home, others of the man beside a car, and another of Juliette at the wheel of a natty little sports job. There were also holiday snaps at various sunny locations that didn't look to be in Britain. And of Juliette in a bikini that didn't leave much to the imagination. By her look and pose, she knew it. Still, she had a nice figure, so he didn't blame her for showing it off.

Cantelli said, 'There are some more pictures of her singing, again it looks to be on a cruise ship. There are pictures of her on a sunlounger on deck. She must have resumed her singing career after Nathaniel died, except she didn't file a tax return.'

'Perhaps she was on a cruise as a passenger and volunteered to give a performance.' Horton rose. 'I'll send a request to the European database for a check on her.' He didn't know when he'd get an answer. Sometimes the information came back within minutes, other times it could take hours or days.

As he keyed it in, he thought of Harriet Ames, who had worked for Europol until recently. Now she was working in the same force as him. It had been a shock to see her in

July, and a little uncomfortable for him to find her working so close. She was in Southampton, but that was only twenty-five miles along the motorway to the west. She'd had no further news on her father, Lord Richard Ames, who had disappeared from his yacht on a foggy April night after Horton had seen him — only he hadn't told Harriet that.

He liked her a great deal, but there could never be more to their relationship than friendship, because Horton had learned on that April night who his father was: the late Viscount William Ames, Harriet's grandfather. Horton had also discovered his mother's fate following her disappearance when he was a child. Viscount William Ames had killed her. Only four people knew that: him, Andrew Ducale of the intelligence services, and Gordon and Richard Ames, the viscount's sons. Harriet's father, along with his brother Gordon, had disappeared into the Solent after Horton had learned the truth and heard a gunshot on board. Neither man had been found on the drifting yacht, nor any blood. Someone — Horton suspected the intelligence services — had cleaned the craft.

He peeled off the wrapper on his sandwiches and, while eating them, sent the request. Then he checked through his messages. He responded to a couple of urgent ones. He thought of those betting shop robberies and the lanky youth who'd legged it pretty rapidly that morning. He called up the reports and carefully reread them. Three betting shops had been targeted in the last two weeks. All had taken place around closing time, at 10 p.m. There had been two men, and the witnesses had claimed, from their voices and the way they moved, that they were quite young. They had worn balaclavas and gloves and had carried machetes, which they used to threaten the staff, who, in accordance with policy, had rapidly handed over the money. Cash, it seemed, was still king in the betting world, at least in Portsmouth. Walters was overseeing the case. Horton called him in.

'I was just heading out to Citizens Advice before they close, and then the Samaritans.' Walters thrust his arms into his jacket. 'Another law firm has phoned in to say they've never heard of Juliette. That leaves two to get back to me, but she might have made her will online, using one of those will-writing services.'

'I think we might have seen one of our betting shop robbers today.' Horton described the man they'd scared off outside the block of flats where Sheila Cranley lived. 'The description about the protruding eyes fits. Ring any bells with you?'

Walters shook his head. 'Could be any of the lowlifes, they all seem to merge into one. Same stance, same look, same smell.'

'I'll ask Sergeant Wells to circulate his description. One of the community police officers might recognize who it is.' Horton would also ask Billy Jago, an unofficial informant, who might have picked up some news on the streets about the robberies and recognize the description of the youth.

Angie had sent over the funeral services for Georgina Barlow, Norman Cranley, Roy Whiteman and Gideon Nichols. Horton settled down to read them.

CHAPTER SIX

He started with Cranley's. It was like a fairy tale, so little of it rang true. He shook his head in wonder. Cantelli would love it. Had Juliette believed it? Did it matter if she hadn't? She'd been paid to deliver it.

He envisaged her looking down at the solemn faces of the mourners, most of whom knew the thing was a lie. Yes, Cranley had been born in Portsmouth and had been taken into care and had had a tough upbringing, but then so had he and he hadn't turned out a villain. The difference was that Cranley's parents had been villains and had spent most of their adult lives in prisons. Norman Cranley had carried on the family tradition. There was mention of him getting into trouble as a juvenile, then how he had pulled himself together and tried to go on the straight and narrow and that unfortunate circumstances had led him to being accused of theft and arrested — wrongfully, of course. Horton gave a cynical smirk. No mention there that he'd actually been caught on the job. And no mention of his prison sentences and crimes, just what a fun-loving man he had been, and a devoted husband. But then Cranley hadn't had much time to be anything other than devoted; as he and Cantelli had discussed earlier, he'd hardly been at home.

There was some other guff about how he'd been well known on the manor, which was true. And how Sheila had been a loyal wife, which wasn't, but no one was going to dispute that and risk having their private parts tattooed. There was no video of photographs at this funeral. They'd be hard put to find any that weren't on the police file. He chuckled at the choice of song while they reflected on Cranley's life: Willie Nelson singing "Don't Fence Me In".

He was interrupted by a phone call, not connected with Juliette, and dealt with it before returning to the eulogies. Georgina Barlow had been a loving wife and mother with a son and daughter. Her husband had been a tax collector for the Inland Revenue. Not an occupation popular with many. On his retirement he and Georgina had spent time travelling around Britain and the continent in their cherished campervan. His children had given readings. The video of pictures celebrating her life had been shown to the tune of one of her favourite country and western artists.

Roy Whiteman was next. A decent man, much loved, as he and Cantelli had gathered from their interviews that morning. The service gave details of his time with the Blue Boys, as Greg Harrison had told them, and how Roy loved his music, especially the piano and harmonica, and how he'd been a big fan of Bob Dylan and had even managed to see him performing at the Isle of Wight Festival in 1969, a memory he cherished and talked about so often that Alice, his daughter, could recite it by heart. He felt sympathy for Penny Whiteman and Alice Rails.

The final funeral, held on the morning of Juliette's death, was that of Gideon Nichols. For this, Juliette had taken a different stance, perhaps at the suggestion of one of the family. Instead of a chronological account of the deceased's life, she'd asked friends, relatives and colleagues to describe Gideon Nichols in one word, and had then gone on to match the description with key markers in the man's life.

'Funny' was demonstrated by a couple of pranks Gideon Nichols and some old friends had got involved in in their twenties. 'Clever' and 'resourceful' were shown by the fact that he had set up his own business as a sound engineer in 1971. 'Efficient' in that he had expanded the business into a highly successful events company, handling major tour management and logistics, and many other aspects of the entertainment industry, and which his son, Lee, and his granddaughter, Tiffany, had taken over on his retirement, although he remained a director. 'Loving' was chosen by his wife of forty-three years, Edwina. He was 'fit' and 'competitive' according to a couple of friends who he enjoyed squash with, and he loved sailing his 36-foot yacht, which he kept at Haslar Marina, Gosport. And here was a name Horton recognized: Don Winscom, who had said Nichols had been 'generous'. Don was the founder and chief executive of Go Ahead, a sailing charity that helped traumatized veterans and juvenile criminals to adjust, and in the latter case rehabilitate them if possible. If it hadn't been for Don, Horton would never have discovered his love of sailing as a teenager. It had eased his troubled mind and given him the space and peace he needed as well as the adrenalin rushes he craved. It still did.

In return, Horton had volunteered as a skipper on one of the charity's yachts many times before the trauma of the rape allegation and his marital break-up had consumed all his time, along with his quest to discover the truth behind his mother's disappearance. Now that was over, maybe he should volunteer again.

The service included a video collage with music — in this case rock — and two readings, one from Lee, the other from Tiffany. Horton suspected that Don would have attended the funeral, in which case he'd be a very good person to ask about the man in the yellow shirt. He might also be able to tell him something about Juliette. Horton was tempted to call him but changed his mind. He'd go there tomorrow after the funeral that he and Cantelli were scheduled to attend.

He studied the details: Joshua Fells had been a widower with two sons. He'd been a prominent Portsmouth

56

businessman, owning a fleet of taxis and a private car and van hire business, and was a big Pompey fan, like Cranley, but Joshua got to see the matches live, instead of behind prison walls. He was also a director of the football club. Horton imagined his funeral would play to a packed house.

He joined Cantelli in CID.

'We've got a sighting of Juliette on Tuesday morning,' Cantelli said. 'PC Gregory has placed her buying petrol at a garage in Milton Road. She was a regular and the cashier remembers chatting to her. There was nothing different about her manner and she didn't say where she was going after that. Clive Delamore has also returned my call. He expressed the usual shock at Juliette's death but claims he didn't know her, except in a professional capacity. He never heard her mention children or relatives, strictly business, but if he recalls anything he'll let me know.'

'I've got the eulogies through. I'll send them over to you. You'll particularly enjoy Norman Cranley's. It's highly imaginative.'

'I could do with a good book at bedtime.'

Horton smiled. 'Yes, if you're into fantasy.'

'Better than reality most of the time, so Marie tells me, but then she reads everything and anything.'

Marie was Cantelli's third child of five, and very bright, like her eldest sister, Ellen, a genius at IT, who at eighteen had been headhunted by GCHQ and was now undertaking a sponsored apprenticeship with them in Cheltenham.

He returned to his office thinking of Emma's choice of books. He didn't know them all, only the ones she had brought with her on their sailing holiday in August. As well as Enid Blyton they had included some modern authors he had never heard of, which wasn't surprising as he had spent so little time with his daughter over the last two years, because of Catherine's obstinacy. Now, with Emma being a full boarder, he wouldn't be able to make that up. But there were still holidays, if Catherine didn't attempt to deprive him of those too. He was convinced that she had persuaded

Emma it was best for her to board full-time because her daughter might cramp her style with her soon-to-be husband, multi-millionaire Peter Jarvis who wouldn't want a kid in tow while they were jetting off around the world. It meant he might get to see more of Emma, unless Catherine's parents stuck their noses in.

He knuckled down to some work. Before signing off for the day he checked to see if anything had come through on the European database. Sure enough, Juliette Croft had been clean. No criminal record. That didn't mean to say whoever she had lived with wasn't a former criminal, *if* she had lived with someone. But there was no reason to suppose her partner had been a crook.

He went in search of Billy Jago. It didn't take long. He found the skinny little man with the sallow complexion and darting eyes in one of his regular haunts, an amusement arcade just off the city centre. He noted Jago had seen him. Horton slipped outside to wait in their usual place, the war memorial by the Guildhall. Jago joined him a couple of minutes later.

'Do you know a tall, lanky youth about eighteen, with pop-eyes, a bullet-shaped head, dark slicked-back hair?' asked Horton without preamble. 'Wears designer jeans and T-shirts and trainers, hangs around Vernon House, Portsea.'

'Sounds like Damien Cranley, cocky little sod.'

Horton should have known. Damien must have been visiting Granny.

'He has street cred on account of his grandfather, Norman, and his dad, Frankie. Been in trouble tons of times. You look him up, Mr Horton. I'm surprised you don't know him. Goes around with another lad, dark-skinned, short and stocky.'

Horton hadn't run into Damien — or run him in — and neither had Cantelli or Walters or they would have recognized him. That could be on account of Damien's previous being petty crime, but Jago's words were a reminder to check out not just Damien's record but also if Frankie and his brother, Isaac, had other offspring who were following in their father's footsteps. There might be a family likeness in the eyes.

'Keep your ear to the ground, Billy. I think Damien's involved in these betting shop jobs, the description fits. If you get any hint something's going down, pass it on.'

'Righty-ho.'

'I'd also like to know anything you pick up about Norman Cranley's funeral. It was expensive. I'm curious to find out who paid for it.'

Jago ran a bony hand under his nose. 'Cranley never stashed noffink away from that last job, not that I heard anyways. Maybe Sheila had a whip-round.'

It would have been a very big one, running into several thousand pounds, most probably. 'I'd especially like to know if any big-time villains were at the funeral.'

'That'll be extra.'

'I'll give you a bonus, but only if the information is worth it.'

'Have I ever let you down, Mr Horton?'

'Frequently. And if you can get anything on our elusive Milton burglar and keyless car thieves in the same area, two other cases we're very eager to clear up, I'll give you a double bonus.'

'Off my patch, but you're on.'

Horton watched Jago swagger off in his usual brash style, then returned to his Harley.

He waited until he was on his boat before checking the police computer. Jago was right. Damien, aged nineteen, had a string of offences behind him: petty theft, antisocial behaviour, car theft, shoplifting. And it looked as though he might have stepped up a couple of gears by adding robbery with menace.

That night he mulled over Walters's theory about Mark Lindley. He just couldn't believe it. He thought it far more likely that Juliette had set that suicide scene herself after taking some drugs earlier. Not all drugs acted instantly; in fact, many didn't. She could have swallowed something hours beforehand, got rid of the bottle — possibly off the premises, ditto her laptop and phone — returned home, and, after placing the items on the table, lain down and fell into a coma. Yes, that could fit. Tomorrow, Dr Hobbs would have the results of the post-mortem, so they might be a shade clearer on that. And perhaps tomorrow the man in the yellow shirt would show up at Joshua Fells' funeral and they could ask him about his fascination for the dead woman.

CHAPTER SEVEN

Friday

'Nothing.' Cantelli pulled off his black tie as they made their way to the crematorium car park. He plucked a colourful one from his pocket and deftly tied it. Horton hadn't worn a tie of any colour but kept in the background, watching the undertakers and funeral directors from a discreet distance, and, as Cantelli said, no one matched Yellow Shirt in clothes or appearance. They'd spoken to the crematorium staff before the mourners had arrived. And, as Horton had expected, they hadn't seen the man they were looking for, nor had they had received any enquiries specifically about Juliette Croft or the Lindley funerals.

Walters had reported that Juliette hadn't contacted the Samaritans or Citizens Advice, and one of the two outstanding legal firms had returned his call of yesterday to say they hadn't been instructed by Juliette to draw up her will. There had also been no response from the website appeal, or Leanne's Payne article in the local newspaper.

Cantelli made for Gosport, where they'd agreed he was to call on Mr Barlow while Horton spoke to Don Winscom at Haslar Marina. If Don wasn't there then Horton would wait in the marina-side café for Cantelli's return. He was in luck.

'Andy, lovely to see you.' Winscom sprang up from behind his cluttered desk in his cramped, untidy office with the alacrity of a thirty-year-old rather than a man in his mid-sixties. He pumped Horton's hand with a dry, vice-like grip and a broad grin on his big, malleable, weather-tanned face.

'Great to see you too, Don, and looking so well.' Horton meant it.

'And you. Is this business or pleasure? I note the motorbike jacket and helmet are missing, so deduce it must be business.'

'A bit of both. Sergeant Cantelli dropped me off on his way to interview someone.'

'How are the sergeant and his nephew, Johnnie? I was so glad that terrible business of him going missing turned out all right — for them, at least.' Winscom gestured him into a seat after removing a pile of paper from it.

It had been disturbing case. Johnnie's life had been held in the balance by a crazed killer who thought he and his mates from years back held a secret that would damage his career. Fortunately, Horton had found Johnnie in the nick of time, before he'd suffered the same fate as his friends.

'He's doing splendidly,' Horton replied. 'Racing yachts all round the world — and winning.'

'I'm very glad to hear it. One of our success stories, although they don't all have to be as spectacular as that. If sailing helps some of these young people to adjust to life and keep them crime free, then it's a job well done. So, how can I help you? Got another young tearaway you want me to take on? Or perhaps you've come to tell me you're coming back to help us, as a skipper.'

'That's the pleasure bit. I'd like to if you'll have me.'

His face lit up. 'Of course. Delighted. When can you start? Sunday? I've got a team needing to be taken out. Three veterans and two young people, only one of them has sailed before.'

Horton laughed. 'Let's get the business over with first. I believe you knew the late Gideon Nichols.'

'I did.' Winscom's face fell. 'His death was a great shock. Very sudden. Brain aneurism. Why do you ask? There was nothing suspicious about it. Or was there?' he added, worried.

'No. But there might be about his funeral.'

'Ah, you mean the celebrant not showing. Has she disappeared?' He joked.

'No, she's dead.'

Winscom's mouth gaped. He frowned and ran a hand over his thick grey hair. 'I'm sorry. I had no idea.'

'She was found dead in her house on Wednesday morning by Mark Lindley. Suspected suicide. I can't go into details, Don, but a few things have made that questionable.'

'But her death can't have anything to do with Gideon, or his funeral, surely?'

'I take it you attended.'

'I did, along with a hundred or so other mourners. Gideon was well-liked and respected. A good man. I've known him for years. We met when I was organizing a charity night to raise money for Go About at the Castle Sailing Club during Cowes Week, decades ago. Gideon's company were there providing sound equipment and staging for the various events. We got talking about sailing and he's been a generous supporter ever since.'

'I didn't come across him when I was volunteering for you.'

'He always kept it low-key, didn't want to be mentioned. He gave generously both in monetary terms and by providing equipment free of charge at our various charity dos. I wanted him to be a trustee but he declined. Too busy, and said it wasn't his style. Modest man, never one for the limelight.'

'Modest' hadn't been a word that Juliette had picked up on in her eulogy, but then there wouldn't have been time to include everything.

'We're trying to locate Juliette's next of kin, would you have any idea who that might be?'

'None. I didn't know her, although I spoke to her over the phone to give my tribute to Gideon. She asked me to sum up Gideon in a couple of words. Mine were "generous" and "considerate", although I could have said a lot more.'

Other words she hadn't used.

'I'm pleased to say that Gideon's son, Lee, is continuing to support us, and his granddaughter is also carrying on the tradition. Tiffany's a volunteer. Lots of experience on her grandad's yacht. A very competent sailor.'

'I wanted to know if you saw a man at the funeral, mid-fifties, distinguished looking, wearing a yellow shirt.'

Winscom puffed out his cheeks as he considered this, then slowly shook his head. 'Doesn't ring any bells. As I said, the funeral was packed. Aside from the immediate family, who I know, and a couple of local business people, the rest were strangers to me and I didn't really take any notice of them, not to that extent.'

'You didn't see any man hanging back behind the mourners after you all came out of the chapel? Or anyone on their own before you went in?'

'I can't say that I did. Why are you asking?'

'He seems to have been at recent funerals where Juliette Croft was acting as the celebrant and we'd like to talk to him.'

'Can't you put out a statement asking him to come forward? Sorry, teaching grandma to suck eggs here.' He beamed.

'We might have to,' Horton answered, although he doubted they would do so. The description was vague enough to stimulate countless responses, all of which would tie up resources and lead nowhere. 'If you do remember or hear anything, Don, give me a call.'

'I will. Is that the business over with?'

'It is.'

'Good.' He clapped his hands smartly. 'I've lost two skippers recently — not overboard,' he joked. 'But they've moved away with their jobs. Now, with you and Harriet I'll be back up to strength.'

'Harriet? You don't mean Harriet Ames?' Horton said, stunned.

'Yes. She was very keen to get involved now she's moved here from Europe. We met, if you remember, when Johnnie went missing. She came to see me in August, during Cowes Week. Our team was competing, as were she and her brothers, not in her father's yacht though.' His expression fell. 'Sad business about Lord Ames. I suppose you know his body's never been found; it's been almost five months. His yacht was discovered drifting off the coast of France, no one on board.'

Oh, Horton knew all right. He'd also been told by Ducale of the intelligence services that they believed Richard Ames had been shot by his brother, Gordon, on board that yacht. Harriet didn't know that, nor did her family, not unless Ducale or someone from the service had told her, which he very much doubted. The Ames family secret would be protected at all costs, and he wasn't about to expose it. He hadn't expected to come into contact with Harriet through Don's charity. And he might not. They could be volunteering on different days, and certainly sailing different yachts. Go About currently had two.

Winscom was saying, 'Harriet and her family have donated Lord Ames's yacht to us. Yes, it surprised me,' he added to Horton's startled expression. 'No strings attached. We can sail her or sell her and use the money in whatever way we wish for the charity. It's here now, do you wish to see it?'

No, Horton instantly thought, then changed his mind. 'Yes.' Not that he could glean anything from it.

Winscom locked his office and they made their way across the marina entrance. 'It's moored up just beyond our two boats.'

Horton could see it at the end of one of the pontoons. On board, he'd learned that Gordon Ames had had an affair with his mother, Jennifer, at the same time as she'd had one with his father, Viscount William Ames. Her aim was to infiltrate the viscount's ultra-right-wing organization. He knew Gordon wasn't his father because he was sterile. The viscount had arranged a meeting with Jennifer on board his yacht, taken her out into the English Channel and disposed of her. It hadn't been long after that he'd jumped overboard rather than risk being exposed as a fascist traitor and a killer.

Horton wondered how he would feel on seeing the boat again. He stood before it. There was no anger, no bitterness, no sadness — that had all been spent. But there was also no real closure. For Harriet and her family, not knowing if Richard was alive or dead, there would always be that yawning space, that question hanging over them. For Horton too. Although he tried hard not to think about it. He wasn't sure how he would feel if he came into contact again with either Gordon or Richard.

'What will you do with it, Don?' *Just don't ask me to sail her*, thought Horton.

Don scratched his chin. 'I've been wondering what Lord Ames would have wanted. It seems insensitive using it after what happened. They say he got caught in the fog and was knocked overboard, or slipped and fell. Are you superstitious?'

'I think we all are to an extent.'

'You wouldn't sail her?'

'No, and I can't see Harriet doing so either. Did she bring it over?'

'Yes, but she made it quite clear she wouldn't sail her again. I'll put her up for sale.'

Horton had been thinking of buying a bigger yacht — now that Emma wouldn't be staying with him quite so often as he had hoped and anticipated, meaning he didn't have to rent a flat for her sake — but he could never buy this one.

'The money will help keep our two yachts well equipped and we can run more sailing courses for our youngsters and traumatized veterans.'

Horton was relieved. Harriet would be too.

'Do you want to go on board?'

'No.' Horton was adamant.

They walked back down the pontoon. Winscom said, 'That's Gideon's yacht.' He pointed to one on the next pontoon. 'Hello, there's someone on board.' Horton saw a slender, long-legged blonde in her early twenties. 'That's Tiffany Nichols. Would you like me to introduce you?'

Horton said he would and they made their way towards the boat. Winscom greeted Tiffany warmly. She looked harrowed, understandably so given the recent death of her grandfather. Winscom made the introductions, omitting Horton's rank and that he was a police officer, saying instead that he was one of the charity's volunteer skippers.

'I'm sorry to hear about your grandfather,' Horton said. 'Don's told me a lot about him.' He hesitated, wondering if it would be insensitive to ask her now about the funeral, but after all this was an unforeseen opportunity. 'In fact, I came not only to tell Don I'd like to volunteer my skipper services again but because I had a question about your grandfather's funeral.'

She looked alarmed.

Horton quickly reassured her. 'I'm a police officer. I don't know whether you've heard, but Juliette Croft was found dead on the morning of your grandfather's funeral.'

'Oh, yes. I see. Mark told us.' She climbed off the boat and joined them on the pontoon. 'I felt awful when I found out because I was so angry when she didn't show up to conduct the funeral, and so upset. Grandma was in pieces. Rachel, from the funeral directors, stepped in and it was OK but we felt so let down by Juliette. We'd come to know her so well. She spent hours and hours with Grandma and my dad going over everything, and looking through photos, talking about him.' She pushed a hand through her hair as the wind whipped it across her unblemished face. Her nails were bitten right down, the fingers raw. 'This is Grandpa's boat. I loved sailing with him.' Her blue eyes welled up. 'I slipped out of work to come here to be near him.' She pulled herself together with effort. 'But why are the police involved? Mark told us it was suicide.'

'We're having difficulty tracing her next of kin.' He didn't see the need to tell her more. 'Did she speak about her family?'

'Not to me. She might have done to Dad and Grandma. You can ask them but Grandma's pretty upset, as you can imagine.'

'I won't trouble them unless it's absolutely necessary; maybe you could ask them for me?'

'You can ask Dad yourself, here he comes.'

Horton turned to see a wiry man in his early fifties striding up the pontoon with a worried look on his gaunt, lined face.

Don quickly introduced Horton. After offering his condolences, Horton asked if Juliette had mentioned any family.

Lee Nichols shook his head. 'All she said was that she was widowed and knew what grief was like. It's hard to believe she took her own life. We had no idea she was feeling so desperate, she never gave any hint of it.'

'Do either of you recall seeing a man at Mr Nichols' funeral — mid-fifties, distinguished looking, greying streaks in brown hair, dressed in black but wearing a yellow shirt?'

Tiffany answered first. 'I don't but it was all a bit of a blur. Dad?'

'I knew everyone who came — Dad's friends, our staff, clients and relatives — and there weren't any strangers. Tiffany, I need you at work.' She pouted. To Horton, Lee said, 'We're busy, and Dad wouldn't want us to let down any of our clients. He built the business up from nothing. I've not only lost a father but a great business partner.'

Horton got the impression that Lee Nichols wasn't very sure of himself. Maybe he'd lived in the shadow of his energetic and successful father for so long that it had chipped away at his self-confidence. Or perhaps he hadn't been born with a large dose of his father's vigour. But then Horton was seeing him at a highly charged time. Tiffany and Lee both carried the burden of grief heavily.

Tiffany said she'd lock up and Horton left them to it.

'She's a nice young lady,' Winscom said. 'Gideon's death will leave a gaping hole in their lives. You'll let me know about Sunday?'

'Yes, later today, after the results of the autopsy on Juliette, in case there's any immediate action I need to take.'

'I understand.'

They shook hands. Winscom waved to Cantelli, who had pulled in by the car park. Behind him Horton could see a sports car with a personalized number plate that he judged to be Tiffany's, and beside it her father's silver van boasting the name of the company, Nichols Event Management.

'How did you get on with the Barlows?' Horton asked, reaching for his seat belt.

'Neither Mr Barlow nor his son or daughter-in-law remember seeing the man in the yellow shirt. There were about fifty mourners. Georgina Barlow was well known at their local church and had been a member of the Women's Institute until her stroke nine months ago. Mr Barlow had been trying to cope with her care at home, with the aid of carers, but it all got too much for him, especially as he's not in the best of health. Georgina moved to a nursing home three months ago. He met Juliette there when she was singing to the residents. When Angie Lindley mentioned her being a celebrant, he was happy for her to officiate.'

'Don doesn't recall Yellow Shirt either, and I've spoken to Tiffany and Lee Nichols — they were here. Gideon's boat is in the marina. Both are pretty cut up, as you can imagine.'

'Same with the Barlows. Neil, the son, said they were all too emotionally charged to note everyone and could easily have missed him. They only really acknowledged those who came up to them after the service. I remember that at Dad's.'

Toni Cantelli had been a very well-respected Portsmouth businessman and was much loved by his family and friends.

'You don't really see anyone when you're following the coffin inside, you're too uptight and distressed. Then, after it there's a whoosh of relief. You've been on a kind of adrenalin rush, taking you through the funeral, and it's still there afterwards. I was busy talking to people, some of whom I hadn't seen for years, relatives who had come over from Italy, and I was looking out for Mum, making sure she was OK. You might note the occasional person you haven't seen before, perhaps someone from the hospital or a care home, or an old work colleague or neighbour, but before you can really register them they're gone.'

Horton remembered that feeling at both his foster parents' funerals. Bernard's had been packed with former and serving police officers, and Eileen's, not long after, with many friends whom Horton hadn't known.

'Mr Barlow said that Juliette was very empathetic and easy to get along with but they know nothing of her personal life.'

'The same with Tiffany and Lee.' Horton's phone went. 'Walters.' He put it on loudspeaker.

'We've got a result, guv. Wilde and Straw Solicitors have called to say they drew up Juliette Croft's will. They're in the High Street in Old Portsmouth. Ms Straw, who prepared it, says she can see someone at two. Do you want me to go?'

'No, we'll head there now. Anything come in on Juliette?'

'No. Any joy with Yellow Shirt?

'None. Let's hope we get some with the will.'

CHAPTER EIGHT

'Mrs Croft was most insistent that no copy of it was to be kept by us.' Ms Straw waved them into seats in her poky, old-fashioned, cluttered office in a narrow listed building in Old Portsmouth, squeezed between a public house and a convenience store. Her small, rotund figure was almost submerged by the folders, papers and books piled on her desk, as well as on the mantelpiece and the floor. Not everything, it seemed, was on computers these days, although there was one on Ms Straw's desk — state of the art by the look of it, thought Horton, which made him again wonder about the whereabouts of Juliette's laptop. It might be a mystery they'd never solve. Despite Ms Straw's diminutive stature, she was no shrinking violet, more like an old-fashioned sergeant major with her short, square-cut, iron-grey hair on a square, stern face. About mid-fifties, Horton guessed. Her greeting had been curt but not hostile, and behind her similarly square-shaped tortoiseshell spectacles there was a lively glint. She and her partner didn't handle criminal law, so they were unknown to Horton.

'Isn't that unusual?' asked Cantelli.

'It is, but not unheard of. I take it you being here means it wasn't among her possessions?'

71

'No.'

'She might have kept it at the bank.'

'Possibly, but most of the high-street banks — if you can find one — don't have safe deposit boxes anymore.'

'Didn't she tell her executor where it was kept?'

Horton answered, 'He believed it to be in the house, and he's unaware of its contents.'

'Well, he'll need the original for the probate application. I suppose she could have deposited it with another law firm, although I doubt that, given I drew it up.'

'What happens if it can't be found?' Cantelli asked.

'The executor will need to apply to HM Courts and Tribunals with the death certificate and evidence that he's the executor.'

'What kind of evidence?'

'A copy of a letter, text or email from the deceased asking him and/or confirming it.'

Horton didn't think Mark Lindley had that, from what he recalled of his conversation with him and with Angie. They said that Juliette had asked, face to face. No mention that the request had been backed up in writing. 'But you can bring evidence, Ms Straw, to say she told you who she wanted her executor to be, hence you put it in her will.'

'I can, but how do we know that the will she asked me to draw up is the final one? She might have changed her mind two days or two weeks later and made a new one.'

'When did she make this one?' Horton needed to check if the timing fitted with what Angie Lindley had told him.

'End of June.'

Angie had said two months ago, so that seemed about right. He doubted Juliette would have changed it that quickly.

Ms Straw said, 'You could check if the will is registered with the National Probate Registry in Newcastle. You, or the executor, can search for it online, for a fee, but as there isn't any debate that a will was made there's probably no point in you doing that.'

'Her executor is Mark Lindley.'

She tapped into her computer. 'Yes. That's who I have named, but he isn't the beneficiary.'

'Who is?' Cantelli got there before Horton.

She peered at them. 'Under normal circumstances I wouldn't be able to say, client confidentiality and all that, but as Mrs Croft is not a client, except for having paid us to draw up her will, and as you say the will is lost, then I don't see why I shouldn't tell you. First, though, why the interest? Are you treating her death as suspicious?'

'We're keeping an open mind until we have the results of the autopsy,' Horton answered.

'Being cagey, eh? Fair enough.' She again scrolled down the file on her computer. Looking up, she said. 'Her sole beneficiary is Rodney Pierce.'

Unfortunately for them, Pierce was a common enough name, thought Horton. 'Did she specify how she knew him, or why she'd named him?'

'Nope.'

'Any address?' asked Cantelli, pencil poised.

'She didn't know it.'

'Why not?'

'She didn't say and I didn't ask her. None of my business.'

Perhaps at the time of making it she didn't know his whereabouts. He could have been travelling for his job. He could have been living and working overseas. Portugal came to Horton's mind. Could Pierce have been her partner there? But why would she leave him her estate, especially if she'd left him at the beginning of last year when she returned to live in Portsmouth?

'She gave me a date of birth, so you can probably trace him,' Ms Straw added. 'The second of February 1970, which makes him fifty-two.'

A vision of the man in the yellow shirt flashed into Horton's mind. He knew it had crossed Cantelli's too, although he gave no sign of it.

'There was nothing else in the will. It was very simple.'

'Who witnessed it?' asked Horton.

'My secretary and my partner; Aynsley Wilde.'

Horton heard a telephone ring in the outer office. 'What happens if we, or her executor, fail to find Mr Pierce and a will?'

'Then the rules of intestacy will come into play. If there is no spouse, or civil partner, which seems to be the situation here, then next in line are children.'

'There's no record of her having any. Would a stepson inherit?'

'Stepchildren don't benefit under the laws of intestacy.'

So Rodney Pierce couldn't be the stepson because his surname would have been Croft.

'However, legally adopted children and their descendants do benefit.'

'No record of that either.'

'I take it there are no living parents?'

'No. We have their death certificates.'

'OK, so if there are no children and no parents living, then next in line are brothers or sisters, or any living descendants of deceased brothers or sisters, such as nephews or nieces.'

'None of those either,' said Cantelli.

Ms Straw tapped her pen on the desk. 'Any living half-brothers or half-sisters, or any living descendants of deceased half-brothers or half-sisters, such as half-nephews or half-nieces?'

'Not that we've unearthed so far. But I suppose there could be,' Cantelli answered doubtfully.

'If there are no living grandparents — which in this case there can't be unless they're superhuman — next in line are living aunts or uncles, or living descendants of deceased aunts or uncles, or any living half-aunts or half-uncles, or living descendants of deceased half-aunts or half-uncles.'

'It sounds very complicated,' Cantelli said, smiling. He'd ceased making notes.

'And time-consuming, which is why probate hunters exist.'

And Horton knew one who had helped them recently on a case, Nicola Bolton.

'If there are none of these then the whole estate goes to the Crown.'

'I think we'd better try and find this Rodney Pierce,' Cantelli said pleasantly. 'Be a shame for the Crown to benefit.'

Horton said, 'Juliette might have given him her will and he's unaware of her death.'

'Well, if you don't find a will then the courts and tribunal service will consider the evidence in the applications procedure for a lost will. If the application is successful, the executor will be able to apply for probate; if not, that brings us back to intestacy,' said Ms Straw.

'So Rodney Pierce will have a strong reason to find the will, if he doesn't already have it.'

'Yes. And he'll need to prove that he is *the* Rodney Pierce who Mrs Croft intended to leave her estate to. His birth certificate should confirm that, unless there are two, or more, men with that name and that date of birth, alive or deceased, because if the real Rodney Pierce is deceased then his beneficiaries would inherit. I hope you have both made your wills.'

'I have,' Cantelli said firmly.

'Me too.' Horton had updated his after his divorce, and again after Catherine had hitched up with Peter Jarvis, changing it so that Emma got everything. There was no need to make sure Catherine was provided for. On her forthcoming marriage she would have more money than she would know what to do with.

'What can you tell us about Mrs Croft?' he asked.

'Pleasant, friendly, but not chatty. She wanted to get down to business and that was fine by me.'

'What made her come to you? Were you recommended?'

'She said so, but I don't know by whom.'

'How did she pay?'

'I'm not sure. I'll ask my secretary.' She rose and crossed to a door. 'Zoe, can you come in a minute?'

Zoe confirmed that Mrs Croft had paid by debit card. It was from the same bank they had noted, to which they could apply for access to her accounts if the autopsy found homicide.

There was nothing more that Ms Straw could tell them. Outside, Horton immediately rang Walters. 'See what you can get on a Rodney Pierce, born second of February 1970. He's Juliette's sole legatee. Get on to it right away. We're heading back.'

'Righty-ho.'

As they walked along the High Street towards the car, Horton said, 'Ms Straw has confirmed a point that's been nagging at me. Don't you think it strange that there was no will in that document folder yet all the other documentation was there?'

'I do. Who would have an interest in taking it?'

'Someone who hopes the estate will be intestate, who doesn't want Rodney Pierce, or that will, to be found. Who does that suggest to you?'

'Walters hasn't had any luck in finding a relative.'

'And it's not our job to do so, not unless that person killed her to inherit.'

Cantelli unlocked the car. 'This will could have replaced an earlier one with a different beneficiary who was told he or she would be cut out of the new one. Or Juliette might have made another since June, which is why we can't find it. She destroyed the one Ms Straw drew up.'

'And we'd be very suspicious if someone suddenly pops up waving it.'

'They might not be very bright, hence the botched job with the champagne, glass and tablet bottle. This person could have nipped upstairs and taken the new will after Juliette's death. Or perhaps they took it some time ago when in the house on a friendly visit. Did it strike you that Rodney Pierce's year of birth puts him in the age bracket for Yellow Shirt?'

'It did.'

Cantelli turned the vehicle round and headed north.

'I wonder how much her estate is worth,' Horton pondered. 'There's the house, of course, unless she has a mortgage on it. And she could have other savings.'

'From ill-gotten gains in Lisbon?'

'We don't know that. Everything points to her being a decent, law-abiding citizen. The trouble with us is we're just naturally suspicious.'

'Goes with the job.' Cantelli grinned.

'Yellow Shirt could be connected with her in Portugal and finally tracked her down.'

'Where to? I mean us. Back to the station?' Cantelli said hopefully.

'And your sandwiches.'

'I'm hungry and it's way past feeding time.'

Horton's phone rang. 'Dr Hobbs.'

'I've completed the autopsy on Juliette Croft and sent tissue samples for analysis,' he said. 'There's something I'd like to discuss with you. Are you able to get over here?'

'We'll be there in ten minutes.' To Cantelli, Horton said, 'Your sandwiches will have to wait — that is, if you still feel like eating them after a visit to the mortuary.'

'Better than eating them before.'

CHAPTER NINE

'It looks to be a case of death by natural causes,' Hobbs declared.

Then why are we here? thought Horton, as the smell of the mortuary churned his stomach. He stared at the naked, lacerated body of Juliette Croft, trying hard not to compare it with the lively, attractive woman he'd seen in those photo albums. That person had long since departed this life.

He looked up at Hobbs the other side of the slab, a small man in his mid-forties with sharp, intelligent eyes and a keen expression. Brian, Gaye's favourite mortician, was clattering some instruments in the background, whistling 'Surrey with the Fringe on Top' from *Oklahoma*, his favourite Rodgers and Hammerstein musical, and making a good job of it. It seemed a bit out of place, but then Brian worked here, and Hobbs didn't seem to mind.

'As you can see, and as you noted at the scene, Inspector, there are no obvious signs of foul play, no blunt-force trauma, no stab wounds, and no evidence of asphyxiation. She was a very healthy woman, especially for her age. Some signs of arthritis in her hips, the left one in particular, some in her left foot but negligible. And although I said cause of death looks to be from natural causes, there are no obvious signs of that. For example, there is no evidence of cardiac arrest, or that she suffered an aneurism or stroke. There are also no obvious signs of poisoning. I say "obvious" in that there was no swelling of the limbs or liver inflammation, but many poisons only show up in the tissue, blood and urine analysis, and I won't have those results until Monday at the earliest. I understand an empty bottle of tablets was found beside her.'

'Yes, but we have no idea what they contained, unless our forensic expert has found traces inside and can identify it.'

'I also understand there was an empty bottle of champagne beside the deceased.'

'Yes.'

'Then I can tell you she didn't drink it. There is no trace of alcohol in her system.'

'We suspected that because of the absence of smell in the room and on her clothes. Did you find anything significant about her clothes when she was undressed?' Horton could see them on the bench behind the body.

'No. And I agree, no smell of alcohol on them. No traces of blood on the clothes either. We've taken fibre samples. The clothing wasn't soiled or stained in any way, but your forensic expert might be able to get more from them and the fibres. There was nothing under her fingernails or in her hair, but again scrapings and samples have been taken in case something shows up under closer examination.'

Cantelli was jotting down some points while he chewed his gum.

'There are no needle marks. She wasn't raped and neither had she had sex recently. But there is evidence that she'd had a full-term pregnancy.'

Horton glanced at Cantelli, who ceased chewing. He knew they were both thinking alike. Juliette's legatee — Rodney Pierce?

'Any idea how long ago?' Horton asked.

'No, but given her age, and the fact the pitting isn't as sharp as it might be on the posterior surface of the pubic bone, it could have been fifty years or so.'

Again that fitted with Pierce's age. Horton said, 'Did she have more than one pregnancy?'

'Impossible to say for sure, but probably not, given that her overall health, and bone and muscular condition, is good. As to time of death, I've taken samples of the fluid behind the eyes, which could pinpoint it more precisely once it's analysed. Flies have laid some eggs, and lividity is well established. The contents of her stomach were partially digested. I'd therefore estimate time of death anywhere between twelve and sixteen hours before she was found, which I see from the report was three fifteen Wednesday afternoon.'

Horton did a quick calculation. 'She died then some time between eleven thirty Tuesday night and three thirty Wednesday morning.'

'It could have been earlier but not later than that.'

'And being dark, and night, no chance of anyone being seen entering and leaving the house, *if* they did.'

'They might have done and administered poison, but not by force. There's no evidence of that around her mouth and throat. If poison shows up to be the cause of death then it wasn't an agonizing one, because there are no facial contortions. I also understand there was no sign of her having thrashed about in that room.'

'Correct,' answered Horton. 'How do you account for those items being laid out so neatly on the table, with no prints and nothing in them?'

'She might have taken a substance earlier, and voluntarily. Before it could take full effect, she set the scene, wiped her prints from the items, lay down and slipped away.'

Exactly as Horton had conjectured. 'Then it was suicide.'

Cantelli looked up. 'But why bother with all that?'

Hobbs shrugged. 'That's just a theory, and we'll need to wait for the full analysis to confirm it. But one thing makes it less likely.'

Horton listened eagerly.

'There is bruising on the back of her shoulders.'

80

'Couldn't that have been caused by a fall?' Cantelli asked. 'She took the drugs, staggered and fell before collapsing on the sofa, after previously setting the scene.'

'No. Because these bruises are post-mortem.'

Horton eyed him, baffled. Cantelli stopped chewing. 'You're saying that someone moved her after death?' Horton said.

'Yes.'

'And that person set the scene?'

'That's for you to establish.'

Cantelli said, 'But how can you tell they were made after death? I'm not doubting your expertise, Doctor, but could they have been caused by changes in the body?'

'No offence taken, Sergeant,' Hobbs answered brightly. 'They're valid questions. And you're right, it's not always easy to correctly interpret bruising in a cadaver. It might be caused by the post-mortem changes, as you indicated. I therefore needed to consider whether the tissue disruption was before or after death. Let me explain: Bruises should not occur after death because many of the bodily process have stopped, right?' Cantelli nodded. 'But a heavy blow after death can cause blood vessels beneath the skin to rupture and bleeding to occur. In living tissue the bruise will contain a large number of white cells, part of the body's immune system to combat infection and help the healing process. In a bruise that occurs after death there are a lot fewer leucocytes or white cells. I conducted a microscopic examination; there are hardly any white cells.'

Horton's mind raced. 'Could she have been struck after death?'

'Difficult to say, but there was no sign of impact or damage to the brain or skull, and no broken bones in the shoulders.'

'Could someone have physically held her down using his or her hands and caused the bruising?'

'Again hard to say. The bruising is across the back of her shoulders; it looks as though she was dropped against

81

something while being carried, but not far, as there are no hand or fingerprint marks under her armpits.'

'So she couldn't have died upstairs and then been carried or dropped down the stairs?'

'No, there would have been a great deal more bruising over a wider area. From the photographs taken at the scene, I'd say she was lifted on to that sofa and, in the process, was dropped, possibly against the edge of the coffee table.'

'Lifting a dead body takes some doing.' Horton rapidly considered this new and puzzling piece of information.

'Yes, and while she wasn't a big woman it would still have taken some considerable effort, especially to lift her up and put her on the sofa.'

'It's a low one,' Horton said, recalling its modern style and metal legs. 'They wouldn't have had to lift her very high. Nevertheless, it must have been someone very strong, or possibly two people were involved.' And did they kill her first by doping her? It would explain why the items on the coffee table had been wiped clean, and the absence of fingerprints on the table. But why not leave some champagne in the glass and bottle?

'She could still have drugged herself voluntarily, then someone found her dead and moved her out of sympathy,' Hobbs suggested. 'They realized their prints were on the items, and in the room, and didn't wish to be implicated. And, of course, we don't know yet that she was drugged.'

'But she died of something,' Cantelli offered.

'Yes. And although it's rarer in women than in men, she could have died of sudden death syndrome. However, I didn't find any evidence of thrombus, plaque rupture or erosion, or haemorrhage into a plaque or critical coronary stenosis in the major coronary artery.'

Cantelli blinked. He didn't bother jotting down this medical jargon in his notes.

'And neither does she fulfil the criteria for a different type of sudden death, i.e. alcoholism, obesity and hypertension-related cardiomyopathy, or primary myocardial fibrosis.

That doesn't mean she didn't die of it. We need to wait until we have the results of all the tests. I'll do my best to fast-track them. I'll let you have my full report in due course, and I'll also send it over to the coroner.'

Outside, Cantelli looked flummoxed. 'Well, that's a turn-up for the books. Why on earth would someone move her and set that scene so clumsily? And they took a chance on not being seen, although I admit it was dark at the time of her death. Could this Rodney Pierce have done it?'

'If he's Yellow Shirt then the description of him doesn't suggest a strong man; no one's said he was big and muscular. But he sounds as though he's fit. Distinguished with a good bearing suggests he could be a military man, or a veteran, and maybe because of that moved around a great deal, which was why Juliette had no idea where he was living.'

'Do you think he's her son?'

'I'd say it's a possibility, but why take the will?' Horton stepped around a group of doctors in conference in the corridor.

'Maybe he didn't. Juliette had already ripped it up, and now he'll come forward. He doesn't have to wave a will, just claim he's her son and DNA will prove it.'

'If so then he badly needs the money.'

CHAPTER TEN

'He doesn't,' Walters announced on their return, after Horton had updated him. 'Rodney Pierce made the *Sunday Times* Rich List a few years back and for all I know he could be on this year's.'

'Are you sure you've got the right man?' Horton said disbelievingly, while Cantelli paused in the middle of eating his sandwiches.

'Positive. I checked out his birth certificate. Parents Joseph and Alma Pierce from the Isle of Wight. His birth was registered in Portsmouth under the name of Rodney, the date of birth tallies. I thought I'd do a search for him on the internet and bingo, there he is in all his glory, worth millions.'

'He might have spent it all,' Cantelli said, munching again.

Walters eyed him disdainfully. 'Unlikely. And he wouldn't have gambled it away, because it's those suckers he made his fortune from.'

'Don't tell me he owns a chain of betting shops and online gambling sites,' Horton said, peeling off the plastic film on his vending machine sandwiches, thinking of their spate of robberies.

'No. He founded a computer games company way back in the Stone Age. Developed some very successful games that he then sold or licensed, not sure which, and amassed his first fortune. After that he teamed up with a guy called Bob Spiley, expanded the business, developed more successful games, sucking in the punters, getting them hooked and making themselves megabucks.'

'Seems easier than rushing into a betting shop with a machete wearing a balaclava.' Horton bit into his ham and cheese. 'How do you know it's our Rodney Pierce?'

'There's an article on his rise to fame and glory on a techie website. It says he was born and raised on the Isle of Wight, left there at seventeen to seek his fortune in London, and it gives his month and year of birth — not the actual date, I admit, but it has to be the same man.'

'OK, we'll go with that for now. Go on.'

'He sold out to one of the big boys in the States eight years ago and made even more megabucks. Spiley died of a heart attack a month before the deal was done, so never got to spend the fruits of his labour. I guess Pierce took it all, unless Spiley's will left the shares in his company to his relatives. But you can't keep these techy geeks down. Pierce set up another company almost immediately, specializing in developing holograms and artificial intelligence. He's probably well on his way to making yet another fortune.'

'And us all redundant,' muttered Cantelli. 'Robot police.'

'They've already got robot police dogs and drones in some countries,' Walters replied.

Horton said, 'Then it won't be long before they get a robot DC Walters who won't even need to stop work to be fed every half-hour.'

'I'm not the one filling his face with sandwiches,' Walters quipped, good-humouredly. 'To get back to Pierce: his company website reads like a sci-fi movie, but from what I could grasp they're involved in providing holographic services and products based on augmented reality technology and artificial intelligence.'

'What's augmented reality when it's at home?' asked Cantelli.

'I'm sure Ellen would be able to translate,' Horton said, thinking of Cantelli's eldest daughter. 'But as she's not here Walters can enlighten us, because he must have looked it up.'

'Didn't need to. I understood that bit at least. Augmented reality's been around for a while, Sarge. It takes something from the real world, say South Parade Pier, and enhances it with computer-generated visual elements, sounds and other stimuli.'

'Smell?'

'Probably. It'd be fish and chips at the end of the pier.'

'Or seaweed or sewage.'

Walters rolled his eyes. 'Instead of, or as well as, seeing a couple of people walking down the pier, you could see, and hear, a giant shark rising up over the railings, about to gobble them up. Jaws hits Southsea.' Walters chuckled. 'We've had interactive computer games for a while, which is what Pierce and Spiley successfully developed. You can get augmented reality headsets, and they're developing contact lenses that display AR imaging.'

Cantelli shook his head sorrowfully. 'The mind boggles.'

Walters continued. 'Pierce's new company takes it further. As I said, they specialize in the development of holographic AR entertainment products, which they say on their website is going to be the next big thing. They're developing an interactive virtual reality holographic-imaging system based on artificial intelligence technology; translated into English, that means the holograms are so real you'd be hard put to know that it's a hologram.'

Horton finished his sandwich. 'It makes *Star Trek* look positively ancient. And it doesn't fit with Pierce botching a phoney suicide.'

'Not unless he wanted to make us think it was a stupid or careless person,' Cantelli ventured.

'I can't see someone like him going to all that trouble.'

'Maybe he employed someone not very bright to do it and they cocked up,' Walters suggested.

'Or maybe he was nowhere near there because we've got the wrong Pierce, or because if we have the right one he certainly wouldn't need Juliette's inheritance. I suppose he lives in London.'

'He might have a place there but his main residence isn't far from here. I got his address from the electoral roll and Companies House. It's Chidham Creek House, Chidham, West Sussex. I looked it up on the internet, and, as expected, it's a ruddy great mansion that runs down to the Bosham Channel into Chichester Harbour.'

Horton knew it and the harbour well, having sailed there many times. On the opposite side of Chidham was the ancient, small and highly popular village of Bosham, once the home of smugglers and fishermen, now primarily that of the wealthy and second-home owners. It had a popular and elite sailing club, a pub, a couple of art galleries, and a Saxon church where King Canute's eight-year-old daughter was buried in a Saxon coffin, having drowned in the Brook Stream there.

Cantelli said, 'Could Juliette have given him up for adoption? Things were very different in the 1970s. She would have been under pressure.'

But Walters was shaking his head. 'The birth certificate is a standard one, not an adoption certificate.'

Horton consulted his watch. It was just after four. 'We'll give it an hour and then see if he's at home, either virtually or in reality.'

'He might offer you cocktails,' Walters joked. Then more seriously, 'He might not be at home. Maybe you should telephone him, guv.'

'How? Is his personal number on the website?'

'No, guess not. But he could be in the office in London.'

'If he is, and if he was available to speak to me, then telling him Juliette is dead is hardly the sort of thing you'd discuss over the telephone. For all we know they could have been very close. If he's not at Chidham Creek House then it might involve a trip up to London tomorrow.' Horton could ask the Met to speak to Rodney Pierce, or the West Sussex police as Chidham was their patch, but that meant he wouldn't be able to see Pierce's reaction. And they wouldn't know the right questions to ask. He probably didn't know them himself, but they would come to him when he spoke to Pierce. He also decided to postpone telling Reine about this development, and of Dr Hobbs's findings. He wanted to speak to Pierce first to be certain they had the right man.

Just over an hour later, he and Cantelli headed east out of the city towards Chidham. The early evening had clouded over and it looked like rain. He called Don on the way to tell him that he'd be able to skipper his crew on Sunday. Cantelli was duty CID and there wasn't anything they could do on the Juliette Croft case until they had the results of the tissue and blood tests. Walters said there had been no response to their appeal on the website and Leanne Payne's silence indicated she had nothing from her article, unless she was keeping something up her sleeve for a follow-up piece.

The roads were choked with traffic. An accident on the dual carriageway approaching the town of Havant held them up for a considerable amount of time. Horton was tempted to put the blue light on but held back as they were soon due to turn off from the worst of it, which stretched on towards the cathedral city of Chichester.

Some forty minutes later, following Horton's instructions, Cantelli indicated right into a country lane with fields stretching out either side of them. A left turn took him down a single-track road set deep in the fields surrounding it. It was a dead end, which Horton knew from the map on his phone and from his knowledge of the area. It culminated in the creek. Before they reached it, though, a sign on their right announced the private road to Chidham Creek House. There were no gates or intercom. They probably didn't need it, thought Horton, it being a secluded location.

After about three-quarters of a mile of beautifully manicured trees and hedges bounded by pasture and meadows, the house came into view. Cantelli gave a low whistle. 'Walters was right, I don't think Mr Pierce is short of a bob or two.'

Horton had half expected an ultra-modern building, given Pierce's high-tech background. Instead he was looking at a new house built in traditional red-brick, designed in the manor house style with a stone-pillared entrance and stone steps leading up to a stout, carved oak door with an arched window above it. Either side of the door were two large bay windows. On the first floor, six sash windows were separated by a large arched window above the porch, and there were four more windows in the roof. It was beautifully proportioned and graceful. Perhaps this was an antidote to modernism. Inside might be state of the art.

Cantelli drove around the circular flowerbed, complete with statuette, and pulled up at the entrance. To the right of the house was a garage complex with what Horton assumed was also living accommodation, judging by the windows above the doors. Parked in front were a Ferrari, a Maserati and an Aston Martin. Goodness knew what high-end vehicles the other two garages contained.

'They can't all be his,' Cantelli said, climbing out.

'By their personalized number plates I'd say they are. Perhaps he uses a different one depending on what day of the week it is.'

'Do you think a butler will answer the door?'

'Probably, but he might be a hologram or a robot.'

He was neither, and he was a she. A small Filipino woman in her late thirties dressed in a maid's uniform, complete with frilly apron and white cap, eyed them warily. Cantelli blinked as though in shock, while Horton quickly made the introduction with a show of his warrant card and asked to speak to Rodney Pierce before Cantelli could say, *Is your master at home?*

'I'll see if he's available, sir.' She pushed the door to, leaving them standing on the top step.

'Have we arrived at a fancy dress party?' Cantelli said, sotto voce. 'Or perhaps we've entered one of Pierce's time warp holograms. I've only seen maids dressed like that on TV period dramas. We could be on camera.'

'We probably are.' Horton looked around. Nothing obvious, but there was bound to be CCTV somewhere.

The woman returned, followed by another in her mid-forties, extremely well groomed with perfectly highlighted blonde hair, immaculately made up, with a sharp-featured face and penetrating, hostile grey-blue eyes.

'I'm Mrs Pierce. That will be all, Selina.'

The maid scuttled off. Horton had half expected her to curtsey.

'We'd like to speak to your husband, Mrs Pierce.' He noted the expensive jewellery and well-fitting blue dress that showed a figure of gentle curves in all the right places. Nothing off the peg here. He also suspected the high-heeled shoes were handmade.

'He's busy and we're expecting guests for the weekend at any moment.' She consulted her diamond-encrusted wristwatch to stress the point.

Pleasantly, Horton continued, 'We won't keep him long.'

'If it's concerning business then you can return during office hours.'

'It's not.' Horton didn't elaborate, and held her hostile gaze.

'Then what is it about?' she snapped.

'We need to speak to Mr Pierce.'

Her eyes narrowed and her lipsticked mouth tightened. Then a wary expression, tinged with suspicion, crossed her face. Horton could guess that she was rapidly trying to calculate what her husband had done that warranted such secrecy and the presence of two detectives.

'I'll see if he's available. You'd better step inside,' she said with ill grace. They did, and she closed the door behind them. 'Wait here.' She clip-clopped away on the tiled floor.

'I should have doffed my hat,' Cantelli whispered.

'You're not wearing one.'

'If there was a mat I'd wipe my shoes. This hall is bigger than my house and my neighbour's put together. Must cost a bundle to heat.'

'I don't think they're worried about their heating bills, or any others come to that.'

'How many rooms do you reckon it has?'

'Hundreds.'

'I'm disappointed about the butler.'

'He's probably in the kitchen, polishing the silver.'

'Look out. Here he comes. Pierce, I mean, not the butler. Well I never.'

Horton knew what Cantelli was alluding to. Walking towards them was a man in his mid-fifties, brown hair flecked with grey, clean-shaven, about five feet eleven, slender, distinguished looking, wearing casual clothes of excellent quality. Save for the absence of a yellow shirt he fitted the description of the man at Juliette's funerals to a T.

'I'm Rodney Pierce and I'm very busy. What is it you want?' He didn't offer his hand.

'Is there somewhere we can talk, Mr Pierce?'

His eyes narrowed. He looked as though he was tossing up whether to say it's here or nowhere, but turned and opened a door to their right. Cantelli raised his eyebrows before following Horton into the vast room with strategically and artistically placed modern furniture, exquisite rugs on a parquet floor, expensive artwork on the walls, and a white grand piano in the wide bay window overlooking the grounds at the front. Pierce didn't invite them to sit, but stood just inside the room in expectation that they would soon be leaving. Cantelli removed his notebook and pencil. Pierce glared at the items.

'Is that necessary?'

'Memory's not what it used to be, sir,' Cantelli said jovially. 'I expect you have to write notes too.'

'I can't see that anything I have to tell you would be worthy of writing down. Well, get on with it.'

'Your date of birth is the second of February 1970?' said Horton.

'Yes, so what?' he snarled. 'This isn't about identity fraud, is it?'

'No, sir, it's about the death of Juliette Croft.'

'Who?'

'She lived in Portsmouth and was a celebrant at funerals.' Horton watched him carefully, knowing Cantelli was doing the same. Pierce gave nothing away. His face was a mask of harsh blandness.

'What has that to do with me?'

'She named you as a beneficiary in her will.'

'You've got the wrong Rodney Pierce. I don't know anyone called Juliette Croft.'

'We're quite certain, sir, and your date of birth confirms it. It's extremely unlikely that there are two gentlemen with your name and date of birth.'

'But not impossible. I have no idea who she is.'

'Then why should she name you?' Cantelli asked, giving his best dumb copper impression, while pointedly chewing his gum.

Pierce's gaze was withering but Cantelli didn't budge an inch. 'Maybe she picked me off the internet and managed to get hold of my date of birth. It's not impossible, you know.'

'Why should she do that?'

'You're the detectives, not me.'

Horton answered. 'Yes we are, sir, and that's why we're here. Mrs Juliette Croft, a widow, was found dead on Wednesday. There are some questions surrounding her death that need further investigation. One of them is that she named you in her will, which suggests she must have known you, and we're trying to discover her next of kin and more about her. Could she have been a former employee of your company?'

'No.'

'Or a freelancer you used for something connected with your business — computer games, isn't it?'

'I sold that business years ago. And no, she has never been a freelancer.'

'Perhaps you met her at a funeral,' Cantelli suggested.

'I didn't.'

Horton had another go. 'Could she be someone you helped in the past by giving a donation to a charity she worked for, or was involved with in some way?'

'How many time do I have to say it? I've never heard of this woman. Now, I have things to do.' He opened the door, but Horton stood firm, Cantelli by his side.

'She might have been a friend of your parents?' said Cantelli.

'She wasn't.'

'Are they both living? Perhaps we can ask them.'

'They're not. So you can't.' He marched into the hall, expecting them to follow.

Horton walked slowly after him, Cantelli trailing in the same leisurely manner. 'She was also a singer at care homes and retirement complexes. Could she have come across you then? Perhaps you have a relative in a place like that, or your wife does.'

'Neither of us do. If you have further questions, although I can't think what they would be, then call my PA and make an appointment.' He wrenched open the door.

Mrs Pierce crossed the hall, looking thoroughly out of sorts. 'The first of our guests are arriving, Rodney.'

'These police officers are leaving.'

A car was pulling up in front of the garage complex.

'We're sorry to have troubled you, sir, madam,' Horton said. 'It's always disturbing when someone dies in suspicious circumstances, and we have to get answers from many people connected with Juliette Croft.'

Coldly, Pierce said, 'I was not connected with her. You've made a mistake.'

'Perhaps your wife knows her?'

'She doesn't.'

'Mrs Pierce?'

'I've told you she doesn't.'

'I was asking your wife, sir.'

'I have no idea who she is,' insisted Mrs Pierce.

Pierce looked as though he'd like to shove them down the steps. Horton could see a couple in their forties by a Range Rover parked next to the Aston Martin. The man was looking at the car, the woman towards them.

'Aren't you curious about how much she left you, Mr Pierce?' Cantelli asked.

Mrs Pierce dashed a startled glance at her husband.

'Do I look as though I need money?' he snapped.

'I guess not,' Cantelli laconically replied, letting his gaze roam over the house and grounds and coming to rest at the garages. 'Nice cars.'

The couple in front of them waved. Mrs Pierce made to move.

'Oh, just one more thing,' Cantelli continued in his best police manner, 'do you own a yellow shirt, sir?'

Mrs Pierce stalled. Her husband blinked hard and looked stunned. 'No, I bloody don't.' He swung back into the house, while Mrs Pierce glared at Horton and Cantelli before beaming at her guests and striding towards them.

Cantelli took his time getting into the car, while Horton did the same. Mrs Pierce was chatting to their guests and, Horton thought, deliberately keeping them back until they left. He saw them all look their way. He wondered what she was telling them, and why Pierce hadn't gone to greet them.

Cantelli started up. 'I had an incredible urge to say, "Goodnight, sir, sorry to have troubled you, sir," in my best grovelling PC Plod voice, and salute as though I was in *Dixon of Dock Green* with my helmet on.'

'They'd have taken it as genuine. Make a hash of driving off as you go round that statue.'

'Why? To annoy them?'

'Partly. I want to see their expressions.'

Cantelli stalled the car. The guests looked amused. Horton wasn't sure of Mrs Pierce's expression. There seemed an element of smugness about it, but he could be mistaken.

Cantelli started up again and they drove slowly down the road. A Bentley coupé was heading towards them. 'Bet he reverses before I do.'

The driver did so with an expression of irritation. Cantelli, with his window down, gave a royal wave as they passed him at the entrance.

'Not very friendly, the Pierces,' he said, heading towards the main road. 'About as welcoming as Sheila Cranley but without the swearing.'

'We came at a bad time.'

'Huh! Is he our Pierce?'

'I'd say so, wouldn't you? Although I admit there's only his date of birth to indicate that.'

'Was he lying about not knowing Juliette?'

'If he wasn't then why did she choose him as her legatee? She couldn't have picked his name at random.'

'He looks remarkably like our yellow-shirted man. But I can't see him going to funerals. He'd be far too busy and important for that. And as for driving to Portsmouth in one of his expensive cars, getting into Juliette's house — even if he was invited — and setting that scene . . . no, it doesn't ring true. He's too clever to make a hash of it — unless, as we already said, he did it deliberately to make it look like it was someone stupid. But I still can't see why he'd bother. Not unless he wanted desperately to get his hands on that will, to obliterate all contact between himself and Juliette.'

'It's a good point, but a man as intelligent as Pierce would know that taking the will wouldn't be enough. He'd reckon that both the executor and the lawyer who drew up the will would know his name and would be able to locate him.'

'He didn't ask how she had died or express a single ounce of regret. A cold fish, I'd say,' declared Cantelli.

'Yes, a hard man. Maybe that's what helped him to become so successful. That's not a crime, and neither might Juliette's death be, except for someone moving her body and failing to report it.'

'But did they? Mark Lindley could have moved her. Maybe there's a connection between him, Rodney Pierce and Juliette. Lindley says he hasn't seen the will and doesn't know who the beneficiary is, but that could be a lie.'

Horton recalled his conversation at the pub with Lindley. He had seemed genuinely concerned and harrowed, which could have been the result of a trying day. Lindley had requested the meeting; was that in order to lay a false trail? No, he was ninety-nine per cent certain Lindley had nothing to do with Juliette's death, save reporting it.

Cantelli continued, 'Pierce didn't like it when I asked about Juliette being a friend of his parents, or if they were still living. I know he was itching to get rid of us by then, but he didn't even blink.'

'Are they dead?'

'Don't know. We haven't checked. I'll see what I can get tomorrow.'

Although Cantelli was duty CID, that didn't mean he had to be in the office, only on call. 'Leave it until Monday, Barney. He might have fallen out with his parents a long time ago, and if he did it's not our concern. And nor is Juliette naming him as her legatee. But I'd like to know who moved her body even if the test results come back positive that it was a drug overdose, which could have been self-administered, according to Hobbs's findings.'

'And if they come back negative? Then what did she die of?'

Horton shrugged. He was curious to know more about Rodney Pierce. His copper's instinct told him there was something wrong about the man, and he didn't mean just his bad manners. There was one person who could tell him, or find out for him: Mike Danby, ex-job, now running his own security and close protection company for wealthy and high-profile individuals, and Pierce was certainly the former. Yes, a call to Danby might prove informative.

CHAPTER ELEVEN

Saturday

'Do you know a Rodney Pierce?' Horton asked Danby early the following morning after his run.

'No, should I?'

'He's seriously wealthy and I'd say has need for security. But I suspect he already has some, although there was nothing obvious at his property.'

'Are you looking for a referral fee?' Danby joked.

'No, information.'

'I might have known.'

'Fancy a coffee?'

'Can't you tell me more over the phone?'

'I can but I'd rather see your ugly mug.'

'Where?'

'Haslar Marina café in forty minutes.'

'Might as well, seeing as I've got nothing else to do except run a very busy and profitable company.'

'Then it'll do you good to take a break. See you in the café.'

Horton got there before Danby but only just. Yes, he could have told Danby what he wanted over the phone, but he preferred to do so face to face. And he had been going to Haslar Marina anyway to familiarize himself with the yacht he was to sail tomorrow for Go About. Earlier, he'd called Don, who'd said he would leave the boat's keys in the marina office.

Danby was carrying a little more weight than when Horton had last seen him, and his hair was thinning, but he looked fit, well and affluent.

'A few more grey hairs, I see,' Horton teased him when they had coffee in front of them. The café was quiet.

'What's left of them. And I'd have more grey ones if I'd stayed in the job. Better start counting yours unless you're keen to come and work for me. I'll make sure you don't get the contract for Jarvis. I hear he and Catherine are getting married in December.' Danby handled the security for Jarvis's numerous properties and sometimes provided bodyguards on his superyacht when sailing in more precarious waters.

'You hear right.'

'They seem to be happy.'

'I'm sure they are.'

'And Jarvis seems to be doing well with all his investments, at least well enough to keep paying us. Catherine's going to be working for him, or *with* him, I should say.'

That was news to Horton, as he guessed Danby knew it would be, and there was no point in pretending otherwise. 'She's giving up her marketing director job at her father's company then?'

'Yes. End of October, and the house is going up for sale, which you probably know about already.'

'First I've heard, but then I don't have a stake in it. She got the house, I got to keep my pension, if I reach that age. No reason for her to tell me.' He spoke casually but felt that knot of sorrow tinged with anger inside him. It wasn't the divorce — he'd reconciled himself to that a while ago — it was the loss of what had once been his home, even though he hadn't set foot in it for two years. It was what it had represented. Now it would be a final break with the past. For a while he, Catherine and Emma had been happy there. But there was no point in dwelling on that. It couldn't be changed.

'Have you heard anything more about Richard Ames?' Danby asked before Horton could get down to business. He might have known their conversation would turn in that direction because Danby's company provided security for the Ames family. He'd also provided close protection for Richard Ames when he had been on overseas trade missions.

'No. You?' Horton said lightly, although his pulse beat a little faster. Danby had been a good cop and was shrewd. He could smell lies.

Danby shook his head and drank some coffee. 'You know Harriet is working for the Hampshire and Isle of Wight Police?'

'Yes. She came to the station in July to talk to Cantelli about a case she was reviewing.'

'It's against her family's wishes, and it makes it difficult for us to protect her.'

'Do you need to?' Horton asked, alarmed.

'She's not in any obvious danger, but if it's known who she is she could be a target for kidnap and ransom demands. I know that doesn't happen often in this country but there are some nasty bastards out there, as you and I well know. And if they find out she's rich, the daughter of a peer of the realm — or I should say sister, when Alastair inherits the title — and she's a copper, then some evil sod might lick his lips, rub his hands and think he's on to a winner.'

Horton's stomach lurched at the thought.

'And she's living in that big house all alone on the Isle of Wight,' Danby added. 'Oh, we've got security on it but it's isolated in terms of its location. And if I was a villain, which thankfully I'm not, then I'd approach by sea.'

Horton shifted uneasily as he envisaged the pontoon that led to a very private shore and the back wall of the property with a gate in it — secured yes, and, as Danby said, with cameras and sensors, but what if Harriet turned them off or forgot one night? It must be incredibly lonely for her there. He felt an urge to talk to her, but what would he say, *Make sure you lock all the doors and windows*? Hardly. She was a copper and an intelligent one at that. And he could scarcely suggest she'd be better off living somewhere smaller. It was none of his business.

Danby was saying, 'I think she's only staying there because Alastair's adamant she should chuck in her job and return to the family pile in Wiltshire.'

Horton didn't like the sound of that. It smacked of bullying on her brother's part. 'And do what?'

'No idea. It looks as though Alastair will get a Declaration of Presumed Death on his father. He's had favourable feedback on his application. He filed it on behalf of his mother shortly after Richard disappeared, so it should be through by October.'

Horton wondered if the intelligence services would have a quiet word in the judge's ear to make sure it was approved.

'I don't think Richard killed himself,' Danby continued. 'He was mad to go out in that fog. It was an accident waiting to happen. Once he's officially declared dead, Alastair can apply for probate. He's the executor as well as main beneficiary.'

'Doesn't it all pass to his mother, Lady Isabel?'

'No. Alastair inherits the title, the estate, all its properties and everything in it. There is a trust for Lady Isabel providing an income, and she can stay in the main house until she dies or until they come to another arrangement. But as you probably know, she's wealthy in her own right as well as being a successful and sought-after interior designer. Richard's shares in his companies go to Alastair and Louis equally.'

'Doesn't Harriet get anything?'

'I think she's the main beneficiary in her mother's will.'

'And in the meantime?'

'Alastair will make her an allowance, no doubt.'

'On a certain condition,' Horton said acidly. No wonder she had looked so angry with her brother when Horton had by chance seen them together at Oyster Quays in late July. 'That she quits her job. She won't do that.'

'Well, that's their business.'

'And how do you know all this?' Horton didn't think Harriet would have taken Danby into her confidence.

'The Ameses are my clients.'

'Yeah, and you're telling me confidential information about them.'

'Hardly. The will is in the public domain. So too is Alastair's application to formerly declare his father dead. Don't you read the papers?'

'Not if I can help it.'

'What do you want to know about Rodney Pierce, and why do you want to know it?' Danby was changing the subject, Horton thought, to avoid telling him who had leaked inside information on the Ameses' affairs.

'Tell me what you've got first.'

Danby gave a crooked smile. 'You probably already know it, but, seeing as you bought coffee, I'll oblige.'

He relayed what Horton had already learned from Walters' research, adding that Rodney Pierce was well on his way to earning more zillions with his latest company.

'OK, now tell me what's he done to grab the attention of CID.'

'Nothing except be named in the will of a dead woman as her sole beneficiary. And he denies knowing or having heard of her.'

'You've interviewed him?'

'Yes, at his house at Chidham. He wasn't exactly welcoming.' He told Danby about Juliette.

Danby looked puzzled. 'He certainly doesn't need the money. I don't know who handles his security but I can find out. Did you see any security personnel there?'

'No, but then they'd hardly be in uniform patrolling with dogs. Times have changed. All I saw was a maid, and she didn't look like security in disguise.'

'He's probably got a chauffeur as a bodyguard.'

'He's got some expensive cars. There are no gates to the grounds.'

'He must have sensors and alarms linked to a company that can be there in minutes if needed. The police would take far too long to respond.'

'Oh ye of little faith.'

Danby grinned. 'I can't see him being involved in anything like covering up a suicide, or participating in murder, if it proves to be that. What would be his motive? It's too risky.'

'He must have taken risks in business.'

'Yes, but not the kind that would put him in prison.'

'Not even financial ones?'

'I'll ask around, see what I can pick up — discreetly, of course.' He drained his cup. 'Funny things, wills. They can often bring out the worst in people. Not everyone is fair when it comes to legacies, especially where their children are concerned. That is, if the other half has gone first. Families fall out, as we well know. And the rich and famous often do things differently.'

Horton thought of Harriet. 'Has Pierce got kids?'

'Don't think so. But you can check.'

They would.

Danby said, 'There could be a reason why Juliette named him and why he denied knowing her: he was adopted.'

'He wasn't.'

They parted company with Danby promising to be in touch. Horton made his way to the charity's yacht. It was larger than his own but easy enough to handle, especially with a crew. Don had sent him their details. He had three veterans: two ex-army — one of whom had had some experience of sailing, which would be a help — the other ex-navy. They would be fit, able and willing to do as instructed. The other two were young men aged nineteen and twenty-one, both of whom were on community service but had shown a willingness to reform. The boat had all the latest equipment. The weather was set fair for tomorrow with some cloud, bright spells and a moderate south-westerly. Horton spent some time looking at the chart plotter, deciding where to go. He wanted a sail with enough to make them work, and with a reward in sight, which meant a pub lunch, no alcohol. Yarmouth or Cowes on the Isle of Wight.

He thought of Harriet taking out this yacht, or the other one the same make and size as this. She was a highly competent sailor. He could see Ames's yacht across the pontoon, and wondered how much influence she'd had in donating it to the charity. Richard Ames's will seemed quite unfair, but Horton didn't see her accepting an allowance from her brother; she was too strong-willed, independent and proud for that. Why hadn't Richard bequeathed her something, a lump sum perhaps, even a small legacy or allowance? Had she annoyed her father so much that he had cut her out, if she had ever been included in the first place? Was she excluded because she was female? Surely those days had vanished with the Victorians — or was it still practised among the gentry, with the first son getting the main share, the other sons diminishing amounts or property, and the daughter nothing? After all, it was expected she would marry well and have a dowry settled on her. Yes, those days were long gone, except where Richard Ames had been concerned, it seemed.

As Danby had said, wills were funny things and many a family fell out over them. Would Harriet fall out with hers? It wasn't his business whichever way he looked at it. Was Juliette's will his business though? Possibly.

CHAPTER TWELVE

Monday

'Rodney Pierce's mother is alive,' Cantelli declared as Horton walked into CID.

'Is she now?' Horton put his helmet on the desk beside the sergeant.

'What's more, she's living in a care home about two miles from him. With all his money, you'd think he'd have put her in one of those rooms in that big house.'

'She might have complex nursing needs that prohibit that.'

'She might, but from the Inlands Care Home website it doesn't look as though they specialize in that. They have thirty residents, and also provide respite care. Alma Pierce receives her state pension, which is how I got her address, after establishing there was no death certificate for her. The rest of her care is paid for privately, not by social services.'

'Then Pierce could be funding it. He lied to us because he doesn't want us to disturb his mother by questioning her.'

Cantelli looked dubious. 'Then he should have said. I've also discovered that he has no brothers or sisters.'

'And his father?'

'Died in 1987. Death registered on the Isle of Wight, that's as far as I've got.'

'Not bad going for eight o'clock.'

Cantelli grinned. 'It was bugging me on and off all weekend. I was awake early and it was going around my head, so I thought I'd come in and do some digging.'

'That's usually my problem, the not sleeping. For a change though, I've had two good nights. Must be all that sea air.'

'The sailing went well?'

'Brilliantly.' After the initial problems of awkwardness and some sulks on the part of one young man, the team from Go Ahead had settled in well on Sunday. He hoped the rest of their week went well with another of Don's more regular volunteers. Horton hadn't realized how much he had missed skippering a crew. 'I spoke to Mike Danby on Saturday morning. He's going to see what he can pick up on Pierce, even though it's not really our concern. It's not Pierce we're investigating. And it's nothing to do with us who Juliette left her estate to, unless she was drugged, and that might have been self-inflicted. Nor is the fact that Pierce lied to us about his mother being alive any of our business.'

'Then we don't pay her a visit?'

'No need to. On the other hand . . .'

Cantelli smiled. 'She might be able to tell us more about Juliette and why she named Alma's son as her beneficiary.'

'Which in itself is not—'

'Our concern,' Cantelli repeated jokingly.

Walters meandered in. 'Anything happen over the weekend, Sarge?'

'Very quiet. For us, that is. Uniform were pretty busy with the usual — fights, domestics, antisocial behaviour. I didn't get called out once, no betting shop robberies.'

'Maybe you and the guv put the frighteners on Damien Cranley when he saw you at Granny's, if he's involved. Just don't ask me to go and interview her. I'd like to hold on to my—'

'I know.' Cantelli held a hand up.

'I was going to say hearing.' Walters smiled. 'But I can get Damien's address and, if he's not shacked up with Grandma, I could go and have a nice quiet chat with him and find out where he was on the nights the betting shops were targeted.'

'He'd only lie to you,' Horton replied. 'Let's see if Jago comes back with something more concrete first. Check if anything's come in on Juliette, or if Leanne Payne has been contacted by anyone. Cantelli will tell you about our meeting with Rodney Pierce on Friday and what he's discovered.' Horton addressed Cantelli. 'We'll give the Inlands staff a couple of hours to get their residents up, washed and fed. I'm going to grab some breakfast.' He had skipped it, opting instead for a run along the blustery promenade. Dumping his jacket and helmet in his office, he saw from the window that Uckfield's BMW was in the car park. Uckfield had been leading a murder case in the New Forest. He found the super in the canteen tucking into a full English. Horton bought the same and took the seat opposite.

'You look tired, Steve.'

'So would you if you'd been up all night. Worth it though, got a result. Picked the bugger up three hours ago. Won't say a dickie bird until his lawyer arrives, which will be later today; they don't come out after dusk or at the weekend. Meanwhile, he's sticking to his story like glue: yes, he was inside that house, but he had already left before the victim was killed. Someone must have gone in there after him. But an eyewitness saw him leaving at the critical time, and we have a motive — thwarted love. He found out she was having an affair with his best friend, who corroborates it.'

'Congratulations.'

'I'll accept that once he's owned up to it. Which might not be until the "guilty" verdict, and then the bugger will still proclaim his innocence and say it's a police fit-up. But that poor woman deserves justice and so too do her family. I've left DI Dennings and DCI Belmont to handle it.'

Belmont headed up Southampton CID.

Uckfield pushed his empty plate away. 'I only came in to see what I've missed while wallowing in the depths of Southampton and the New Forest.'

'We have a suspicious suicide.' In between mouthfuls, Horton told him about Juliette Croft, the post-mortem bruising, the difficulty in finding a next of kin, Rodney Pierce, and that they were awaiting the results of blood and tissue tests.

'It all sounds a bit weird, but then everything does after thirty hours working non-stop.' He scraped back his chair. 'My head won't cope with anything more complicated than simple emails. I don't know why I came in anyway.'

'Because you love us,' Horton said.

'Yeah.'

Horton returned to his office, where Walters told him Leanne had had no response to her article. 'She might be telling porkies, keeping any news to herself for a bigger story. She pressed me for more information and asked what the autopsy results were. I fobbed her off but I'm sure she'll ring you sometime.'

Sure enough, she called in the car when Horton and Cantelli were heading out of Portsmouth to the care home ten miles east of the city. Horton repeated what Walters had already told her, and said he'd let her know as soon as they had something to report. She also asked him about the betting shop robberies, to which he replied that they were pursuing certain leads.

The early morning traffic had eased and it wasn't long before Cantelli indicated left off the main road by an impressive church spanning the corner of the small yet ever-more sprawling village of Southbourne. A hundred yards down on the left, he pulled into a car park and drew up in front of a modern building in good condition with gardens either side of the driveway and trees screening it from the road. A skinny woman in her mid-twenties with red-rimmed eyes, a nose ring, tattoos and an anxious look answered the door. Horton made the introductions and they showed their warrant cards. He asked to see the manager, and they were shown through a clean and pleasantly furnished bright hallway to an open door on the right.

'Kerri, these men are police officers.'

The woman was in her forties with long dark hair swept back off a round, kindly face into a ponytail; she looked wary and weary. After scrutinizing their warrant cards, she gestured them into seats the other side of a low table in the corner of her office. She nodded at the care assistant to indicate she could leave, and gently pulled the door to behind her but didn't close it.

'We'd like to speak to one of your residents concerning a possible friend,' Horton began. 'We're unaware of the state of her health and don't wish to alarm or distress her. The matter is confidential, but if she requests your presence then we're more than happy with that.'

'Which of our residents is it?'

'Mrs Alma Pierce.'

Confusion crossed the young woman's face. 'Alma? I'm sorry, you can't.'

'We'll do our best not to upset her.'

'It's not that. I'm afraid she can't speak to you.'

Horton wondered if Rodney Pierce had got here before them and told the manager that no one, especially the police, was to speak to his mother.

'If her son has given you instructions—'

'Her son? Are you sure it's Alma Pierce you wish to see?' Kerri looked bewildered.

Cantelli answered. 'Date of birth, the third of April 1939.'

'Yes, that's her. I'm afraid Alma Pierce passed away last night.'

Horton's shock was reflected in Cantelli's expression.

'I'm sorry to hear that,' he said, quickly recovering, while his head was spinning with suspicious thoughts. But he told himself it was expected. She had been frail, hence her being in the care home. Their timing had been unfortunate. They were just a little too late. 'Was she very ill?'

'She had a pacemaker and various health issues but nothing to indicate her passing so suddenly. She was such a lovely lady. Even though she hadn't been with us long, she was a delight. A quiet, kindly and patient lady. Very spry too. Everyone loved her. It's all been a dreadful shock.'

That explained the red eyes and harrowed looks. Before Horton could speak, Kerri was ploughing on. 'I think the outing yesterday must have been too much for her. She never had any visitors but yesterday a man called for her.'

Horton's ears pricked up at that and Cantelli stiffened.

'Her son, Rodney?' Horton thought he must have come here after they'd seen him on Friday in order to tell his mother to lie for him.

'She didn't have any children,' Kerri said, confused. 'She lived on the Isle of Wight for years. Her son was killed in a car accident there when he was seventeen.'

Horton resisted a glance at Cantelli.

'She was as surprised as we were when she had a visitor yesterday. He took her out for afternoon tea.'

Why was Horton getting a bad feeling about this? Cantelli must have been too, as he was frantically jotting in his notebook.

'Did she know this man who took her out?'

'Oh, yes.'

It had to be Rodney Pierce. She had told the care home staff he was dead rather than suffer the embarrassment of him never visiting, writing or calling her. Now he'd been forced to do so by their visit to him, fearful they would find out he had lied about his parents being dead. But why should that matter so much? Can't lock a man up for that.

'Can you describe him?'

'I didn't see him. Yvonne, one of my staff, told me about him.'

'Do you have his name?

'Yes. Trevor Dorne.'

So Pierce had used a false name. But then Horton did a double-take — why would he have done this, and why should Alma have gone along with it?

109

'Is Yvonne working now?'

'Yes. She's very upset about Alma's death, as are we all.'

'Can we speak to her?'

'But why are you so interested? I don't understand.'

'It's difficult to explain at the moment.'

'I'll fetch her for you.'

'This is a rum do,' Cantelli said once she'd left. 'Could it be Pierce?'

Horton didn't get a chance to answer, as Kerri returned almost immediately with the same thin young woman who had admitted them.

Horton said, 'We won't keep you a moment, we just wanted to ask you about Mrs Pierce's visitor yesterday.' He invited her to take a seat. She perched on the edge of it and Kerri took the one next to her. 'You haven't done anything wrong,' he reassured her. 'We'd only like some information. Can you describe this visitor?'

'He was tall, brown hair, going grey.'

She seemed to dry up. Cantelli took over. 'What was he wearing?' he asked in a light, kindly manner.

Horton thought she wasn't much older than Ellen, and the sergeant had identified with that.

'A blue polo shirt and cream-coloured trousers.'

'Was there a logo on the shirt?'

'It wasn't Ralph Lauren, or a sporty one like Nike or Adidas. It looked a bit like a trumpet. He had a good watch on though — dunno the make but looked expensive. He spoke nicely, not loud or bossy like some you get. Very friendly.'

That didn't sound much like Pierce from their encounter, but then he could have put on an act to see his mother.

'Did he show you any identity?' asked Horton.

She shifted. 'No. He just said his name and would I ask if Mrs Alma Pierce would see him. She was over the moon. I was so pleased for her because no one ever came to see her and she was such a lovely lady. I'm sorry . . .' Tears rolled down her face and she dashed them away with her hand. Kerri put an arm round her shoulder.

'I'm sorry to upset you,' Horton said gently. 'It must have been a terrible shock for you.'

'It was. Alma was absolutely no trouble. Always pleasant and chatty. She was my favourite lady. And the first time she has a visitor, and he takes her out, she comes back and dies. It's as though she was waiting for that moment, and when it came she was happy and just let go.'

Maybe, thought Horton, if she had been reunited with her son, but he wasn't certain it was Rodney Pierce. 'What happened when you showed him in?'

'She was standing up. She smiled and asked if he would like some tea and said that I would get them some, but he said no, he'd take her out to tea if that was allowed. She laughed and told him she wasn't a prisoner. I helped her on with the cardigan and coat.'

'Did they speak while you did so?'

'No. Then Mr Dorne offered his arm and she left with him, looking that proud and as pleased as punch, and to think . . .' The tears sprang up again.

Horton said, 'Just a few more questions, Yvonne. What time was this?'

'About four o'clock or thereabouts.'

'And she came back when?'

'Just before six.'

'Had Mrs Pierce mentioned Trevor Dorne before?'

'No.'

'Did you see which car they got into?'

'No. They walked down the driveway. His car must have been parked in the road.'

'How was she when she returned?'

'Tired. But happy. I asked her if she'd had a nice time. She said they had a lovely drive to Bosham and had tea and cake. She said it was perfect.'

'And Mr Dorne, did he say anything?'

'He wasn't with her. He must have dropped her off. Maybe he watched her come in. I don't know because I wasn't looking out of the window. And to come in this morning to learn of the dreadful news.'

'Thank you, Yvonne. You've been very helpful. We're sorry for your loss.'

She rose and eyed them curiously. 'You being here and asking all these questions, does it mean there's something wrong about Mr Dorne?'

'We don't know. We'd just like to trace him. Oh, before you go, do you know a lady called Juliette Croft? Did you hear Mrs Pierce talk of her?'

'Course I know her. She comes here to sing.'

So that was the connection. Juliette was friends with Alma so she left her estate to Alma's son. But Yvonne scuppered that idea. 'Alma couldn't stand her. She said that woman gives herself airs, when she's no right to.'

To Horton, that indicated the two women had known one another. 'Did she say what she meant by that?'

'Thought she was stuck up, I guess.'

'And did Juliette say anything about Alma or speak to her?'

'No. Alma stayed in her room when Juliette was here.'

'What do you think of Juliette?'

She hesitated and flashed a glance at Kerri.

'It won't go any further,' Horton reassured.

'I thought Alma was right. Juliette thinks she's the cat's whiskers, and she's a flirt, especially with the men. Is that all? Only I've got to get back.'

Horton could hear voices outside. He thanked her and she slipped out. He turned to Kerri.

'What are your views of Juliette?'

'I haven't really got any. She has a powerful voice and knows how to charm an audience. The residents love her. I didn't know that Alma didn't like her. But why are you interested in Juliette Croft?'

'I'm sorry to say that she too has passed away, and we're struggling to find her next of kin. We believed there was a link between her and Alma Pierce.'

Kerri looked stunned. 'Was there? That's news to me. But then I'm not told everything.'

'Did Mrs Pierce leave a will?'

'Yes, but I don't know its contents, you'll have to speak to her solicitor, Charles Dingwall, at Emsworth. I haven't got around to telling him about Alma yet, there's been so much to do. There might be a copy in her belongings. I haven't gone through them.'

'But you must have details on file about who to notify in the event of her death.'

'Yes. Her solicitor.'

'No next of kin?'

'No.'

'How long had Alma been a resident?'

'She first came here at the end of March for two weeks, to see if she liked it, and moved in permanently at the beginning of June. As I mentioned, she had lived on the Isle of Wight.'

Cantelli looked up. 'Why did she move here? Why not a care home on the island?'

'She said she had always liked this area and that everyone she had known on the island had gone now. By that she meant they were deceased.'

'Who helped her to move?' Cantelli again.

'No one, as far as I know. The approach was made via St Mary's Hospital on the Isle of Wight by one of their adult social care team. Alma had suffered a heart attack in January and didn't wish to go on living in her home on the island. She arrived in a taxi with two suitcases. And stayed.'

'Do you have the name of the social worker?'

'I can look it up for you.'

'While you do, is it possible to see her room?'

'Of course. I'll take you there.'

'Who found her?' Horton asked as they made their way down the corridor to the rear of the building.

'Carol Chatlow. She works nights. She came to wake Alma at eight o'clock, as usual, just before she went off duty. I'd just come into work. I live locally.'

'Can you describe how you found Alma?'

'She was lying on the bed. She looked very peaceful, as though asleep. I could see instantly that she was dead, but I did all the necessary, checked for a pulse, then I called the doctor's emergency number and Dr Goodson came out, that was about eight fifteen.'

'And the doctor issued a medical certificate of death?'

'Yes. She'd seen her recently and there was a history of heart disease.'

'Could you give us the doctor's contact details and that of the solicitor?'

'I'll have them ready for you before you leave. This is Alma's room.' Kerri took some keys from her pocket and unlocked the door.

'You're welcome to stay,' Horton said.

'No need, I trust you, and I have a lot to do. We're always short-staffed.'

CHAPTER THIRTEEN

The bedsitting room was neat, clean, decorated in soothing colours and equipped with modern furniture. It looked very much like a respectable hotel room, Horton thought, glancing out of the single patio door into the pleasant garden, where he could see a couple of the residents seated. A door on the left of the room gave on to the bathroom.

Cantelli voiced Horton's thoughts. 'Bit of a coincidence Alma dying now, don't you think? I know it happens but this looks highly suspect to me. For a start, why did she move here from the Isle of Wight when there are perfectly good care homes on the island? If it was to be near her son then why didn't he help her to move, or admit to us she was here? And why not visit her? She's been here since June.'

'And Juliette entertained the residents but Alma never went to her concerts and didn't like her.'

'And why did Rodney Pierce use a different name, and one she recognized? Was it some kind of code?'

'God knows, but even if Juliette's death comes back as natural causes I'm not sure I'll believe it.'

'Me neither.'

'And I'm not sure Alma's was a natural death either. There was something crooked going on with these three:

Juliette, Pierce and Alma. What strikes you about this room, Barney?'

'No photographs of a baby, child or young man. Only the one on that small table of her and her husband on their wedding day.'

'She was very pretty, quite delicate.' Horton studied the shy young woman with a proud smile on her fair face beside a good-looking, muscular man. 'If she loved her son and lost him so tragically in a car accident, why not have at least one picture of him?'

'Because that was a lie.'

'Did you check to see if Alma and Joseph had more than one child?'

'No, but I will.' Cantelli crossed to the wardrobe while Horton tackled the chest of drawers.

'Not much here, just clothes and some jewellery.'

'Same here. No photos, letters, scrapbooks, nothing. It's as if she didn't have a previous life,' Cantelli said, baffled. 'Surely she must have kept something for conjuring up happy memories.'

'Maybe she gave them to a friend or relative for safe keeping.'

'Then why didn't they come to visit her? I know it's expensive travelling across to the mainland from the island but it's not that extortionate.' Cantelli reached to the top shelf of the wardrobe, from where he retrieved a suitcase. 'I wonder what her previous address was on the island. I didn't get that from the Department for Work and Pensions.'

Horton crossed to the bathroom. 'Kerri will have it. Nothing in there,' he continued, coming out. 'All her medication would be with the staff.'

'The suitcase is empty.'

Horton opened the bedside cabinet and found a novel, some handkerchiefs, a pen and a notepad. He flicked through it — nothing.

'It must have been a wrench getting shot of so many possessions.' Cantelli turned down the covers of the bed and ran his hand under the pillows. 'I'm assuming Alma had a house or flat and some furniture and ornaments.' He straightened up. 'Mum is thinking of moving. She says now that Dad's gone the house is too big for her and she's not getting any younger. She has happy memories there and I asked her if she would be sad to leave. She said the memories would go with her wherever she went and that she'd take those things that were precious with her, but as she gets older the tangible things mean less and less. Maybe that was how Alma felt. Mum said it's what's in here' — Cantelli tapped his forehead — 'that matters. Fortunately she's all there, but it's not so with some poor souls. Alma doesn't seem to have brought anything precious with her save that picture. Perhaps her memories were all inside her.' His face fell. 'I hope she had some happy ones.'

Horton did too. He locked the room and they returned to Kerri's office. She wasn't there but they waited while someone fetched her.

'I told Mum she could stay with us now that Ellen's moved out,' continued Cantelli. 'It would be a bit of a squeeze but both Charlotte and I said we'd manage. Mum won't hear of it though. She's considering one of those retirement flats. My sister, Isabella, is trying to persuade her to go and live with her, or at least stay for a while, but Mum is very independent.'

Kerri bustled in. 'Sorry to keep you waiting. Did you find anything that can help you?'

'Not really, especially as we're not sure what we're looking for,' Horton replied in a light tone. 'We're surprised Alma had so few personal belongings.'

'Yes, she said she wasn't sentimental but I'm not sure about that. She looked wistful many times, as though lost in her memories. She didn't speak of her past, which is unusual as most of us do as we get older and the past becomes more alive to us than the present. We used to ask her about it, to get her talking — and because we're interested, some people have fascinating tales to tell — but Alma never would. What's past is past, she'd say, and change the subject.'

'And that wedding picture is the only one she kept.'

'Yes. No. I'm sorry, I completely forgot. There is another one.' She opened a desk drawer. 'I didn't know if I should put it back in her room. Then I thought . . .' She looked downcast. 'I thought that maybe she would like to be buried or cremated with it. It was in her hand when she died. Dr Goodson found it.'

Horton took it. Joseph had his arm round Alma. She was wearing a chunky knee-length winter coat with a big collar and buttons. A beret was perched on her fair hair and a large handbag was draped over her gloved hand. Joseph looked smart in his collar and tie underneath his winter coat. He was wearing a felt hat. Behind them were the Christmas lights of what looked like Regent Street, London, judging by the buses and the display in the window of Hamleys toy shop. They looked happy. They must have asked a passer-by to take the picture. Maybe the trip to London was to mark a special occasion. It obviously meant something to Alma. They looked to be in their early thirties and, by the cars, he'd say the picture had been taken some time in the sixties. There was nothing written on the back.

Kerri said, 'Alma must have kept it in her drawer or in a handbag. She never showed it to us or mentioned it.'

'Can we take it? We'll give you a receipt.'

'Yes, of course.' She looked puzzled at the request.

While Cantelli wrote out a receipt, Horton said, 'If Mr Dorne gets in touch, can you get his contact details and let us know?'

'Certainly.'

'Was her body taken to the Portsmouth mortuary or to Chichester?'

'Portsmouth.'

Good, Horton wouldn't have to request it be moved then. Kerri gave them details of the solicitor, the hospital adult social care worker and Alma's previous address, which was in Carisbrooke, Isle of Wight. Horton requested that Alma's room be kept locked and that nothing be touched.

Kerri said, 'It wouldn't be anyway, not until the solicitor, or Alma's executor, instructs us.'

Outside, Cantelli said, 'Interesting that Alma never wanted to speak of the past.'

'Some people don't. But this picture found in her hand is curious. What does it indicate to you?'

'That she made a special point of getting it from wherever it was usually secreted. Why was it hidden away? It seems a perfectly innocuous picture, a happy one at that.'

'Yes. Was she reliving happy memories? Does it mean she had a presentiment of death or—'

'Took her own life,' Cantelli interjected, sorrowfully. 'No one mentioned drugs. She couldn't have ditched them in her room or we or the carers would have found them.'

'Perhaps she took them before returning to the home and they were slow-acting ones.'

'You mean Dorne could have supplied them?'

Horton shrugged.

'Why hold that picture? Why not her wedding one? This is getting more curious as we go. Where to now? Rodney Pierce to ask him about Alma?'

Horton looked at the time. 'No. We'll leave him until we get more from the solicitor. Pierce might be mentioned in Alma's will. Let's see if we can speak to Dr Goodson.'

Cantelli drove the short distance to the surgery, a modern building with a chemist attached and a car park facing onto the main road. He pulled into one of several empty spaces. Inside, Cantelli performed the introductions to the receptionist and a few minutes later a slender woman in her late forties wearing a well-fitting green dress and high heels greeted them in her consulting room. 'I was just grabbing some lunch. I understand you have some questions about Alma Pierce. Please sit down.'

'Did anything strike you as unusual about her death?'

'If it had I wouldn't have issued a medical certificate of cause of death.'

'Heart failure, I understand.'

'Yes. She suffered from pulmonary arterial hypertension — high blood pressure in the blood vessels that supply the lungs — and she'd already had two heart attacks. Both had hospitalized her.' She tapped into her computer. 'The last was in January. She was on the anticoagulant medication warfarin. I saw Mrs Pierce five days ago, last Thursday, when she experienced dizziness and angina. The staff called me out. Her angina was caused by overexertion. She'd been out on her own — which is fine, independence is good and exercise is to be encouraged, and she said she had only walked down the road. Even so, it was obvious she had overdone it. She seemed to have recovered as I wasn't called again until this morning.'

What Dr Goodson had just told them went some way to explaining why Alma had died earlier that morning. The unexpected visitor had created more excitement, which her heart couldn't take. But Horton was still cautious. And that picture in her hand bugged him.

'How long had she been dead?'

'A carer checked on her at eight thirty last night. Alma seemed in good health and spirits, although she said she was tired. Rigor was well established when I saw her, which means she had been dead from two to four hours. The carer found her at eight a.m. It's possible she died in the early hours of the morning, but I can't be precise.'

'So you had to prise the photograph from her fingers?'

'Yes. It was in her right hand.'

'And there was no sign that she had taken any drugs, other than those prescribed and administered by the staff?'

'None. Alma Pierce did not take her own life, if that is what you're implying.'

But how could she be so certain? Now for the delicate part of the conversation. 'I need to speak to the coroner, Dr Goodson, to request a post-mortem. I'm not doubting your diagnosis,' he quickly added at her dark look, 'but we need to be sure in light of the circumstances prior to her death, and another death that could have a connection with her.'

Her brow knitted.

'What I'm going to tell you is in the strictest confidence, but it will help you to understand why we're so cautious. Alma Pierce had a visitor yesterday afternoon, and neither we nor the care home know who he is. Yes, we have a name, and we will check it out, but it was the first visitor she'd had since living there, and she went out that afternoon with him. She seemed pleased when she returned home, but tired.'

'Then that could have overtaxed her and brought on the attack,' she said smartly.

'We have also discovered that she's the mother of a man called Rodney Pierce and yet she denied having a son. Mr Pierce, who we have spoken to, also denies having a mother in a care home, or alive come to that. What's more, Rodney Pierce is named as the sole beneficiary in a will made by Juliette Croft, whose death in Portsmouth is being investigated by us. Mr Pierce also denies knowing Juliette.'

Dr Goodson's cross expression was turning to one of intrigue.

'There has been a forensic autopsy on Juliette Croft and we're awaiting results of tissue and blood samples.' He wasn't going to mention her body being moved after death.

She sat back, considering this. 'You think Alma could have been drugged or given something to induce her heart attack and, feeling unwell, grabbed that photograph, which was obviously dear to her, but didn't pull the cord to alert the staff?'

'It's an option that we have to consider.'

Briskly, but not coldly, she said, 'In that case I agree regarding a post-mortem.'

'Thank you. Can you tell us, did Alma have a child or a pregnancy?'

'I don't have her records that far back.'

'Do you have a patient or know of a man called Trevor Dorne?'

'I haven't heard him mentioned. No, he's not listed as one of our patients,' she said after checking.

'Rodney Pierce?'

'He's not with our practice either.'

Horton said they would keep her posted. In the car, he called up the police computer on his mobile. 'No criminal record for Trevor Dorne. See what you can get on him, Barney, and I want to know more about Alma. Contact the hospital adult social care worker. Also, find out how long she lived at her previous address in Carisbrooke.' He punched in a number. 'We might be able to call in to the solicitor on our way back. Alma could have left personal documents with him.'

He was told that Mr Dingwall was on holiday and wouldn't be in until tomorrow. Horton made an appointment for eleven thirty. They had reached the outskirts of the city when Horton's phone rang. It was Joliffe. Horton put it on loudspeaker for Cantelli to hear.

'There's nothing significant on Juliette Croft's clothes save a few hairs that match her DNA and some others that don't. Nor do they match anyone on the database. They could have been picked up from a previous meeting. Nothing from the scrapings under her fingernails to indicate she scratched anyone or dug her nails into a substance.'

'And the items from the coffee table?'

'I was just coming to that,' Joliffe replied, frostily. 'There's no residue in the small tablet bottle. Nothing to indicate that any drugs of any kind had ever been in it.'

Horton glanced at Cantelli. 'It was put there to make us assume a drug overdose?'

'I have no idea *why* it was there, Inspector, that's your province. I can only tell you what I've found.'

Joliffe was his usual tetchy self.

'The champagne bottle had at one time contained what it says on the label — champagne, nothing else — and the glass showed no traces of alcohol. There are some fibres that suggest the latter was wiped by a cloth. Dr Pooley has all three items to see if he can get some prints from them.'

Horton rang off as Cantelli turned into the station car park. He hoped Pooley's sophisticated machines could perform some magic. But even if they got a print, it didn't mean to say the owner of it was on the criminal records, just as the unknown DNA was not on the database. But the fact that there were no prints, not even Juliette's, backed up their theories that this was looking increasingly like murder.

CHAPTER FOURTEEN

Superintendent Reine was not of the same opinion when
Horton sat in his office some ten minutes after his return.
Reine's view was that Juliette had drugged herself after setting the scene and that who she bequeathed her money to was
none of their business. Nor was the fact of Rodney Pierce's
parentage and Alma's death, which must be due to natural
causes. On the post-mortem bruising he said that Dr Hobbs
was probably mistaken. He didn't see any need for a forensic
autopsy on Alma Pierce, but Horton said it had already been
organized so they might as well proceed with it — a lie, but
he wasn't worried about that. Reine wouldn't check. He told
Horton to get his finger out and get some results on their
other outstanding cases, and wittered on about them being
rudderless without DCI Bliss at the helm. Horton refrained
from saying that made little difference and with her steering
they could easily end up stranded on a sandbank.

Nevertheless, as he returned to CID, stopping off to get
a coffee and a Mars bar from the vending machine, he felt a
small twinge of regret that Bliss wasn't there. Perhaps he was
coming down with a fever, he thought, smiling to himself.
He knew from experience that her views on the case would
have been the same as Reine's. But she had her uses. She was

124

good at deflecting the flak from Reine and making them look highly efficient even when they weren't. It wasn't in her interest to do otherwise because it would reflect badly on her, unless she could shift the blame if things went wrong. She had also become so skilled at taking credit, where it wasn't due, that Reine believed all their successes were down to her. But she was extremely efficient when it came to paperwork and number crunching, which cheered Reine up no end.

'I've found Trevor Dorne,' Cantelli reported, triumphantly, as Horton sauntered in.

'That was quick. Where? How?'

'He's dead. He was Alma's stillborn son.'

'He can't be, wrong surname, that would be Trevor Pierce.'

'It's not a surname. It's a middle name. Her baby was registered as Trevor Dorne Pierce.'

'So where does this lead us?' Puzzled, Horton flopped into the chair beside him and opposite Walters as he tried to fathom what was going on. 'That name was used for a reason and clearly with Alma's blessing.'

'There's more. Trevor Dorne Pierce's date of stillbirth is registered as the fifteenth of November 1969. The certificate was issued at Newport Register Office. As we know, Rodney Pierce's birth certificate shows his date of birth as the second of February 1970, issued on the tenth of March 1970 from Portsmouth Register Office, born to Alma and Joseph Pierce. Even in Walters' calculations that makes it the fastest pregnancy in human history.'

Horton took a bite of his Mars bar, considering this surprising information. 'They replaced their dead child with another.'

'Seems like it, and got away with it.'

'A baby snatch?' posed Walters.

'Could have been abandoned,' said Cantelli. 'Juliette would only have been seventeen. And you are talking about the early 1970s. A lot of stigma was attached to illegitimacy then.'

'I'd say Alma knew Juliette when both were pregnant. This new fact could explain why Rodney Pierce lied to us about not having a relative in a care home, which wasn't a lie because he knew Alma wasn't his mother. And he wasn't going to admit that Juliette was his birth mother because he was ashamed, or embarrassed, at the perjury.'

'He didn't come across as the type to have those emotions,' Cantelli said.

'Anger can be a cover for both. Juliette didn't know where her son was, hence no address, but she knew his date of birth all too well. And from what Yvonne at the Inlands Care Home told us about Alma never going to Juliette's performances, it indicates that Alma didn't wish to see Juliette, or was afraid to face her, because she didn't wish to be reminded Juliette was Rodney's birth mother.' Horton took another bite of his chocolate bar.

'How does it fit with Rodney Pierce calling on Alma on Sunday and using the name of her stillborn child?' asked Cantelli.

'A reconciliation?' suggested Walters.

Horton answered. 'Pierce doesn't seem the placating type, but I might be misjudging him.'

Cantelli said, 'It makes some kind of sense though because if he did know where Alma was, with us showing up saying Juliette had named him in her will and was dead, he was forced into visiting Alma. Maybe to tell her, or ask her, if she knew that Juliette was dead, and to agree what they should say to the police, knowing the birth certificate was a forgery and Alma had perjured herself.'

'According to the care home staff she didn't seem anxious or upset, quite the opposite.'

'Because it had brought Rodney to her door. Maybe that was why she moved there, to be close to him, hoping for a reconciliation, as Walters said. Perhaps using the name of her stillborn boy was a sign that he had something important to tell her, or he wanted to patch things up.'

Walters added, 'And that could fit with him being Yellow Shirt. He went to those funerals to see Juliette from a distance, perhaps out of curiosity. Or perhaps because he wanted to make contact with her but baulked at doing so.'

Horton frowned. 'I'm not sure I see him as the baulking type either.'

'Or the murdering kind?' asked Walters. 'Remember, I haven't met him.'

'We don't know that Juliette was murdered, as Reine was at pains to tell me. It's possible Pierce found her dead and then moved her to make her death look more dignified.' Horton finished his Mars bar. 'Although I can't see him in that role either. But he needs re-interviewing. We'll ask him tomorrow. He's not named as Alma's next of kin, so no need to rush round there, and the solicitor might be able to tell us more tomorrow morning. Pierce could be a beneficiary, and his birth certificate and that of the real Trevor Dorne are lodged with the lawyer. What do you make of that photograph found in Alma's hand, Walters?'

'I'd say they'd gone to see the Christmas lights in London as a rare treat, because travelling from the island to London would have been expensive.'

'It's not their wedding anniversary because the wedding photo shows a tree behind them in full summer leaf.'

'It's not their birthdays either,' said Cantelli.

'We'll probably never know.' Horton rose. 'I'll call the coroner.'

The forensic autopsy was agreed and Horton arranged with Dr Hobbs for it to be conducted on Thursday. He then rang Kerri to inform her. His third call was to Mark Lindley asking if he could call in to their office on his way home from work. Lindley said that he and Angie would be there until seven.

Horton settled down to his other cases, then just before seven made his way to Milton, where Angie offered him refreshment, which he declined. 'I won't keep you long,' he said, as Mark appeared from one of the offices off reception. Horton updated them on what they had discovered from

Ms Straw. He didn't say where Pierce lived, what he did for a living or how wealthy he was.

'I've never heard Juliette mention anyone called Rodney Pierce.'

'Me neither,' Angie concurred.

'Did she come here to meet her clients?' asked Horton.

'Occasionally for the initial meeting. Some people like to assess the celebrant on neutral ground, so to speak. Then, when they feel they've made the right choice, the celebrant visits them in their home.'

'Did she view the deceased in the chapel?'

Mark answered. 'Yes, always.'

That meant she had access to the rear of the building and the offices. Horton thought of Walters' comment about her stumbling across something that enabled her to black-mail Mark or Angie. He didn't think that likely but it had to be considered. He studied them to see if something was troubling them, but there was nothing other than bemuse-ment. Neither looked particularly sorrowful, but that was to be expected; they didn't know Juliette intimately.

Mark said, 'Should I contact Rodney Pierce? Being the executor.'

'Not yet. We have some further investigations to make. But by all means contact Ms Straw. She'll advise you on what to do if the will isn't found. Juliette's maiden name was Inglis and she came from Portsmouth. In fact, she was brought up in this area, does that mean anything to either of you?'

Mark shook his head. Angie looked thoughtful.

'It sounds familiar. I'm from round here. Perhaps my parents knew hers but that's a long time ago. And I can't ask them because they've both gone now.'

'I'll need to do something about her funeral,' Mark said.

'I'll let you know when we can release the body. We're waiting on some test results. There was one interesting thing that came out of the autopsy: Juliette's body was moved after her death.'

They both exhibited genuine shock and bewilderment. Mark eyed Horton keenly. 'Does that mean someone killed her?'

'No direct evidence of it, which is why we need the test results. Someone could have done it because they thought it more dignified. Tell me again what happened when you arrived.'

Lindley went over the events; they didn't differ from what Horton had read in his statement. 'Has anything new occurred to you since we last met?'

'No. And I haven't seen this man in the yellow shirt again, although there have been some mourners resembling him. I can't be one hundred per cent sure I would recognize him without the yellow shirt.'

Horton had one more question to ask. 'Do you know or have you heard of an Alma Pierce or a Trevor Dorne Pierce?'

They both looked at him blankly.

He'd got as much as he could, and he returned to his boat, convinced they weren't involved. Juliette had named Lindley as her executor because he was an outsider and the only person she knew competent enough to handle her affairs. Maybe she'd planned to make another will at some stage. Or perhaps she had been planning her own death, and that was why she'd named him. No friends had come forward after Leanne Payne's article, and no one had contacted them to say they were worried about not hearing from Juliette. It seemed to him that any friends she'd had must be in Portugal. Perhaps her stage presence — if he could call it that, performing at the care homes and at funerals — hid a shy, lonely woman who had found it difficult to adjust to living in England again. Was he wrong then to keep harping on about her being murdered?

He changed into his running gear, switched off his phone and went for a run even though it was getting dark. The lights were on along the prom. The night air was chill and the wind slight. He put all thoughts of Juliette and Alma from his mind, but as he saw the lights on the Isle of Wight across the starlit sea he couldn't help thinking of Harriet. He'd like to have seen her and perhaps talked over this case with her. Then there was Gaye, who would have been as intrigued as he was about Juliette and Alma's deaths.

Reaching his boat, he switched his phone on, to see he'd missed a call from Mike Danby. He rang him back.

'Pierce's security is handled by Kingston Meyer. Ed Kingston is ex-Met and Justin Meyer ex-army intelligence. They're a good company. I've spoken to Dave Hallet. He acts as Pierce's chauffeur and personal bodyguard.'

'He needs one?'

'Pierce obviously thinks so. Hallet lives on the premises, by which I mean Chidham Creek House.'

'So—'

'How do I know this? Hallet approached me last week asking for a confidential chat. He's keen to move on.'

'Why?'

'Why not? He needs a new challenge and my company do have an excellent reputation.'

'You could have told me this on Saturday morning,' grumbled Horton.

'I could, but why make it too easy?' Danby smirked.

'And you wanted to sniff around a bit more.' Horton stepped down into the saloon. 'What else did he tell you?

'Pierce, a difficult man at the best of times, has got worse in the last three months. Hallet said he's fed up being nursemaid to a sociopath. He has an office in London but often works from home, as do most of his staff of six, plus a private personal secretary, Miranda, who arranges all his travel, meetings and correspondence, and liaises with a management consultancy Pierce retains to advise him, who are also London based. Hallet's a former SAS officer with experience in intelligence.'

Horton hadn't seen him on Friday but perhaps he had seen them.

'Oh, there's one more thing that might interest you. I spoke to Louis Ames about Pierce — just dropping his name in casually, nothing to raise any suspicion.'

'Harriet's brother. Why?'

'He runs a software development company.'

Horton had forgotten that. Harriet had mentioned it once.

'He knows Pierce well. But from what I gather he doesn't like him. That could be because they're competitors of a kind, although Ames admits Pierce is streets ahead of him. But he hinted that Pierce's business methods might not always be as pure as they ought. He's cut-throat when it comes to deals, and he's had trouble with staff in the past. There's been some criticism of his manner towards them, not sexual but being heavy-handed.'

'Bullying?'

'It could be jealousy talking.'

And maybe not, Horton thought. Pierce was ruthless, cold-blooded and very clever; that was based on only one meeting, but then sometimes one was all it took.

CHAPTER FIFTEEN

Tuesday

Horton's phone rang as he was locking the boat to leave for work. He was surprised to see the caller was Danby. 'Short-term memory playing you up, Mike? You only phoned me last night. You can't have got more for me in this short space of time.'

'Rodney Pierce is dead.'

Horton froze.

'You still there?'

'How? When?'

'Hallet found him half an hour ago on the shore. Nothing obviously suspicious, no gunshot wounds, no blunt-force trauma, but Hallet didn't examine him. He checked for signs of life, found none and called Ed Kingston and then the police.'

Horton wished to God he had interviewed Pierce yesterday as Cantelli had suggested. He couldn't even begin to contemplate what this startling discovery meant. 'What alerted Hallet to the fact Pierce was missing?' Horton made his way to his Harley.

'Hallet usually does the rounds of the outbuildings and grounds first thing in the morning between six and six thirty.

There was no sign of Pierce in the pool or gymnasium, which was unusual because he has a swim Tuesdays, Thursdays and Saturdays at that time.'

'He was a creature of habit?'

'It appears so.'

'Don't tell me, he worked out on the other days, Mondays, Wednesdays and Fridays.'

'You've got it. No sign of him, so Hallet assumed he was in his office suite. Pierce is always up early, usually at five, and often doesn't go to bed at all. He's one of those people who only need about four to five hours sleep and then not every night, especially if he's working on something new. There was no sign of him in his office. His mobile phone was on one of the desks. His day bed in his office wasn't disturbed, and his bed in the house hadn't been slept in. Bridget Pierce is at their London apartment. They have separate suites. Pierce hadn't said he was going anywhere and no alert had sounded.'

Horton nodded a greeting at a boat owner, while still trying to assimilate this latest news.

'Next he checked the cars. All present and correct. Then he searched the grounds and found Pierce on the shore, dead. Hallet said Kingston would break the news to Bridget. I imagine they're both on their way down. I asked Hallet to keep me updated. Hold on, he's just texted me. Uniform have arrived.'

'Tell Hallet I'm on my way. I know West Sussex is not my patch, but Pierce is involved in one of my investigations.'

'I'd join you, only I'd be treading on Kingston's toes. Besides, I've got a client meeting. Update me when you can, Andy.'

Horton said he would and rang Cantelli.

'This is beginning to become a habit. A sad and suspicious one at that,' was the sergeant's response.

'I'm heading there now. I might need you to visit Alma's solicitor, but I'll see how things develop at Chidham Creek House. I'll keep you posted.'

He weaved his way through the early morning rush-hour traffic and within thirty-five minutes was at the private road that led to Pierce's house. He drew up at the request of the uniformed officer. A patrol car was parked to his right.

Horton showed his ID and was duly admitted. He was told that Detective Sergeant Curran and the doctor had just arrived and were with the body. Horton pulled in beside two vehicles in front of the house that were obviously theirs. A fit muscular man in his late thirties, with a strong rugged face, close-cropped hair and powerful hands, strode across from the direction of the garage complex. Hallet, Horton presumed. He was correct. His handshake was dry and firm, his grey eyes probing and curious.

'Mike Danby told me you were on your way. I'll take you to where I found him.'

'Slowly,' Horton said.

Hallet smiled. They headed across the immaculate, expansive lawn in the direction of the harbour, some half a mile away eastwards. To their right, south, was a row of evergreen trees, and the same to their left. Horton could hear the faint hum of traffic on the main road to the north.

He said, 'Mike told me how you found him. Is it usual for Mr Pierce to walk down to the shore at night? Does he keep a boat there?'

'Yes, it is usual, and no, he doesn't keep a boat. He's into flying. He has a light aircraft at Goodwood. At night he'd occasionally walk to the shore, taking a torch, but I didn't see one by the body. It could be under it. It looks as though he had some kind of attack, lost his footing while standing on the bank above the shore and fell.'

'How was his health? I understand from Danby that Pierce was a bit of a fitness freak.'

'And a health one. Popped vitamin pills as though he had shares in them. All his food had to be freshly cooked. He wasn't a vegan or vegetarian, nothing like that, but his meat had to be British and organic, same for his vegetables, although he did stretch a point on fruit. Can't grow everything in our climate.'

There was a small hut to their right that looked like a bird hide. Horton halted. 'He's a birdwatcher?'

'No, that's just for show and for any guests to use if they're twitchers. They're usually not and they're usually Bridget's guests. Pierce preferred his birds on a plate or in the air with a gun in his hand. He sometimes did a bit of grouse shooting in Scotland.'

'You sound rather scathing of him.'

'He was arrogant, cold and spoilt. Always used to getting his own way, and when he didn't he could be brutal. Not violent but cutting.'

'Not the best of epitaphs.'

'Whose fault is that? He was very determined and focused to the point of shutting out everything and everyone. Guess that was why he was so successful in business. He was emotionless, like one of his robots.' He gave a twisted smile.

'He had them in the house?'

'You'd have thought so, wouldn't you? But he didn't. Aside from the security system and lights he had remarkably little technology, save for in his office suite, but that's connected with his work.'

'Any children?'

'Good God, no! Messy creatures like that had no place in either his or Bridget's lives.'

Horton smiled despite thinking he'd have loved to have had Emma's mess around him.

'No stepchildren either, not that Pierce has been married before, but Bridget has.'

'Staff?'

'There's a housekeeper-cook, Diane Samson. She lives in but she's on holiday this week. Bridget won't cook for Rodney because nothing is ever good enough for him. She gets it in via a cordon bleu agency. Their London apartment is fully serviced. The cleaners and grounds people here are all contractors, the latter overseen by me and the former by Diane. They come in Mondays, Wednesdays and Fridays.'

'I met a maid here on Friday in a frilly cap and pinny, the works — a small Filipina woman about late thirties called Selina.'

135

'Hired for the occasion. They had house guests for the weekend, some London friends of Bridget's. When there's anything like that on, she hires a company that specialize in providing private dinner parties with a cordon bleu chef, catering and waiting staff.'

'Were you on duty?'

'Yes. And I saw you and the other man arrive.'

'Detective Sergeant Cantelli.'

'As you were admitted to the house, I thought it was none of my business what you were doing here, and Rodney didn't call for me.'

Hallet looked as though he'd like to know the purpose of their visit. Horton might reveal that later.

'I keep out of the way when Bridget has one of her parties.'

'Hers not theirs?'

'Rodney would live like a hermit if he could. He didn't have friends. The guests stayed for Sunday lunch and left mid-afternoon. That's when Pierce went out, about three forty-five.'

Horton's pulse quickened. Alma had left the care home with Dorne about fifteen minutes after that, according to Yvonne. He halted. 'Do you know where he went?'

'He could have gone to Goodwood to his light aircraft. When he came back he was in a foul temper. Nothing unusual in that, only he seemed worse than usual. I was in the house and I heard him and Bridget having a row. Rodney didn't usually do rows, just cold sulks before marching off. But this time he raised his voice. Bridget was accusing him of being rude to her friends and he was telling her what he thought of them. Then he told her to belt up. I couldn't be bothered to listen to any more.'

Was Hallet exaggerating? Horton would reserve judgement on that until he could speak to Bridget Pierce. He wondered how she was taking the news.

'What time did he get back?'

'Six twenty.'

That also tied in with Alma's return to the care home.

'He shut himself in his office complex and didn't come out again until Monday morning. He's got an en-suite, kitchen and day bed. He spends more time in there, or I should say spent, than anywhere else around this place.'

They had reached the bank. Below them, a uniformed officer stood next to a stocky woman in a waterproof jacket and trousers and a lean man in a Barbour bending over the body — the doctor, Horton presumed.

Hallet said, 'If you need anything more just come and find me, or call me.' He relayed his number.

DS Curran looked up with a scowl on her lined face. Horton scrambled down the rough path in the bank and quickly introduced himself with a show of his ID. Curran reciprocated but with a curious stare. 'Is the deceased known to you, sir?'

'His name has come up in connection with an investigation. Detective Sergeant Cantelli and I were here on Friday evening interviewing him.' His expression said he'd go into details later. She interpreted it correctly and didn't press him.

Horton addressed the doctor. 'Have you moved him?'

'I rotated his head to test for rigor, which is evident in the face and neck, and lifted his left arm, which doesn't show signs of rigor.' He straightened up. 'I'd say he's been dead about four hours, some time in the early hours of this morning, around three or four.'

Pierce was lying on his right-hand side, his right arm curled up close to his body, his fist closed. His left arm was stretched out, fingers open. His face was clenched as though an attack had taken him suddenly. He was wearing casual trousers, a grey sweatshirt and trainers. No jacket, but then the night hadn't been wet or cold. Horton could see an expensive wristwatch. It felt strange seeing him like this when three days ago he had been so commanding and in control. Not anymore. Horton was still trying to grasp the significance of this death following so swiftly on from Juliette's and Alma's.

The doctor continued. 'No obvious signs of foul play. It's an unusual time to take a walk but I don't know him; it might have been his habit to do so or he could have been an insomniac.'

'A workaholic. His chauffeur says it was normal for him to spend nights in his office complex and take walks at night.'

'That's more than he told me,' Curran grumbled.

She probably hadn't questioned him, and had instead been in too much of a hurry to view the body. Horton couldn't see a torch. Could it have fallen from his grip and landed in the sea? High tide had been at 2.42 a.m. but it wasn't a spring tide, and judging from the waterline it hadn't reached where the body lay. The clothes too were dry.

The doctor looked at his watch, impatient to be off. 'I can't issue a medical certificate because he's not my patient and I've no idea how he died. If there's nothing more, I need to get back to the surgery in Chichester.'

Curran thanked the doctor. To Horton she said, 'I'll check his pockets.'

Horton turned to the uniformed officer. 'Take a look around the shore, see if you can find a torch.'

'Nothing, not even a tissue.' Curran straightened up.

'I'd like our SOCO team to attend, rather than yours in Sussex,' Horton said. 'We have a suspicious death in Portsmouth, a woman called Juliette Croft who named Rodney Pierce as her beneficiary, not that he needs the money. When we questioned him on Friday he denied knowing her. We believe she was his birth mother, while another lady, Alma Pierce, named as his mother on his birth certificate, died in the early hours of Monday morning at a care home two miles from here. None of the deaths might be suspicious, but Juliette's body was moved after death and a forensic post-mortem is being conducted on Alma. I'd like one to be carried out on Pierce.'

'Sounds interesting,' she said, keenly. 'I'll need to square it with my guvnor, DCI Boyce.'

'Go ahead. If he or she . . .'

'He.'

'If he needs to speak with me, just put him on.'

While she stepped away to do so, Horton gazed around. He didn't think there would be much Taylor and his team could get from here — there was just mud, sand, shingle, shells and seagrass — but he would like the body and the area photographed. This was turning out to be a curious case, if there was one to answer. Three people all connected who had died within days of each other was surely stretching coincidence too far. And if Pierce hadn't visited Alma and wasn't Dorne, or the man in the yellow shirt, then it was looking increasingly probable that this Dorne could be involved in causing three suspicious deaths.

Why had Pierce come to this spot? Was it just an early morning walk? Or had it been to meet someone on the high tide? There was no jetty or pontoon and no marks that he could see of a RIB, or some other small flat-bottomed boat, having come ashore, but the high water could easily have washed away the evidence of that. And this was the only accessible part of the house and grounds that wasn't monitored or equipped with sensors. Nor was it screened by high trees like the other perimeters.

He peered down the Bosham Channel, which fed into Chichester Marina to the east and the Solent to the west. Across the creek further south, he could see the tower of the ancient church in Bosham as well as the sailing club on the south-eastern edge. Several boats were moored on buoys in the channel. If someone had come here by boat, on or before the high tide, how would they have known that Pierce would take a walk? Hallet had said that Pierce often walked the grounds at night. Had someone been monitoring his habits? Or had someone notified this person that Pierce was on the prowl in the early hours of the morning? That suggested Hallet being in league with this other person, but Horton had no reason whatever to think that. This could be natural causes, as could Alma's death.

'DCI Boyce wishes to speak to you, sir.' Curran handed over her phone.

Horton repeated what he had told Curran and answered a few questions. 'There's nothing on the surface to say this is murder,' he added, 'so I don't believe we should treat it as such at the moment and ramp up the investigation. I think an initial examination by SOCO will be sufficient at this stage, and I'd like the forensic post-mortem to be conducted by Dr Hobbs to ensure continuity.'

'I'm happy with that, we've got a lot on our hands. DS Curran will remain with you until the body's been removed and SOCO have finished. Could you keep her informed of progress?'

Horton said he would. He handed back Curran's phone.

The uniformed officer returned with negative news. No torch, and nothing else that didn't look to belong to the shore.

Horton called Taylor, who said he and Beth would be there within thirty minutes. Next, Horton called Mark Lindley and requested the services of his company. 'The deceased is Rodney Pierce, Juliette's legatee.'

'Blimey. That's a bit of a coincidence.'

There was that word again.

'So, who gets her estate now?' Lindley asked.

Who indeed? Would a distant relative pop up to claim it? Was that Dorne, who hadn't been Pierce, and who had tracked down Juliette with Alma's aid? Could Alma have got Juliette's contact details from one of the care home staff? Or perhaps Juliette had left a business card or flyer lying around that Alma had picked up and given to him. No one had visited her, not until Sunday, but she could have met someone outside the care home at any time. Something Dr Goodson had said nudged at him. She had seen Alma last Thursday when she'd overexerted herself walking to the church and back. But perhaps she'd gone further. Had she perhaps posted that flyer and a letter to Dorne? He'd check that out later.

He climbed up the bank. 'It looks as though Pierce stood here, or someone else did,' he said to Curran. 'The grass is slightly flattened. But I can't see any skid marks where he might have slipped.'

'There's more shingle on the shore here just below you,' Curran replied, 'but that could have been there for some time.' She looked at the body. 'The position looks fairly consistent with a fall and not as though he was pushed. If he had been, he'd have fallen on his face.'

'He could have been moved after death and repositioned.' He thought of Juliette. 'I'll take a walk along this perimeter to the south. You take the north, see if there's anything that suggests he could have been moved or a boat could have come up here last night.'

They both drew a blank, and by the time they reconvened Phil Taylor and Beth Tremaine were heading towards them with Hallet. Horton introduced Curran to the team and briefed them on what was required, including photographs, then, leaving the uniformed officer with them, he headed back to the house with Hallet and Curran. Hallet reached to his ear and then consulted his watch, which Horton could see contained a screen. 'The undertakers have arrived.'

It had started to drizzle. As they reached the gravel drive, the undertaker's grey van with blackened windows drew up. Mark climbed out and Horton exchanged a few words with him, requesting that when Taylor had finished they were to take the body to the Portsmouth mortuary, not the Chichester one. Hallet gave them directions to the shore, which were straightforward enough as it was dead ahead. Then he consulted his watch again. 'Ed Kingston's here.'

CHAPTER SIXTEEN

A sturdy man with a round, rough-hewn face and a powerful body climbed out of a Range Rover and glared at Horton.

'Who the hell are you?'

Horton knew he didn't look much like a detective so wasn't surprised at the greeting, although he had expected something more civil. Still, it wasn't every day you lost a client in this manner. 'Detective Inspector Horton, Portsmouth CID, and this is Detective Sergeant Curran from Sussex. You must be Mr Kingston.' Horton showed his warrant card.

Kingston's brow furrowed. 'I didn't expect undercover.'

'I'm not. I always look like this.' Horton smiled to show there was no ill feeling at the abrupt greeting, but didn't get one in return.

'I see the undertakers are here, and the white van. I take it that's SOCO? I'm ex-Met.'

Horton didn't let on that Danby had told him who Mr Kingston was because it wouldn't go down well that Danby had gossiped about the security arrangements, and he didn't wish to get Hallet into trouble with his boss.

'I brought them in as a precautionary measure. Mr Pierce's death doesn't look to be suspicious, but it's best to be on the safe side.'

'Hallet said there were no signs he'd been attacked.'

'On the face of it, it appears not. He could have been taken ill and slipped or fallen onto the shore.'

'Then what are you doing here? You're a long way from home, Inspector.'

'Mr Pierce features in a case I'm handling in Portsmouth.'

Kingston looked stunned and then mistrustful. 'What kind of case?'

'It's best I speak to Mrs Pierce first.'

'She'll be here any moment. In fact, here she is.'

A slick Mercedes coupé drew up in a slew of gravel in front of the garage complex. 'I'll just have a quick word with her to explain who you are.'

She was as impeccably dressed as when Horton had previously seen her, with a short, tight-fitting, light-grey dress under a smart jacket, and wearing heels so high it was a wonder she could drive in them. Her blonde hair was immaculate, as was her make-up. She looked cross rather than upset as she removed her sunglasses with her slender hands. Horton watched as they conferred. Kingston seemed to be reassuring her. She shook her head, waved her hands about and tossed Horton a hostile stare, almost as though he was an unnecessary intrusion. But perhaps he was judging her too harshly.

'She's wondering what all the fuss is about,' Hallet interpreted in a low voice.

Curran opened her mouth, then closed it. Horton guessed she'd been about to retort, *Her husband has just died.* But maybe on closer examination of Bridget Pierce Curran had thought twice about it. This was no bereaved widow, unless she was suffering from shock and disbelief. Even then, Horton would have seen traces of that.

Her gaze travelled beyond him and he turned to see Lindley and his colleague heading towards them with the body on the trolley. He held out his hand to still them. He stepped forward to greet Kingston and Bridget.

'Please accept our condolences, Mrs Pierce, we know how distressing this must be for you.'

'Bridget doesn't wish to see him,' Kingston said curtly. 'Can I?'

'If you wish, although Mr Hallet has made the formal identification. Perhaps DS Curran can go with Mrs Pierce inside the house.'

'No, I'll wait,' Bridget snapped. She moved closer to the house, trying to smooth down her hair, which the drizzling rain was beginning to mess up.

Lindley unzipped the body bag to reveal the face. Horton watched Kingston study it expressionlessly.

'Yes, that's Rodney.' To Lindley, Kingston said, 'You can take him away.'

Lindley looked at Horton, who nodded.

Heading towards them were Taylor and Tremaine. They hadn't been at the scene long, but then Horton hadn't thought there would be much for them to find, if anything. All he could see in the evidence bags were scrapings from the shore and some seaweed. No torch. Taylor would also have taken photographs of the ground where the body had been. Behind them was the uniformed officer.

'Is all this really necessary?' Bridget said sharply. 'There's been no crime here.'

'It's just a routine precaution, Mrs Pierce. It's an unexplained death that we need to investigate. Shall we step inside for a moment, out of this rain?' suggested Horton.

She looked as though she'd like to refuse, but turned and marched towards the house. Horton threw a glance at Taylor, who shook his head, indicating he'd found nothing or very little, as Horton had already surmised. He asked Curran to tell the uniformed officers they could leave.

Inside the hall, Bridget rounded on Hallet. 'You should have prevented this. It's your job.'

Kingston restrained her. 'We'll go over that later. You can leave now, Hallet.'

'I'd rather Mr Hallet join us,' Horton said.

Kingston's lips tightened. Curran slipped into the hall.

Petulantly, Bridget said, 'Can we get this over with? There's a lot to do.'

'I won't keep you long.'

She led the way into the room on their right. The same one he and Cantelli had been in previously. She sat but didn't offer them a seat. Curran took out her notebook at a sign from Horton. Kingston stood almost protectively at Bridget's side.

Horton began. 'How was your husband's health?'

'Sound. It should have been with all the vitamins he took. I think he was determined to work through the alphabet from A to Z. Doesn't seem to have done him any good.'

'And his manner? Had that changed recently?'

'If being more irritable and frigid than usual counts, yes. I put it down to your visit and our houseful of guests who Rodney couldn't stomach. But then there's nobody he really likes. He wasn't sociable. He prefers . . . preferred talking to a computer. Artificial intelligence in the form of a robot or a hologram was perfect for him.' Her tone was acidic.

'Bridget,' Kingston cautioned.

'Oh, let's face it, Ed, I can't play the grieving widow, not the way they expect me to. I'm not going to collapse in a quivering heap. Rodney and I were estranged, Inspector,' she tossed at him, her fingers playing with her expensive rings. 'Apart from the fact that we lived in the same house and went through the motions of a marriage, we had absolutely nothing in common.'

Except money, thought Horton.

'It suited us both that way. We'd come to an arrangement.'

'And did that include romantic entanglements on his part?'

She gave a bitter laugh. 'Delicately put, Inspector. No. He wasn't interested in women in that way, only in their intellect and programming skills. And he wasn't gay either. He was too focused on his work to bother with sex. Work was all that existed for him, aside from his cars and his light aircraft, which he flew alone. I hate the thing, which was just as well because I was barred from it — and his office.'

And Horton would dearly love to see inside it; Hallet had said Pierce's mobile was there. But at present there was nothing to indicate he needed to.

'I'd appreciate it if you could leave his office untouched for now, until we have the results of the post-mortem.'

'It makes no difference to me.'

'I understand he went out on Sunday afternoon?'

'Yes. That wasn't like him. He never went out Sundays, said there were too many morons about.' Her voice was sharp with bitterness. 'He left in the Jaguar immediately after the last of my guests had gone.'

'And that was?'

'About three thirty, four o'clock.'

That tied in with what Hallet had said.

'Do you know where he went?'

'He wouldn't confide in me,' she said sardonically. 'He was bad enough after your visit on Friday and even worse when he got back on Sunday, just after six. Usually I'd ignore him. I perfected the art over years. But I'd had enough. I was furious at the way he'd behaved all weekend. Cold, distant, silent. He'd made it plain that he didn't want our guests here. Although I say "our", they were mine. Rodney doesn't . . . didn't have friends. And those who started off as friends soon got dropped, or became enemies when he tired of them or they had served their purpose. He said they were boring. Them! I told him to take a good long look at himself. He'd had a personality bypass at birth. That got him. He went purple with rage, told me to shut up and stormed out. That was the last I saw of him, and good riddance.'

'Bridget, I don't think—'

'Well, I do, Ed.' She rounded on him. 'It's about time people knew what he was really like. Hallet will confirm what I'm saying.'

Hallet looked stoically ahead. Curran looked slightly bored, which Horton knew was an act; she was probably spellbound. Kingston looked uneasy.

'I need a drink.' Bridget Pierce jumped up and crossed to a table in the far corner. There she poured herself a brandy. She didn't offer them one. Perhaps she knew they would refuse, although Horton thought it probably hadn't crossed her mind to ask. He was pleased to get more background on Pierce than he had expected. What she said could be coloured with bitterness and hate, but it confirmed what Hallet had told him and Horton's own impression of Pierce.

She tossed the brandy back and then poured another generous measure. She turned her hard gaze on Horton.

'I was sick of making excuses for Rodney's behaviour. I've always had to do that. But everyone forgave him because he was a "geek" and they act differently to normal people, don't they? Rodney was far from normal. He was obsessed with everything being just so and with getting his own way. How his staff put up with him I'll never know, but then they were lucky enough to work remotely. If they didn't do what he asked, or if they didn't produce results, they'd be out before you could say P45.' She took a swig of her drink.

Horton could see that her fury had been simmering for years. The shock of her husband's death had opened a release valve. He wondered later if she would regret pouring it all out. Kingston looked as though he did now but he couldn't stop her. No one could, and Horton certainly had no intention of doing so.

'Rodney's PA, Miranda, is efficient and pleasant enough and worships the ground he walks on, but she didn't have to live with him or hear him sneer about her and say nasty things behind her back. She's the one who'll weep and wail at his departure. My trouble was I wouldn't kowtow to him.'

She retook her seat and nursed her drink, while Kingston, who hadn't moved, looked down at her. This time she gestured Horton into a seat opposite, across a low coffee table. He took it. Curran remained standing with Hallet beside her.

'He'd order me about, say hurtful things to make me feel small. It took me a while to learn not to respond but to just look at him.' A mocking smile played at her lipsticked mouth.

'He didn't like that. At first he lost his temper and threw tantrums. I remained unmoved. I didn't even argue back. I just let him bellow and storm out, slamming doors like a five-year-old. I went off and did my own thing. When he cottoned on that I wasn't going to be bullied he left me alone, which suited me fine. How do you think he made his fortune? Not by being nice, I can tell you that. His former partner, Bob Spiley, would tell you the same if he were alive. Rodney drove him to a heart attack just before they sold out to the Americans, very convenient for Rodney. He got all the money and kudos. Bob wasn't married and all his shares were left to Rodney.'

'Did he ever talk about his childhood?'

She gave a hollow laugh. 'I don't think he had one. He was born old.'

'What about his mother? Didn't he ever talk about her?' Horton could feel Kingston's eyes boring into him with curiosity, but he focused his scrutiny on Bridget.

'I doubt he had one. I think he was an alien. I asked him about his family once when we were getting married. He said there weren't any. It became clear that it was a taboo subject. All I know is he was born and raised on the Isle of Wight and left there as soon as he could to work with a software development company in London, which he bought out and so started on his road to fame and fortune, only he forwent the fame. He hated being in the limelight. He wouldn't give interviews and he forbade me to. Not that I was bothered about giving them anyway.' Her bitter tone had eased slightly, perhaps because the brandy was taking effect, or she was running out of steam. Horton had a couple more questions to ask before she dried up.

'Does he have any relatives?'

'No.'

'Have you ever heard of Juliette Croft, née Inglis?'

'Only when you asked him about her on Friday. Who is she?'

He'd been making up his mind what to say, especially as she had opened up so bluntly about her relationship with

Pierce. He wanted to see her reaction. 'We believe she was his mother.'

'My God, then he did have one! The poor woman. Fancy giving birth to that. But maybe she's to blame for the way he turned out, a spoilt brat.'

Kingston interrupted. 'If Juliette Croft, née Inglis, was his mother why was Rodney's surname Pierce? Was he adopted?'

Bridget's hand froze in the act of raising the glass to her lips. 'That would explain why he never spoke of her. He'd have been disgusted and angry at being given away. He'd class that as being a reject, flawed. He hated anything to be damaged. Even if something had a hairline crack, he'd throw it away. And he was thrown away.' She threw back her head and laughed. The sound chilled Horton. If Bridget didn't have an alibi — she was in London last night, according to Hallet — he wouldn't have put it past her to have killed her husband, possibly with the help of Ed Kingston. He'd need their alibis checked out.

Kingston said, 'Is there anything more you need? Only there is a lot to do.' He gave Horton a look that said, *It's time you left, she doesn't know what she's saying.*

'Just a couple of things, Mrs Pierce. Could your husband have been distraught or depressed enough to have taken his own life?'

She studied him as though he'd just declared he was to be the next president of the USA.

'Never in a million years. He was used to obliterating others, not himself.'

Kingston shifted uneasily.

'And your movements last night, Mrs Pierce?'

'You think I killed him? I'd tell you if I had. I left here Sunday about seven. I was in our London apartment from then until now, including all last night.' She glanced at Kingston. 'There's a concierge. He'll confirm that.'

And would he confirm that Kingston had been there too? Because judging by that look and Kingston's manner,

Horton was beginning to suspect there was more than a professional relationship between them. Still, that was their business, unless they had plotted to kill Rodney. Kingston could easily have overridden the security. Hallet too had the perfect opportunity to drug Rodney, then gently push him down onto the shore. But Horton was getting ahead of himself.

'If you could give us the address?'

'I'll do that, Bridget,' Kingston replied.

She wafted a hand in reply as though to say, *please yourself*. Her figure slumped; the brandy and shock were beginning to take their toll.

Horton rose. 'I'd also like the details of Mr Pierce's PA, Miranda.'

'Hallet will give you that.'

'And Mr Pierce's doctor?'

'Giles Weatherby, Harley Street,' Kingston answered.

Horton thanked her but she wasn't listening. As Kingston showed them out, Horton said, 'Do you back up what she said about her husband?'

'He was a cold fish. Clever, cutting and exacting. She's not as hard as she makes out. He made her like that. She's had fifteen years of a frozen marriage.'

'Could your security system have been hacked into and taken down, allowing an intruder to enter the grounds?'

Kingston exchanged a glance with Hallet, who answered. 'It's the best there is and some of the sensors have been devised by Rodney.'

'But someone could take down the system? It being Wi-Fi enabled?'

'It's possible.'

'So if the internet goes down, or has a blip, then it would go offline. Have you checked if it went down last night or early this morning?'

'I have, and it didn't.'

'Unless Rodney took it down himself in order to meet someone by the shore?'

'He could have done but I've got no record of it being down.'

'And when was the last time you were here, Mr Kingston?'

'A month ago, just a routine visit. Pierce wasn't here.' Kingston opened the door and dismissed Hallet, then addressed Horton. 'The concierge will confirm Bridget's alibi, and before you find out second-hand he'll also provide me with one. I was with Bridget all night. We left at the same time this morning when Hallet called me with the news.'

That didn't mean they couldn't have killed Pierce. A drug could have been added to his food or drink before Bridget had left on Sunday.

Kingston added, 'And before you ask, Rodney didn't know of our affair, which has been going on for a year, because if he had done he'd not only have sacked my firm but he'd have made sure that my wife knew all about it. And he would have rubbished my company name so much we'd have been hard-pressed to act as security at the local Co-op.'

'You risked a great deal then.' *Enough to have killed for?* wondered Horton.

CHAPTER SEVENTEEN

Horton asked Curran to telephone the concierge and check their alibis, and to speak to Pierce's Harley Street doctor. Once outside the grounds he called Cantelli, gave him the gist of what Bridget had said and asked him to report to the coroner and organize a forensic autopsy. He just had time to make the appointment with Alma's solicitor and, after that and as he made for Emsworth, he noted the post office sign just past the church at Southbourne. Could she have gone there, he wondered, or had any staff of the Inlands Care Home posted letters for Alma? They could easily check.

He was five minutes late, but Charles Dingwall greeted him affably and enthusiastically. He was a small man with a little grey goatee, shrewd eyes behind overlarge spectacles, flamboyant gestures, and a purple dickie bow.

'I've been given the news about Mrs Pierce,' he said in a rich, deep voice that had a theatrical element about it, as did his gesture for Horton to take a pew. 'Very sad.'

Not so for you, thought Horton. The solicitor would earn a nice fee from being her executor. 'We're trying to trace her next of kin. She told the care home there wasn't anyone, but we know there was one man who was friendly with her and who might have been a relation, a Trevor Dorne. He came to visit her recently, but the home don't have any contact details for him.'

'I can't help you there, Inspector. I've not heard the name. She telephoned, made an appointment to see me, told me what she wanted in her will. I drew it up, she signed it and that was that. In all, I saw her twice. A very clear-headed and intelligent lady.'

'She came alone?'

'She was alone, yes, but she didn't come here. I visited Inlands.' With a flourish, he flicked open the paper folder. 'This was in June.'

Definitely amateur dramatics, thought Horton. 'Can you tell me the terms of her will?'

'It's very straightforward. She left her estate to a children's charity on the Isle of Wight.'

'Had she been actively involved in the charity when she lived on the island?'

'I've no idea, she didn't say. She wished to be cremated and her ashes taken back to the island and scattered from Tennyson Down. I don't know the value of her estate but she left some papers with us — details of her bank and savings account, her birth and marriage certificates, her husbands' death certificates and that of her stillborn son.' He spread them out on the desk.

So Alma had kept that but not the false birth certificate of Rodney Pierce. He had tangible confirmation that their wedding had been on the fifth of June and neither of their birth dates were in December, when they'd visited London and the picture was taken. 'Are there any further documents or letters?'

'No.'

'I'd like copies of these and I'd be grateful if you could put them in a folder.'

Dingwall arranged that and soon Horton was heading back to Southbourne. There he pulled up outside the post office. Twenty minutes later he came out with the news that Alma had indeed posted a letter, and not just one.

He hesitated, but only for a moment, before making for Portsmouth. Instead of the station, though, he made for the Isle of Wight ferry, and just caught the one o'clock sailing. On board he called Cantelli and relayed what he had learned at the post office.

'Alma sent letters to a poste restante address at Yarmouth Post Office on the island. I'm on my way there now. She also received letters from them addressed to her poste restante at Southbourne, one of which she collected last Thursday when she overexerted herself and Dr Goodson was called in.'

'Don't tell me, these letters were addressed to Dorne.'

'Correct. She usually went to the post office once a fortnight on a Thursday, and started posting the letters and receiving them at the end of June. The one from Yarmouth came first. There is no outstanding mail for her, and there were no copies of the letters she received in her room, so she must have destroyed them after reading them. I think the letter she received last Thursday, which caused her relapse, was to tell her that Juliette was dead.'

'Dorne killed Juliette?'

'Possibly. Give me Alma's previous address at Carisbrooke. I'll call on the neighbours while I'm on the island checking out Yarmouth Post Office.'

Cantelli relayed it. 'I've spoken to Dr Hobbs; the forensic autopsy on Pierce is confirmed for Monday. He can't do it sooner. I don't think he expected to be kept so busy. Probably wishes Gaye was here.'

Me too, thought Horton, watching a yacht sail past the ferry's bows.

'I've left a message with the hospital's adult social care worker about Alma. The one she saw must have left because the number connects to a different person.'

'Check to see if Alma had any brothers or sisters.'

Horton bought a baguette and coffee, found a quiet corner and went through Alma's documents. One of them brought him up sharply. Joseph Pierce had committed suicide. Cantelli hadn't mentioned that when he'd checked out

Rodney's parents. Perhaps he hadn't noted it. They hadn't been looking for the cause of death when they'd viewed the certificates on the Register of Births, Deaths and Marriages.

Joseph's occupation was listed as cemetery worker, and he'd died in January 1987. There had been an inquest, and the death was confirmed as carbon monoxide poisoning. Rodney would have been eighteen in the February following Joseph's death, and according to Danby he'd left the island for London at the age of seventeen. One of Kerri's remarks flashed into his head: *She lived on the Isle of Wight for years. Her son was killed in a car accident there when he was seventeen.* Had that been the last time Alma had had any contact with Rodney, who was now effectively dead in her mind? Did she refer to it as a 'car accident' because her husband had died in a car, albeit at his own hands?

He finished his lunch and texted Cantelli to ask him to request the coroner's report. He was curious to know whether Rodney had returned for the inquest; his gut said he had not.

He tucked the documents into his saddlebag, then went on deck to watch the ferry sail into Fishbourne. The drizzling rain had stopped and the grey sky had cleared to give way to a watery blue that Horton knew wouldn't last. His thoughts turned to Lord Richard Ames's house to the west, tucked away out of sight in a private bay. They'd investigated a body found on that shore, that of a private investigator who'd worked with Eunice Swallows, Bliss's friend and holiday companion. Could Trevor Dorne be a private investigator, engaged by Alma to find Rodney Pierce? Had he researched the nursing homes close to where Pierce lived and assisted Alma's move there for the purpose of blackmailing Pierce into providing for Alma? Had Dorne discovered something about Pierce that he could use as leverage to extort money? It was possible. Juliette, his birth mother, had been party to the perjury, but was that enough to make Rodney pay up? Bridget had said he hated anything soiled or broken. And was Dorne responsible for drugging Juliette and moving her body? Did he also drug and kill Alma and Pierce? But if blackmail was his motive, he wouldn't have killed the goose that laid the golden egg — Pierce.

Horton postponed his speculations as the announcement came for them to return to their vehicles. He made the fourteen-mile journey to the small harbour town of Yarmouth, bordering the western Solent, and had to wait in the post office queue while two people were served before him. Fortunately no one came in behind him. He got confirmation that the man who had set up the poste restante address and collected the post was Trevor Dorne. He was chatty, friendly, about mid-fifties, and fitted the description Yvonne at the care home had given them. He had told the clerk that he needed them to handle his post because he was sailing around the island. He hadn't given the name of his boat, but had shown an invoice from Yarmouth Harbour as proof of ID, along with a plastic driver's licence.

Next, Horton called in at Yarmouth Harbour office. The berthing master couldn't remember a boat owner called Dorne, but pointed out that he might not have been on duty when Dorne came in. Horton asked him to check their records for payment. This took a while but eventually, after scrolling back to June, he confirmed that there was no record of a man called Dorne paying the daily visitor, short stay or overnight mooring fee, and neither did Dorne pay annually.

Horton wasn't surprised. The invoice, like the driving licence, was false; the plastic licence card had been overlaid with a photograph of the man calling himself Dorne, and somehow he'd got hold of, or replicated, the harbour's letterhead paper and created his own invoice. This was a clever man with the confidence and ability to bluff his way round any strict ID checks. Did that mean he had criminal tendencies, or was he back to Dorne being a private investigator, possibly an ex-copper?

His phone rang. It was DS Curran.

'The concierge at Pierce's London apartment confirms that Bridget arrived on Sunday night. Mr Kingston arrived on Monday night and left just before Bridget this morning.

I've also managed to speak to the Harley Street doctor, Weatherby. He wouldn't go into details, not without a warrant. But he did say he was shocked at the news; as far as he was concerned, Rodney Pierce was in good health last September on his "annual service", as he called it. Is there anything else you need me to do, sir?'

'Not for the moment. If you could just type up those reports and send them over.' He called Sergeant Elkins of the marine unit.

'Got a job for you, Dai.' He could hear the police launch engine running and the sound of the wind down the line. 'I'm trying to trace a man called Trevor Dorne who, according to the post office clerk at Yarmouth, sailed into the harbour, but the harbour have no record of him doing so. I think he's a fraud.' He gave Elkins the gist of their investigation.

'You want me to check out the other marinas on the island?'

'Yes, all of them: Ryde, Bembridge, Ventnor and Cowes. Ask them to examine their records back to the beginning of June. I don't have a boat name. See if any strangers mooring up fit the description of our man.' Horton gave it, adding, 'I know it's general enough to fit many men, but do what you can.'

'He could have anchored up on a private pontoon or in a bay and used a tender to come ashore,' Elkins suggested. 'In the height of the season he'd have blended in with lots of visitors.'

'If the boat story is true.' Horton knew it wasn't.

He made his way to Alma's former address and was soon turning into a leafy lane not far from the ruins of Carisbrooke Castle. He drew up outside a bungalow that was in the process of having seven bells knocked out of it. It was now after four and the builders had clocked off for the day. Horton would get nothing from the new owners about Alma, save that they had bought the bungalow from her. It was her background he wanted, which meant knocking on the neighbours' doors.

The first he tried, on the right, drew a blank. There was no answer. But the left-hand neighbour's door opened to reveal a woman in her late seventies with chin-length silver hair and steel-rimmed glasses on a round face, which showed a pleasant if cautious expression. He knew he didn't look like a copper. And if he didn't swiftly convince her he was, she might set what sounded like a pack of hounds on him. He was glad she hadn't brought them to the door.

He showed his warrant card and said she was at liberty to telephone Portsmouth CID and confirm his identity while he waited outside. He was making enquiries about her former neighbour, Mrs Alma Pierce.

That drew a worried frown.

'Nothing's happened to her, I hope.'

'I'm sorry to have to tell you that Mrs Pierce passed away on Monday.'

'Oh dear, how sad. She was a lovely lady. Heart, I expect. How can I help you?'

'I'd like to know more about her. We're trying to trace her next of kin,' he lied.

'Then you'd better come in. It's OK, I'll take you at your word. I'm Joyce Snow. Take no notice of the dogs, they're locked in the back garden, hopefully driving the new owners mad with their barking, as they are me with their builders banging and drilling, and their loud music blaring out all day. Anyone would think we were at the Festival and not in a residential area. You know about the Isle of Wight Festival? If the wind's in the right direction, or I should say wrong direction, we can hear the whole thing. I'd better go and tell the dogs to be quiet before madam comes round moaning.' Joyce opened the lounge patio door, which gave on to a good-sized, neatly tended garden with shrubs surrounding a tidy lawn.

Horton took 'madam' to be the new neighbour. He watched her call two black standard poodles to heel. They obeyed instantly. She wagged a finger at them and Horton could have sworn the dogs looked sheepish. With a wave of her arm, she sent them to the opposite side of the garden. They went quietly, sat and remained silent.

'I'm impressed,' he said when she re-entered. 'There must be a bit of a dog whisperer about you.'

'No, just simple bribery. I promised them treats and a walk if they shut up. My husband's fishing. So, tell me about poor Alma. Would you like a cup of tea? You don't look much like a police inspector to me. Oh, I believe your ID, it's just you don't expect one to arrive on a motorbike, not unless they're a traffic policeman, and you don't see many of them these days.'

'I've come from the mainland and it's easier on my bike. And thanks for the offer of tea, but I've just had a drink. I'm trying to trace Alma's relatives.'

'Then you'll be disappointed. There aren't any. Take a seat. She had a lot of sorrow in her life. Did you know her husband killed himself?' She settled herself opposite him the other side of the gas fire.

'Did you know him?'

'No. It happened before we moved here. She told us she was widowed but didn't say how he had died, it's not the sort of thing you talk about, but old Mrs Torren down the road told us not long after we moved in thirty years ago. She's long gone now, so you won't be able to speak to her, unless you're psychic.' She laughed, then her expression assumed a more solemn countenance. 'He went off in their car and gassed himself. The poor man must have been at his wits' end to do a thing like that. No one seemed to know why he did it. Mrs Torren said it came from working in the cemetery — he was a gravedigger — but I don't know about that making him so depressed as to do himself in.'

Horton recognized he had a chatterbox on his hands. He was glad of it, although he might have to steer her back on course a few times.

'Alma lived here ages before we came. This was our dream home, a nice little bungalow with a bit of garden, not far from the shops and quiet, or it was until they moved in.' She jerked her head in her neighbours' direction. 'I don't know why people need to do such things, it's not as

159

if they've got a family, there are only the two of them, but then there's—'

'Did Alma live alone?' he interjected before she could start on the neighbours.

'Yes. Although there was a boy, but he'd left home by the time we moved here.'

That had to be Rodney.

'She was always very smartly dressed, kind and gentle, shy, not one for gossip, kept her own counsel. I thought she must be lonely and I invited her to various things, Women's Institute meetings and events at the castle. Did you know we've got a magnificent castle here? It dates back to the Norman Conquest, although there was something on the site even before then.'

Horton thought he might need to bring her back on track again, but she returned to Alma. 'She said she was happy as she was, only the poor dear never looked happy. She was sort of lost. And her health suffered, probably after her husband took his life, understandably so — her health going downhill, that is. She probably blamed herself, although she had no cause to.' She took a breath but continued before Horton could speak. 'Not that I know the real cause. There was an inquest. I don't know if he left a suicide note.' She looked suitably forlorn and lowered her voice as though there were lots of people listening. 'I asked her once but she said it was too painful to talk about.'

That was probably true, and it was also probably a technique for telling Joyce Snow to mind her own business. 'Did she have many visitors?' he quickly asked, before she could continue in that vein. Cantelli would get more on the suicide from the coroner's report.

'None. No, I'm wrong, there was one, came just after Christmas, in January, and it would have been best if he hadn't come. If I hadn't gone in I dread to think what might have happened. I found her on the floor and called the ambulance. She was in hospital for three weeks. When she came out I made sure she was all right. But she never said who her visitor was, and to be frank, Inspector' — she leaned forward conspiratorially and lowered her voice to a whisper — 'I didn't ask her because I knew it was because of him shouting at her that she'd had the heart attack.'

That couldn't have been Dorne then. With keen interest he said, 'Did you see him?'

'Oh yes, he got out of a taxi.'

Thank heavens for nosy neighbours. 'Can you describe him?'

'About mid-fifties, short brown hair flecked with bits of grey, made him look distinguished, not bad looking but he had a tight mouth. Couldn't see his eyes, he wore sunglasses or lenses that react in the sunlight, clean-shaven, slim, well-dressed, smart but casual, marched in as though he owned the place.'

That sounded remarkably like Pierce, and the man in the yellow shirt. But were they the same man? 'Did you hear any of the conversation?' Horton knew she must have been madly earwigging.

'These bungalows, as you noticed, are detached, so it's no good putting a glass to the wall.' She chuckled.

He smiled. 'But you heard something.'

'Only because I had to go into the garden to bring the washing in and Alma's kitchen window was wide open.'

Oh yeah? 'And?'

'All I could hear him say was, "How could you be so stupid?" Alma talked very quietly, so I don't know what she replied. Then he said, "everything was a lie". Then the dogs started barking and the window was closed. He was in there about ten minutes. He marched out and left in the taxi, which had waited for him. I was worried about Alma, so knocked on her door to check on her.'

I bet, and dying to know what had taken place.

'There was no answer. I knocked again and called through the letter box. I said, "Are you all right, Alma?" But when I didn't get a reply, I let myself in. We had keys to each other's houses in case of emergency and I thought this was one. Good job I did. I called for an ambulance and it was here

161

in a trice, saved her life. That man nearly killed her. And now it's finally happened. God rest her soul.' She sighed heavily.

Horton left a moment's silence. 'When did Alma put the bungalow up for sale?'

'I don't know. One moment she was here, the next gone. You could have knocked me down with a feather when she said she was moving to the mainland two days before the removal men turned up. She'd lived on the island all her life. She said there was no one left here that she knew, and she wanted a fresh start. At her age too! If you ask me, I think she was scared of that man coming back. She could have gone to a care home the other side of the island though. I told her I'd visit her but she was determined. She said she'd write to me when she settled in but she never did. It was as though she wanted to cut off all ties here.'

'Who packed and moved her belongings?'

'The removal men. She came out with two suitcases and said goodbye before she got in the taxi. She looked sad and very tired.'

Horton didn't think she had done all this on her own, although he could be mistaken. He was betting that Dorne had helped her. He must have overseen the selling of her bungalow and her move. Perhaps he'd arranged to have her furniture stored or sold. Then another thought struck Horton. Was Dorne a con man who had manipulated and used Alma, and along the way siphoned off her money from the sale of the house? Dingwall, the solicitor, didn't yet know what Alma's estate was worth. Dorne had wheedled his way into her confidence so much so that she had allowed him to use the name of her stillborn son, maybe even in the misguided hope that he could have actually been him. His body tensed at the thought.

He asked Joyce if she knew the name of the removal firm, the estate agent and the solicitor who had handled the sale. 'Only the removal company. Attridges. They're an island company. There wasn't a For Sale board. It was a massive shock when she left so suddenly. I'd have thought she'd have confided in me, after helping to save her life.'

Horton could see that Joyce still bore a grudge over that. But then he didn't blame Alma for wanting to keep things close to her chest. And maybe she'd been urged to by Dorne. He thanked her warmly, and again expressed his regrets at having brought her bad news, knowing she would bask in the glow of imparting it, and his visit, to all and sundry. He would be able to get the details of both the solicitor and the estate agent from Alma's buyers, which he did after reassuring the woman who answered the door that there was no problem with the transaction.

But it was too late to call on either, or the removal firm. He'd have to leave that for another day. Recalling what Hallet and Bridget had told him about Pierce, he made for Bembridge airport, hoping to find someone still there.

His luck was in. Rodney Pierce had flown his light aircraft in on the fifteenth of January and out again the same day. There were two regular taxi drivers who served the small airfield, and Horton rang the first. He was pleased when his call was answered, even more so when the driver confirmed he had picked up a fare on that date and time and taken him to the Carisbrooke address. After his initial attempt at making polite conversation his fare had told him to shut up and do what he was paid to do. Rude, stuck up and angry was the taxi man's verdict on his passenger.

'Yeah, I waited outside for about ten minutes, then he came out with a face like thunder, slammed the cab door so hard I thought I'd need a new one. I took him back to the airport without a single word being said. Didn't even say goodbye, thank you, kiss my arse, nothing.'

Horton asked him for a description. It was Pierce all right. To add to it, the taxi driver said, 'Wore a nice watch. I noted it when he paid. One of those expensive jobs. A Breitling. Not short of a few bob. And he didn't even give me a tip.'

Horton caught the 9 p.m. sailing back to Portsmouth.

CHAPTER EIGHTEEN

Wednesday

He'd been in his office less than fifteen minutes when Dr Hobbs rang. 'I'm about to make for Swindon, Inspector, where I'm due to conduct an autopsy, but I thought you'd like the test results for Juliette Croft. The class C drug lorazepam was found in her system.'

'That's a tranquilizer, isn't it?'

'Yes to treat anxiety, stress and depression. It's also used for sedation and as a premedication for people about to undergo minor surgical operations.'

'Then she could have got it on prescription.'

'Except she didn't. According to her medical records, her GP didn't prescribe it. She must have acquired it elsewhere.'

'Portugal? She lived there before returning to Portsmouth.'

'I don't have access to those medical records.'

And Horton hadn't heard from the Lisbon police yet. 'But it is class C, which means if she brought it into the country without a prescription, or acquired it here illegally, being in possession would have warranted a fine or even a short prison sentence. How would it have affected her?'

'Its actions are similar to those of diazepam but it's considerably more potent. She'd have become confused and dizzy, and would have experienced problems with her balance before becoming unconscious. If taken with even a small amount of alcohol it would be dangerous.'

'But there wasn't any alcohol in her system.'

'No. But the drug could still have been fatal if she took a massive dose. It can be taken in a few formats, including intravenously, which acts very fast, about three minutes maximum. There are, however, no needle marks on the cadaver. It can also be taken in liquid and tablet form, with the latter breaking down into two formats, either ingested — that is, swallowed — or taken sublingually, which means you put it under the tongue and wait for it to dissolve before swallowing.'

'No trace of any drug was found in that bottle beside her.'

'She might have had another one that she discarded after emptying the tablets onto the table. She took them, possibly with a glass of water in the champagne glass, or in another glass. She got up, washed out the glass, dried it and put it away, thinking she'd have time to return to the sofa, but the drug took effect quicker than she anticipated. She felt dizzy, fell and couldn't get up. She went into a coma and died.'

'How long would that have taken?'

'When taken sublingually, the drug acts quicker. About twenty minutes. Ingested could be anything from thirty minutes to an hour, possibly even longer.'

'Twenty minutes doesn't give her much time to call for help.'

'No, but enough if she was on the floor with her mobile beside her and punched a quick-dial digit.'

'She called someone for help but they arrived too late. All they could do was put her on the sofa, but they dropped or knocked her against the table in the process.'

'It would explain the post-mortem bruising. I've revised the time of death. Originally I estimated between twelve and sixteen hours before she was found, which put it between eleven thirty Tuesday night and three thirty Wednesday morning. I think you're looking at between nine thirty and midnight, Tuesday.'

Horton asked Hobbs to carefully examine Rodney Pierce's body for any signs of an injection, or of having snorted a drug, and obviously to test for lorazepam, and to do the same with Alma Pierce — the latter's PM he was conducting tomorrow, Pierce's on Monday. He heard Cantelli and Walters come in and went out to give them the news, and to update them on his findings of the previous day.

'Juliette's mobile is missing, so whoever moved her took that, so as not to be identified as the last caller. Find out who her phone provider is and I'll make an application for the records.'

'She might not have called anyone,' Cantelli said. 'Before she died she sent an email or message to someone using her computer. This person took both the phone and the laptop. Could be a married man she was having an affair with and it all went wrong. Anyone could have got into that house, the doors were unlocked.'

'Walters, return to Dunlin Way tonight and ask the neighbours if they saw or heard a car that night outside the house, or close by, or if anyone saw a man hanging around or entering or leaving her house.'

'Thought we'd already done that.'

'Well, do it again. See if Sergeant Wells can spare a couple of uniformed officers to help.'

'We still looking at Pierce for it?' asked Cantelli. 'Because if so, what's his motive?'

'Didn't like being told she was his birth mother.'

'But he's had plenty of time to kill her before now. He could have done so soon after Juliette told him in January, which is the reason he went haring off to the Isle of Wight to confront Alma.'

That had bugged Horton on the ferry back, and on and off during the night. The only reason he could think of was that Rodney had paid Juliette to keep quiet. Over time she demanded more money until he felt she had to be dispensed with. He said as much, adding, 'Let's check where he was the night she died.'

'With a Ouija board,' joked Walters.

'No, with a bodyguard.'

Horton, with Cantelli driving, made his way to Chidham Creek House, where Hallet greeted them from outside the garage complex. 'Bridget's gone back to London. She said there's nothing she can do here, all her friends are in town, so too are the lawyers and accountants. Besides, she loathes this place, far too quiet and remote for her. She'll sell it as soon as she can.'

'I'm assuming Pierce left a will, leaving everything to her,' Horton said after introducing Cantelli.

'I wouldn't put it past him to have cut her out of it from spite, but Bridget's been on to the lawyers and she was very happy when she left, so I'm assuming she's his sole legatee. I didn't expect you back so soon. Have you got more on Rodney's death?'

'Not yet but there are a couple of things we need to check with you. How long will you stay on here?'

'I'd go now if I could, but I'm still employed by Kingston Meyer, and Ed's asked me to hang around until the cars are taken to a secure compound. I specialize in close protection work and here I've been nothing more than a security guard and chauffeur to Pierce, and now a caretaker. I need a new challenge.'

'I hope Mike Danby can give it to you,' Horton said lightly.

'Me too. Diane, the housekeeper, has already been given notice by Bridget. She's to leave immediately on her return from holiday.'

'Bit harsh that,' Cantelli said.

'Diane won't shed too many tears, and she's been paid off, handsomely.'

'She didn't get on with her employer?'

'Rodney was very fussy, everything had to be just so — fresh bedlinen every other day, his meals cooked a certain way when he ate in, the timing of them exactly when he said, and his office suite had to be spotless with not a thing out of place. He had an almost photographic memory when it came to that. He hated being there when it was cleaned, so he usually took himself off to the pool, but Diane had to be present. She's a good housekeeper, she'll be snatched up.'

'Why won't she continue to work for Mrs Pierce in London?' Cantelli asked.

'It's a fully serviced apartment and Bridget will want to engage her own staff. She might even be planning to go abroad or move elsewhere. The security here will be monitored remotely. Anything of real value is to be removed. What is it you wanted to know?'

'Did Rodney go out the Tuesday before last, in the late afternoon or evening?'

'Yes. He left at seven and returned just before midnight, then went to his office suite.'

The critical time. But Hallet's next words quashed their idea that Rodney might have driven to Portsmouth to drug Juliette.

'He went to his aircraft at Goodwood, not to take it out, but to admire it most probably, and to eat there. He's a member of the Kennels, Goodwood's exclusive clubhouse. Bridget wasn't here.'

They would check that out. 'Is it possible to see his office suite?' asked Horton.

'We'll go round the back, the tradesmen's entrance.' Hallet smiled. 'There are doors to the kitchen for deliveries, but there's also a separate ground-floor wing with its own external door. Rodney's office suite.'

'Do you know if he was on any kind of tranquilizer or other drugs?' Horton asked as they walked past the swimming pool and fitness complex.

'He didn't like taking anything except vitamin pills and aspirin, said the latter was good for the heart. He liked to be in full control of his faculties. He didn't need much sleep, so it's possible he could have taken something occasionally to help him catch up, but that's just guesswork. This is the door to the office suite.' Hallet pressed something on a small handheld device and the door slowly opened.

'I was expecting a key,' Cantelli said, startled. 'There's a keyhole and the door is a traditional one.'

'Looks can be deceptive, Sergeant.'

Can't they just? thought Horton, looking at Hallet, wondering if he had drugged Pierce.

They entered a large room furnished in a modern style with two huge screens on the wall to Horton's left and another two on an expansive table arrangement facing the large window onto the garden, which was slightly hidden from view by slatted blinds. There were three computers on the table, and beside one a torch. Seeing Horton noticing it, Hallet said, 'It was here all the time. He must have walked down to the shore in the dark. The house security lights would have lit a path some of the way, and he knew the rest by heart, nothing to stumble over or into. Maybe the moon was up.'

'Where's his mobile phone?'

'Bridget took it. I know you said nothing was to be touched, and it hasn't been, but Bridget insisted on coming in here to get his phone. I couldn't stop her.'

Horton wondered why she had wanted it so badly. Reading his mind, Hallet said, 'She wouldn't have got much from it. It's password protected and Pierce changed that regularly. He rarely sent messages from it and cleaned his call log religiously. As I said, he was a creature of habit. I think she took it to make sure he wasn't spying on her. Not that it matters now.'

Cantelli gazed around, chewing his gum. 'There's nothing as crude as a filing cabinet in sight and the desks don't even have drawers.'

There was also nothing on the walls except screens.

'It's very plain,' Cantelli added.

Hallet replied. 'It's not meant for comfort, although, as you can see from the day bed, Rodney often slept here in between working.'

There was also a large L-shaped sofa and a low coffee table. Two doors stood to Horton's right.

'That one leads into the small kitchen, and the one next to it the bathroom,' Hallet explained. 'Pierce used to have all the screens on at the same time, one giving him a view of his London office when he needed a video conference, which was fairly often. And he always worked on three computers at the same time. The servers are in London.'

'Did he drink?' asked Cantelli.

'Alcohol? No. And woe betide any member of staff who did while working. If anyone came into work the worse for wear for drink, or he smelled it on their breath at a meeting, it meant instant dismissal. Obviously they could get away with it on screen to a degree, but he had an uncanny knack of sussing out anyone not up to speed, and if it were drink-related. I was always very careful myself — my tipple is a beer now and again — but Pierce didn't even drink that. He drank copious amounts of spinach water and herbal tea, and the occasional coffee.'

They entered the kitchen. As Horton had expected, there wasn't much to see save for a coffee machine, water cooler, fridge freezer and a built-in microwave.

'No kettle?' asked Cantelli.

'The tap provides hot and cold water. The water cooler is drawn from the mains, filtered, and chilled before dispensing.'

So less chance of anyone drugging him, thought Horton, which was speculation anyway.

'Did he eat in here?'

'He ate, worked and slept here. You can understand why Bridget gave up.'

'Did you come in here?' Cantelli asked.

'Not unless he wanted me to, which was rare.'

'Who else would enter this suite?'

'Miranda, but she hasn't been here for a fortnight.'

'Anyone since Monday?'

'No. Want to see the rest of the house or my rooms?'

If there was evidence of lorazepam it would be long gone by now. And Pierce's alibi would probably check out. Horton declined and they headed back to Cantelli's car.

Hallet said, 'You think his death is suspicious?'

'Do you?'

'If it is then I suppose I'm a suspect.'

'Why would you want him dead?'

'I didn't. I thought he was an awful man, but then he didn't have the monopoly on that. And I could walk away. He wasn't my employer and I wasn't married to him.'

Was he deliberately pointing the finger at Bridget? Horton said, 'You know that Bridget and Kingston are having an affair?'

'That's their business. I can see that you're thinking it gives them a motive for getting Rodney out of the way, but I don't think it was serious on either part, just boredom.'

'Kingston is married though,' Cantelli put in.

'Doesn't mean to say he's not bored.'

'And you?' Cantelli asked.

'Bored, yes. Married, no.'

As Cantelli opened the car, Horton said, 'How's the business community taking the news of Pierce's demise?'

'In shock, according to social media, not much expression of sorrow that I can see. The press will be elaborating on his death in tomorrow's papers. There'll be speculation. A crisis PR company in London has been appointed to handle it by Aldsworth Management Consultancy. Rodney retained them for acquisitions, patents and other business matters. They're taking over the running of the business until Bridget decides what's to be done with it. The buyers are probably already lining up.'

Horton said they would keep in touch and update Bridget after the post-mortem. It wasn't far to Goodwood, only seven miles, and Horton instructed Cantelli to head there. An hour later they had confirmation that Rodney Pierce had been there for the whole of the evening Juliette had died, and alone.

'Do you still believe she was murdered?' Cantelli asked, as they headed back to the station.

'Do you?'

Cantelli thought for a moment. 'Yes.'

That was all the encouragement Horton needed.

CHAPTER NINETEEN

Thursday

Horton stared down at Rodney Pierce's mud-smeared face and still-clothed body, which Brian, the mortuary attendant, had slid out of the freezer for him. He shuddered. Not because of the mortuary chill or because he was horrified by what he saw, but because Alma was laid out on a nearby slab ready for Hobbs to conduct the post-mortem. Horton thought it a cruel irony that they should be united in death. He wished they hadn't been together. He knew it didn't matter now, but to him it somehow did. He wanted Pierce away from Alma as soon as possible, as though he wished to protect her. But that was ridiculous. He only had what others had told him about her to go on. They might have coloured views of Alma Pierce. Somehow, though, he didn't think that. Yes, she and her husband had committed a criminal offence, and yes they had deceived a boy by hiding the circumstances of his birth, but Horton believed they had acted out of desperation, and had given the child a good home. But again he corrected his thinking. How did he know that for certain? Perhaps it was Rodney's upbringing that had turned the boy into a cold, ruthless man.

Cantelli had detailed Sergeant Norris on the island to get all the information he could on Joseph and Alma Pierce before they had moved to Carisbrooke, and if there were former neighbours they could speak to. Norris was also going to interview the estate agent and solicitor who had handled the sale of Alma's bungalow to see what he could get.

Yesterday, Horton had spoken to the removal company on the telephone. They confirmed they had taken Alma's furniture into storage, as well as some ornaments and a handful of books. It was all the property of one of the leading island auctioneers, who had instructions to put it to auction and dispose of that which wasn't sold to a second-hand dealer or charity shop. Those instructions had come from Mrs Pierce, who had signed the documentation. The proceeds, less the auctioneer's fees, were to be paid direct to the children's charity Daisy Chains. He had telephoned them. After some delay, his call had been returned late yesterday, to say that nobody there had ever heard of Alma Pierce.

Elkins had also sent him a message to say they hadn't found anyone by the name of Dorne as a berth owner or visitor to any of the marinas on the island. Horton had been expecting that. It didn't mean he didn't own a boat though. Was Dorne Yellow Shirt? It seemed highly probable.

Cantelli had called the care home and spoken to Kerri, who confirmed they didn't have lorazepam on the premises and none of their residents were on it.

Horton's eyes lingered on Alma while Hobbs prepared himself for her autopsy. It was the first time he'd seen her, aside from in the two photographs. She was just an ordinary elderly lady. There was no sparkle of the woman he'd seen in that wedding picture and the one taken in London, which he had stared at long and hard yesterday, and had mulled over during the night. In the wedding picture she had been pretty, delicate, and happily looking forward to the future with her strong, good-looking husband. In the London one she was still pretty and dainty, and yet there was less confidence about her expression. To him the hesitant smile was tinged with sadness. He felt as though Rodney Pierce had shattered their lives, and yet they had engineered it. He hadn't. And what of Juliette? Her body was also here. The three of them brought together in death.

Hobbs crossed to him. 'As you can see, he hasn't been washed or prepared, because you wished to see him first.'

He sounded a little out of sorts, perhaps because they were keeping him busy, or he'd had a bad day in Swindon yesterday. Not for the first time, Horton wished he was facing Gaye across this cold slab. Last night he'd thought about calling her, but that wasn't fair to her. He'd woken with the resolve to get to the heart of this case even if it turned out that none of the three involved had been murdered.

'I'll let you get on.'

He was about to mount his Harley when Walters rang.

'We've had two calls, guv. The sarge has gone to one. A woman who went to school with Juliette read Leanne's article in the newspaper. She said that she kept in touch with Juliette during her first job on leaving school and saw her again after that. I've just taken the second call. A Mr Dennis Sperryman says he knew Juliette. He's a member of the band Roy Whiteman and Greg Harrison played in.'

Horton remembered Harrison had told him that Sperryman had been on holiday at the time of their fellow musician's funeral, at which Juliette had officiated.

'He thinks he might have some useful information but says we can be the judge of that. It's his morning for volunteering at the Rock Gardens. He'll be there until midday.'

'I'll head there now.'

He made good time and parked the Harley in one of the spaces in front of the gardens that gave on to the seafront. The first man he asked, who he thought could be Sperryman, judging by his age, pointed him to a well-built man with a bulbous nose, a craggy suntanned face and stubbly fair hair turning grey. He was tending a palm of some kind.

Horton introduced himself and made to show his warrant card, but Sperryman said, 'No need, Greg described you.'

Horton wondered what that had entailed but didn't ask. 'I'm sorry I didn't get in touch before.' Sperryman pulled off his gardening gloves. 'But my wife and I only got back from our holiday on Tuesday and I had a few things to do yesterday. I popped round to see Greg last night to talk about how Roy's funeral had gone and he told me you and the sergeant had questioned him about it and about Juliette. I was shocked to hear of her death and thought I'd better get in touch. I'm sorry to drag you down here when you must be very busy. I'd have come in, only—'

'No, it's fine. I much prefer to be out.'

'I can see that.' He eyed Horton's leatherwear and helmet. 'What you got?'

'A Harley-Davidson.'

'I envy you. I used to have a Triumph. Anyway, you didn't come here to talk motorbikes.' His expression became more solemn. 'Do you think Juliette's death is suspicious? Well, you must if you're investigating it,' he quickly added. 'I'm not sure what I have to tell you is of the slightest interest, and I didn't mention it to Greg. It was only when I got home yesterday from seeing him that I thought it over and decided to call the police.'

He stopped as two elderly ladies made their faltering way around the path, stopping to look and discuss various plants.

'Let's walk up to the prom.'

They did so. The main holiday season was over and the weather windy and chilly, so it was relatively quiet. There was a small queue at the coffee kiosk to Horton's left and a handful of people sitting at the tables outside the café to their right. The Solent was choppy in the breeze, with dark patches scudding across it, reflecting the glowering sky. Horton could make out Ryde quite clearly, the downs above the hilly, waterfront town and those to the west, as well as the houses at Seaview and the entrance into Bembridge Harbour to the east. They took one of the seats on the edge of the Rock Gardens slightly below them. They had the place to themselves.

'Greg said you asked several questions about Juliette. I expect you know she used to sing on the cruise ships.'

'Yes.'

'She told me that before she went on the ships she sang backing vocals with a couple of groups and hoped to go on from there but that it never happened. We talked about how tough it was for singers and musicians to break through and that you needed not only talent but also that bit of luck, being in the right place at the right time. She said that was her problem — she was in the wrong place at the wrong time.'

'What did she mean by that?' Horton asked, interested, wondering if she was referring to becoming pregnant. With that, a thought suddenly struck him, one he hadn't previously considered: could her pregnancy have been as a result of rape? Was that why she had given up her baby?

'She didn't elaborate on it and I didn't pry. But I had an idea. She had a powerful voice. A mezzo-soprano. Untrained and gutsy, and she could really belt them out. She knew how to charm an audience too. She was also, how can I put this? Flighty. And that might have helped her to get on, if you get my meaning, but it could also have held her back. Maybe she picked the wrong men,' he said pointedly, eyeing Horton steadily. 'She got caught out. He could have been married. It was an affair that kicked her out of the business and she took to the cruise ships as a means of getting away from him and any flak. That's purely speculation on my part,' he hastily added. 'But it's based on what I saw and knew of her. I know this might sound ridiculous because of our ages, but she was seductive. Yes, everyone would have thought she was past it, but attraction can happen at any age, despite the fact that young people think you've got one foot in the grave when you're over forty and you're veritably ancient at my age. And no, it wasn't me she made a play for, Inspector, it was Roy Whiteman.'

Horton showed his surprise.

'He was the wealthiest of us.'

'She knew that?'

'She could smell it,' Sperryman said, with a sorrowful shake of his head. 'Some women can. Roy was flattered. I told him to watch his step. Penny, his wife, now his widow, is a lovely lady and they'd been happily married for years, but Juliette had a way with her. She must have been a stunner in her youth.'

Horton recalled those photographs of her on the cruise ships. The fashions, make-up and hairstyle looked dated now but he could see how attractive she'd been. He'd realized that on first flicking through the albums.

'I think she was also dangerous — and this isn't just a silly old bugger talking,' Sperryman quickly added. Horton had thought nothing of the kind. He could tell that Sperryman was intelligent and fair-minded. 'I was glad I had a holiday booked for Roy's funeral, not because I didn't wish to pay my respects, I'd loved to have done so, but I didn't want to see and hear Juliette delivering the service when I knew what she had been doing. Thank God she didn't get Roy completely in her clutches, although I believe he was tempted once, maybe twice. I don't know how far it went, nor do I wish to know. In fact, I won't because they're both gone. You won't have to mention this to anyone, will you?' he anxiously asked. 'Especially not to Penny and her daughter?'

'No,' Horton reassured him, recalling them. He could see that Sperryman had been bottling this up and brooding on it while on holiday. He was desperate to confide in someone, thankfully the police.

Sperryman pressed on. 'I've worked with people all my life, Inspector, and I've seen all sorts of things happen, including office romances. I've witnessed marriages destroyed all for a bit of sex. I've seen manipulative women and preying men. I recognized the former in Juliette. And I got confirmation of that without her having seduced Roy. And it's this that I thought you should know about, although it might not be relevant to your investigation.'

'Please do go on. I'm very keen to hear what you have to say. This is all very helpful.'

'We were playing at the Maybeline Nursing Home in Fareham and due to go on after Juliette. She'd finished her bit and we were setting up. I ducked out because I needed to visit the gents. I came out and saw Juliette with a man. They didn't see me as I dived into the corridor. I didn't intentionally mean to eavesdrop but I felt awkward about crossing the hall and them seeing me. And . . .' He looked a little shamefaced. 'I thought this might be something I could use to persuade Roy he was playing with fire. It wasn't that Juliette and this man were lovey-dovey, quite the opposite. He eyed her as though he despised her.'

A dog ran around their legs and they had to wait until the owner had retrieved it with some difficulty and apologies.

'This man said, "Juliette, it's been a long time." She looked him up and down as though she was about to flirt with him, then she must have seen the hate in his eyes because she scowled and drew herself up. He said, "Don't you recognize me? But then you wouldn't as you pushed me off to school and kept me away from my father. I'm Adam Croft, your stepson."'

Horton's interest deepened.

'She tried to look pleased and said, "How nice to see you again after all these years." He said, "I wish I could say the same of you." He was very bitter, Inspector. Then he said, "Who's your victim this time? Aren't they all a bit too old for you here? But then that would suit you because they wouldn't live very long and you can spend their money as you did my father's." This man, Adam Croft, was clearly implying that Juliette was a gold-digger. Does any of this make sense?' he appealed to Horton.

It was beginning to. 'Was he in his mid-fifties, brown hair flecked with grey, clean-shaven, about five feet eleven, slender, distinguished looking?'

'Yes. You know him?' Sperryman asked, taken aback.

Horton was certain it was the man in the yellow shirt who had attended those funerals. 'Please go on, if there's more to say.'

'There isn't. They were interrupted by Greg, who had come to see where I was. They broke up. Juliette left and Croft returned to the residents' lounge, where he sat with an elderly lady.'

'Can you describe this lady?'

'I can, and I can also give you her name.'

Even better.

'She's small, curly silver hair, blue eyes, a lovely smile, about ninety. She was wearing a pale blue cardigan and checked skirt. Geraldine Dyer. Croft stayed for two of our numbers, then left.'

'When was this?'

'Two weeks before Roy died.'

Horton rose and shook Sperryman's hand. 'Thank you. That's been really helpful.'

He called Walters and asked him to do a search on Adam Croft. 'I'll explain when I get back.'

'Where are you going?'

'To a nursing home in Fareham to talk to Geraldine Dyer.'

CHAPTER TWENTY

Two hours later Horton was back at the station, updating Cantelli and Walters about his conversation with Sperryman and his subsequent visit to Miss Geraldine Dyer. Sadly, she hadn't been able to give him any relevant information because she had dementia, but the nursing home manager, Rosemary Chaplin, had provided a wealth of it. Horton now relayed it.

'Adam Croft visits Miss Dyer regularly. He speaks nicely, has no accent, is always polite, friendly and intelligent. He's mid-to late fifties, slender, of good bearing, an engineer of some kind and is either self-employed or retired, she's not sure, but he comes during the daytime on weekdays. She knows he's single but not if he's widowed, divorced or unmarried. He's been visiting Geraldine for three months. She was the matron at his boarding school near Littlehampton.'

'We've got nothing on him. He's clean,' Walters said.

As Horton had suspected.

'How did he know she was in the home?' Walters polished off one of the doughnuts that Horton had stopped to buy for them. He shouldn't have encouraged such unhealthy eating, especially in Walters's case, but now and again they needed a sugar fix.

'He heard it through his school alumni. He told Rosemary that he'd never forgotten Miss Dyer's kindness to him following his father's remarriage.'

'To the gold-digger Juliette,' Walters said.

'According to Sperryman, if he overheard correctly, and I think he did. My reading of him is he's on the level.'

Walters wiped his mouth clean of the jam in the corners. 'I bet she found another sugar daddy to live with in Portugal after Nathaniel Croft died. Then he popped his clogs and she sold up and returned to Portsmouth. Maybe she was hoping to bum off her rich son, and Rodney was having none of it.'

Cantelli said, 'So Adam Croft is Yellow Shirt?'

'Yes. The description fits and I have a photograph on my phone of him taken at the nursing home with Geraldine. I also have a picture of him as a child with a couple of other boys and a young Geraldine. We can compare that picture with the one in the album of his father's marriage to Juliette.'

'I'll fetch it.' Walters waddled off to Horton's office.

'Rosemary also told Adam Croft that Juliette was a celebrant and was conducting the funeral of a resident who had been in the home for three months. This was the same day Sperryman overheard their conversation.'

'Georgina Barlow.' Cantelli clicked his fingers. 'Yellow Shirt showed up at her funeral first.'

Walters returned with the album. Horton turned to the wedding picture. 'That's Adam Croft, all right. The boy in the suit, looking none too happy.' He swivelled it round for them to see and put his phone with the photograph on it beside the one in the album.

'Yep, that's him,' agreed Walters. Cantelli nodded. Horton continued.

'Croft went to Georgina Barlow's funeral. Then he heard of Roy Whiteman's death on his next visit to the home, a week later. Greg Harrison had called Rosemary to cancel their forthcoming engagement and to tell her the sad news. He also told her when the funeral was, in six days' time on the seventh of September. Rosemary relayed this to Croft, knowing he'd be saddened by the news of Whiteman's death because Geraldine had liked the band so much. She mentioned that Juliette was to be the celebrant; Harrison had told her.'

Cantelli said, 'And he didn't need to go to Gideon Nichols' funeral because by then he knew she was dead. But did he kill her? Did he want revenge that badly for being packed off to school?'

'Perhaps his stepmother spent all his father's money, and when he died what little was left went to her. Adam Croft felt hard done by. But is it a strong enough motive?'

Walters picked up another doughnut. 'Depends how much money was at stake. Although, I have to say, I'd have thought he'd have taken his revenge on her before now. And what would he gain by it? She doesn't seem to have had any money.'

Cantelli chipped in. 'There's the house and its contents, and we haven't examined her bank accounts. We also don't know how well-heeled Croft is. He could be in debt.'

'Fair enough,' Walters acquiesced.

Cantelli continued. 'Maybe seeing her, and speaking to her for the first time in years, brought back all his anger and hurt, so much so that it ate into him. At first he planned just to stalk her by attending the funerals where she was a celebrant, but that only made things worse and he began to plot how to kill her. He could have followed her home from one of those funerals and wangled his way into her house, saying he wished to chat about old times, or his father.'

'Maybe apologizing for his harsh words at the nursing home, spoken in the heat of the moment,' Horton ventured. 'She let him in. They had a coffee or two, he spiked her drink. Rosemary told me that none of her residents were on lorazepam, but Croft could have been on it or acquired it from somewhere. When Juliette died he set up that suicide scene, and took her mobile phone and computer in case there was anything on them that mentioned him.'

'Nobody saw a man even on our second combing of Dunlin Way last night,' Walters said.

'Doesn't mean to say there wasn't one.'

Cantelli said, 'Is Croft Trevor Dorne though? If so, how would he know Alma? And why help her?'

'No idea, but his address is in Lymington and the ferry runs from there to Yarmouth on the Isle of Wight. Handy for picking up his post. I'll email his picture to Sergeant Norris. He can show it to the staff at Yarmouth Post Office and to Alma's estate agent and solicitor to see if it matches.' Horton picked up the last doughnut, noting Walters' disappointed look. To Cantelli he said, 'What did you get from Juliette's old school chum?'

'Sharon Rainey said Juliette was a bit wild, liked a good time and the boys, and they liked her. She was never short of boyfriends. It was an all-girls' school where the teaching of secretarial skills was an important part of the curriculum. They were trained to end up in the typing pool or as secretaries. Juliette had no intention of doing that. She left for London as soon as she could, at sixteen, after having worked for a year at a chemist in Fratton. She was determined to make it as a singer. Sharon heard from her a couple of times but then they lost touch. She saw her again though, two years later, by chance. Juliette was heading over to the Isle of Wight for the festival.'

'This was in 1969?'

'Yes. The festival was held in late August then, not in June like it is now. Juliette told Sharon that her singing career was about to take off. She was a backing vocalist for a band, didn't say which one though. Sharon was, to use her term, "gobsmacked" and "green with envy". Bob Dylan was performing along with the Who, Moody Blues, Bonzo Dog Doo-Dah Band, Joe Cocker and Julie Felix. I've looked it up. Everyone wanted to be there.'

'Roy Whiteman was. Harrison told us Roy was a big fan of Bob Dylan's and had seen him at the Isle of Wight Festival in sixty-nine.'

'Could he have first come across Juliette then?' Cantelli asked.

'There must have been thousands there. I'd say the chances were remote. But they had that experience in common, and if Dennis Sperryman is correct, and I believe he is, then maybe that helped Juliette and Roy to gel all these years later.'

Cantelli continued, 'Juliette told Sharon she'd get her a ticket but it never materialized. Juliette said she had to run or she'd miss the ferry. The boys were heading over there to set it all up.'

'What boys?'

'The roadies, Sharon supposed.'

Walters said, 'Could have been bullshitting. She might have been going to sing at a holiday camp or just visiting the festival. She could have been hoping to get a job there and be talent spotted.'

'Sperryman said she told him she'd been a backing vocalist, so maybe it wasn't bullshit. She also told him that she'd never hit the dizzy heights because she'd been in the wrong place at the wrong time. She could have been referring to the festival. Did she get pregnant there?'

'Not unless Rodney was premature,' Cantelli answered. 'If so, the baby would have been in a hospital unit, but where is anybody's guess. We don't know where she lived.'

Walters said, 'Maybe the band manager discovered she was already pregnant and sacked her because they couldn't have a pregnant woman on tour. Or it could have been his kid and he didn't want the responsibility of it, or her tagging along with a baby.'

'Another idea struck me earlier,' Horton said. 'I wondered if Juliette could have been the victim of rape. Perhaps it happened at the festival. She could have been . . .'

'What?' Walters prompted.

'She told Mark Lindley that drinking wasn't her scene because she'd had her fill of alcohol when she was young. She might have got so drunk at the festival that someone took advantage of her, and having a baby would certainly have put her singing career on hold. And it was a traumatic experience for her. But instead of giving up the baby for legal adoption, she gave it to Alma and Joseph. Why? Aside from the fact that they lived on the island, why them?'

'Maybe they met at the festival,' Cantelli volunteered. 'And Juliette stayed with Alma and Joseph. But no, he was a farmhand then on the other side of the island. Norris got that far checking him out. The farm has changed hands and the cottages are now holiday lets. Alma would have been six months pregnant. I'm not sure she'd have been letting it all hang out at a pop festival.'

'If Juliette did hang around on the island, after the festival, she could have met Alma in the maternity ward. Ask Norris to contact the hospital and see what he can get from their records for August 1969 to February 1970.' His phone rang. 'Hobbs.' He put it on loudspeaker.

'There's nothing suspicious about Alma Pierce's death,' Hobbs announced. 'Not unless the blood and tissue analysis come back with something, but I can't detect any obvious signs of poison, or of a drug overdose. There's no bruising or evidence of homicide. No needle marks either.'

Horton was glad of that. He didn't like to think of the elderly lady being murdered.

'She suffered from pulmonary arterial hypertension, which led to right ventricular heart failure and death. Angina, which her medical records say she had, is a frequently reported symptom. My pathological findings are consistent with PAH; parts of the lungs revealed the presence of obstructive and interstitial lung disease. I've asked for the lab to fast-track the blood and organ sample analysis. You should have the results some time tomorrow. They'll contact you direct.'

'I wonder if Dorne knows Alma's dead,' Cantelli said when Horton came off the phone.

'Not unless he's contacted the care home, and Kerri would tell us if he had.'

His office phone was ringing. He went to answer it. It was Reine.

'The chief constable's had a call from Matthew Teesdale of Aldsworth Management Consultancy. They want Pierce's computers from Chidham Creek House. They might contain vital company information and they're concerned about it getting into the wrong hands. The chief has authorized their handover. You're to be there when it's actioned. Matthew Teesdale is on his way now. Ensure everything goes to plan. I understand there's a security guard.'

'From Kingston Meyer, yes.'

'They've also been informed and will liaise with you.'

Ed Kingston's number was flashing up on Horton's mobile. He rang off and immediately returned Kingston's call. Kingston said he had informed Hallet. 'I've instructed him not to let anything go until you're on the premises. I'll be glad to get shot of them because that's all Hallet is there for now, guarding them, and the cars, which will shortly be moved. I can employ him elsewhere.'

'I'm on my way.'

He stopped off only to tell Walters and Cantelli where he was heading and to say that he would call into the Inlands Care Home on his way back to show them the photograph of Adam Croft in case anyone recognized him as Dorne.

As he travelled eastwards, he felt there was something at the back of his mind, something he had missed, but what it was refused to crystallize. He postponed trying to work it out and drew up in front of Chidham Creek House, where a Ford was parked. Teesdale's, Horton presumed as he made for the rear of the house and the office suite. He knew Hallet would have seen his arrival on his watch monitor.

He had expected Teesdale to be in his thirties or forties, but he was mid-fifties. He seemed amiable enough. His hand-shake was firm, his eye contact good and his manner apologetic.

'I'm sorry to inconvenience you, Inspector,' he said, handing over his business card. 'But I need to remove the hard drives and take them away. I understand you've been informed.'

'I have.'

Hallet released the catch on the office suite door. Stepping inside, Horton said, 'I'd have thought you'd have access to all Pierce's information backed up on a server off these premises.'

'We do. This is really a security precaution in case Rodney was working on something privately. And there could also be sensitive information on his personal laptop. I explained everything to Mr Meredew, your chief constable. I'm happy to wait though if you need to contact him.'

'No, that's fine. He's authorized this. Please go ahead.'

Teesdale set to work.

Horton said, 'How well did you know Rodney?'

'Not very. He wasn't an easy man to get close to. He was very secretive. Not a bad thing in his line of business. I doubt that he told his staff, or us, his advisers, everything, which is fine and understandable. It was important that we understood what he wanted professionally and where he was heading, that was all.'

'I only met him once but I can't see him taking advice very readily.'

'He did when it was valid, balanced and appropriate.' Teesdale was unscrewing the back of one of the computers.

'Even when the advice went against what he wanted?'

'That made it more challenging. He didn't always listen to me or my colleagues. Sometimes he got it wrong, sometimes we did.'

'What exactly did your consultancy do for him?'

'We were engaged to monitor the worldwide competition and markets. To examine trends, new developments, social media, to pick up news and information on potential future developments, especially where artificial intelligence is concerned, a rapidly growing and critical technology. We read scientific papers, attended forums and seminars that Rodney didn't go to, which was most of them because they bored him stiff. He wasn't a natural socializer.' He removed the hard drive. 'Do you want me to screw the plate back on?'

'No need as far as I'm concerned,' Horton answered.

Hallet agreed. Teesdale moved on to the next one and continued. 'We also spotted and headhunted talent for him.

We would approach the individual, and if it looked feasible for them to join Rodney's team, then Mr Hallet's company, Kingston Meyer, would take over vetting them from a security point of view.'

'And those who left? Did you continue to monitor them?' Horton threw Hallet a sidelong glance.

Again Teesdale looked up with a knowing smile. 'We track them and make sure they stick to their confidentiality agreement and that nothing the company was working on shows up with a competitor. To date we've not had any problems.' He removed another hard drive and put it in his case along with the first one. Moving on to the third computer, he continued, 'We also advise on possible acquisitions and liaise with his accountants and lawyers.'

'He kept you pretty busy then. I take it you have a team of people working for you?'

'Yes. It's not my company though. I'm a specialist IT senior management consultant. I didn't intend ending up one. I thought I was going to retire but I, in turn, was headhunted. You might think that unusual because I'm older and IT is deemed to be a young person's business, but that's not strictly true. I, and those of my generation, have been in it from the beginning. By that, I mean the early days of the World Wide Web, computer gaming, the evolution of social media and now the latest developments, artificial intelligence, holograms and whatever comes next.' He straightened up. 'This, I take it, is his laptop?'

Hallet nodded.

'His mobile phone?'

'Bridget has it,' Hallet answered.

'What will happen to the business now?' Horton asked as Hallet secured the door.

'I understand there are several potential buyers circling.'

They headed back to the front of the house.

'Why would Mr Pierce have needed three computers?' Horton asked, curious. 'Two I can understand — one open on certain websites or programmes and the other to work on, but three?'

'In case one failed, possibly, although he'd have had his laptop. Or perhaps because he was working on two or three projects at the same time and corresponding with others while doing so.' Teesdale made his farewells.

Turning to Hallet, Horton said, 'Will you leave tonight?'

'Tomorrow morning, after the cars have gone. I'm driving the Jaguar to London.'

'Pity you didn't get the Ferrari.'

Hallet smiled.

On the way back to Portsmouth in the steady rain, Horton stopped off at Inlands Care Home. Kerri hesitated to give a positive ID of Adam Croft being Trevor Dorne from the picture Horton showed her, and Yvonne couldn't swear to it either. There was a similarity, but more than that they couldn't say. Kerri would circulate the picture and ask if the other care assistants and residents had seen and recognized him when he had arrived to see Alma.

He returned to the station in a thoughtful mood, checked his messages, typed up a brief report on Teesdale taking the hard drives and sent it over to Reine. He was leaving when Billy Jago called him.

'Got some information for you, Mr Horton. Meet you in the usual place.'

'Which one? We have a few.'

'Clarence Pier.'

Horton found him at one of the slot machines.

'I got something on those betting shop jobs,' Jago said without pausing his activity. 'And I know who paid for Norman Cranley's funeral.' His narrow, lined face creased up and his bloodshot eyes swivelled away from the machine for a moment. He smirked, showing missing teeth and a blackened one. 'Jackie Alfleet.'

Horton swiftly searched his memory, recognizing the name and trying to place it. Then he had it. 'The armed jewellery robbery in seventy-nine.' It was before Horton's time, but he remembered reading and hearing about it from some of the older officers when he joined the force.

'That's him. Jackie Alfleet and Mikey Weller made off with stones worth a fortune. Mikey died. Very conveniently. But you lot couldn't prove Jackie killed him, although word is he did. Body found the other side of this pier in too bad a way to say what he died of. Jackie went down for twenty years, no remission. Wouldn't say where the stones were. Went abroad when he came out, no one knows where at first, travelled around to avoid the cops following him, flogging off the stones, which the cops didn't find. Ended up in Spain or Portugal, loaded.'

'How do you know all this, Billy?' Horton had registered 'Portugal', but tried not to make any great leaps. Lots of people ended up in Portugal and Spain.

'I have my ways and means.' He winked and tapped his long, crooked nose.

'Then make sure you don't go too far. I'd hate for anything to happen to you.'

'It won't.'

'And the betting shops?'

'They're keeping it in the family, the Cranleys.'

'I suspected as much. Damien?'

'Yeah, and his mate, Ishan. They're doing a job Saturday night, a betting shop in Albert Road, Southsea. Don't know which one. That's the best I can do, Mr Horton. How about my bonus?'

Horton handed over the agreed amount.

'Where docs Jackie Alfleet live?'

'London, I think. But he's been spending a lot of time with a certain widow.'

'Sheila Cranley.' She hadn't let them inside her flat, but that was only to be expected.

Jago just grinned.

CHAPTER TWENTY-ONE

Friday

'Present for you, Andy.' Sergeant Stride marched into Horton's office with a broad smile and an evidence bag. Inside it was a mobile phone.

'Does that belong to who I think it does?' Horton exclaimed eagerly as Stride placed it on his desk.

'Yes. Juliette Croft. Not only does it fit the make and model, according to Mark Lindley, but we've got the toerag who took it breaking into her house last night to see what else he could pinch.'

'He wouldn't have got much — we've got her jewellery, cash and bank cards. He's admitted being there before?'

'Not yet. But given time and your skill, I'm sure he will.'

Horton laughed. 'So what happened last night?'

'A man living at the rear of Juliette's was late going to bed, just after midnight, and didn't put his light on. He looked out of the window and saw a figure scrambling over the back gate. Knowing what had occurred there, he called it in and, seeing as it was peeing down and there were no punch-ups, a unit was available and despatched immediately. Caught in the act. And I've got another little treat for you

— the culprit is Riley Ballantine, and, on searching his bed-sit, we found items that match the description of those stolen in the spate of Milton burglaries. He's currently having a nice little lie-in in a warm, comfy cell.'

'I should have known it was him, but his prints weren't picked up in Juliette's.'

'He's probably learned a thing or two inside. He's only just been released after serving a short custodial sentence for that last lot of robberies at Eastney. He just can't keep his hands off other people's possessions. And that being Juliette's, could he be facing something more serious?'

'Drugging people and manhandling bodies isn't his MO, but I'll ask him just the same.'

'He hasn't had his breakfast yet.'

'Good, maybe he'll talk quicker on an empty stomach. Bring him up to one of the interview rooms. Has the arresting officer filed the report?'

'Yes.'

'I'll read it while Riley cooks up some cock-and-bull yarn. Before you go, one of my informers tells me there's going to be another raid on a betting shop Saturday night in Albert Road. We'll need a couple of units. I'll get Walters onto it with you. Ah, Walters you're just in time.'

'For breakfast?'

'No. We've got a guest. He kindly brought this with him.' Horton pointed to the evidence bag.

Walters peered at it. 'Juliette's?'

'Looks like it, courtesy of Riley Ballantine.'

'Thought he was inside.'

'He will be again soon with luck and a decent magistrate. We're going to have a nice little chat with him.'

'That'll put me off my breakfast.'

'Walters, nothing will do that. Now, give me five minutes to read through the report, and no, you haven't got time to get something to eat. Just check if anything has come in from the Lisbon police on Juliette.'

Horton quickly read the report, which bore out what Stride had told him. One officer, PC Penrose, went to the rear of the premises and nimbly climbed over the back gate while another officer stood by at the front of the property. The window into the conservatory was open. Penrose entered and crept upstairs, where he could hear movement, and nabbed Ballantine, who only put up a token resistance.

Horton picked up the evidence bag.

'Nothing new in,' Walters reported as they made for one of the interview rooms.

'After we've dealt with Riley I want you to liaise with Sergeant Stride. Jago says another betting shop job is organized for Saturday night and you're duty CID this weekend. Hopefully you'll have the pleasure of Damien Cranley's company and his mate Ishan.'

Horton pushed open the interview room door. Seated was a scruffy, scrawny man in his early twenties with several earrings in each ear, a constant sniff and a squint.

After going through the formalities, Horton began. 'Tell us where you got this, Riley, and don't insult us by saying it's yours, or it was given to you, or it fell off the back of a lorry.'

'Don't know what you're talking about, ain't seen it before.'

'It was in your grubby little bedsit. And don't say it was planted because we know it wasn't.'

'I ain't saying noffink.'

'Very well. DC Walters, send the crime scene team into Mr Ballantine's flat, instruct them to take all his clothes and shoes for forensic examination and see that those things he's wearing are also taken away.'

'You can't do that.'

'I can,' Horton sat forward. 'Because I'm about to charge you with the murder of Juliette Croft.'

'Me? I ain't murdered no one!' He sprang back, alarmed.

Horton ignored him. 'After killing her you stole from her. Not content with taking her computer, which you've already sold, and her mobile phone, which was found in your possession, you returned last night to find what else you could lay your thieving hands on. And what's more, we've got one of your prints,' he lied.

'Can't have, 'cos I wore gloves.' His cocky look vanished when he realized what he'd said.

Horton scraped back his chair. 'Good, that will do as a confession. Book him for murder, Walters.'

Ballantine started. 'I didn't kill her,' he bleated.

'Tell that to the jury.' Horton had reached the door.

'She were dead when I got there.'

Horton spun round. 'You expect us to believe that?' he scoffed, hiding his excitement.

'It's the truth.'

'You wouldn't know the truth if it smacked you in the head.' Horton sauntered back to his seat. 'But just to humour you, I'm listening.'

'I got in the back door. It weren't locked. It were dark. I nearly tripped over her. Give me a shock. She were lying on the floor.'

'Where?' Horton asked sharply.

'Just inside the living room. I saw she were dead and scarpered.'

Walters said, 'How did you know she was dead?'

'I put my torch on her.'

'And you checked for signs of life, took her pulse?'

Ballantine eyed Walters incredulously. 'Nah. She were grey and her eyes were open and staring.' He ran a hand under his nose. 'Ain't seen noffink like that before and hope I don't again. I just turned round and ran out.'

'After picking up her laptop and mobile phone.'

He ran a hand under his nose and looked sheepish. 'Yeah, all right, her phone but not her laptop. Didn't know she had one. Her phone was lying on the floor. I thought, she don't need it no more.'

Was he telling the truth about the computer? Horton doubted it. 'And you thought, she's dead, no point in hurrying out now. I can help myself to whatever else is lying around.'

'No, I got out quick. Don't I get a cup of tea and something to eat?'

'When you've told us all there is to tell like a good boy. Then you'll get your breakfast.'

'That's against human rights.'

Horton feigned a concerned expression. 'Is it, Walters?'

'Might be. I could look it up, but that will delay Mr Ballantine's breakfast by about two hours.'

'Maybe we should then—'

'All right, what do you want to know?' Ballantine said sulkily.

'What was on the coffee table?'

'Noffink.'

'Not even her handbag?' Horton had found that upstairs, but he wanted to test Ballantine.

'No. Like I said, I didn't want to hang around in case you lot showed up and thought I'd done her in. I just picked up the phone. No point in it going to waste.'

'He's into recycling now, Constable, to save the planet,' Horton tossed at Walters.

'Maybe he didn't have time to recycle the other things.'

'What other things?'

'What did you do with the bottle and glass?' asked Horton.

'What bottle and glass?' He looked genuinely puzzled.

'The ones on the table.'

'There weren't noffink on it. I told you.'

Although Horton showed no sign of his keen interest, his mind was racing. Walters also looked disinterested, but Horton knew he too was joining some dots.

'What time was this?' asked Horton.

'Dunno.'

Horton glowered at him.

'Just after eleven.'

'How sure are you of that?'

'I saw it on the fancy clock on the wall, when I shone my torch on it.'

'And you didn't feel like stealing that.'

'Looked naff to me and I heard a car. I didn't want to be caught with her lying on the floor. I ran out the same way I come in.'

'And closed the back door behind you?'

'Yeah.'

'Did you see or hear anyone approaching or moving behind you in the alleyway?'

'Nah. I heard a car stopping but I didn't look to see what it was.'

'Where did it stop?'

'Dunno.'

'Come on, you can do better than that.'

'It were down the road, past the bus stop by the path that cuts across the common.'

'You know the area well then.'

'Course I do. I walk round there sometimes.'

'Casing out which houses to break into, no doubt watching the occupants' movements. What made you choose her house to rob the first time? Her car was out the front, you'd know she was in.'

'Yeah, but I thought she'd be asleep upstairs.'

'Why?' asked Walters.

'Why what?'

'Why would you think that?'

'Because her house was dark.'

'So were the others along there.'

'Yeah, but they got burglar alarms and she didn't. And I knew there was an alleyway that ran round the back, and there's no dog. There's one further down but he's a soppy thing, can barely walk let alone bark.'

'How did you know Juliette Croft didn't have a dog?' asked Horton, not sure where this was leading him in respect to Juliette's death but persevering. There might be something more he could get from Ballantine that might help or throw up some ideas.

'I guessed.'

'Riley.'

He sighed heavily with exasperation. 'I seen her before, come and go, and she don't put no dog in the back of her car.'

'When did you see her?'

'Now and again, what bleeding difference does it make?'

'Did you see her go out that evening?'

'Nah.'

'But you saw her return?'

'Nah.'

'Have you seen anyone else go into that house or leave it?'

'Nah. I just saw it was dark, no alarm, no dog, an easy gate to climb over. I hoped there'd be a window I could get through but the back door wasn't locked.'

'And you thought Christmas had come early.'

'Except for her being dead.'

Sternly, Horton said, 'You admit you were in that house. You attacked her, pushed her about, she fell and you—'

'I never touched her. She were already dead. I swear it.'

Horton left a silence. Footsteps passed in the corridor. Someone spoke and Ballantine's stomach rumbled. 'I got gut ache. You're trying to starve me, that's not allowed.'

'You tried to get into her computer?'

'I didn't take no computer, I keep telling you.'

'You checked her phone.'

'Yeah, but there was nothing on it and . . .'

'You couldn't get into her bank information.'

He squirmed.

'So what did you do next?'

'I was going to sell it.'

'To whom?'

His eyes darted about the room and finally came to rest on Horton. 'To a mate, only he got put inside last Thursday so I was left with it.'

Thank goodness this person was banged up, thought Horton. 'What was on the texts?'

198

'Noffink. There weren't any.'

'Oh, come on.'

'Honest there weren't. She must have wiped it clean before she topped herself.'

'How do you know she killed herself?' Horton said sharply.

'I didn't. I just thought she must have done because I didn't kill her.'

'And the call log?'

'Noffink. I swear it. Look, I'm starving. I've been banged up 'ere all night without so much as a biscuit. Do I get my breakfast now?'

'What do you think, Constable?'

'Might help his memory to return.'

Ballantine looked hopeful. Horton waited a moment. 'All right. Take him back to his cell. But before you go, Riley, just one more thing.'

'Ain't there always.'

'How did you get into the house this time?'

'Forced the window in the conservatory and climbed in.'

Horton considered Riley's evidence as he returned to his office. If he was telling the truth — and he might be, for a change — then someone had arrived after him, planted the champagne bottle, glass and tablet bottle, and taken the computer, which must have been upstairs otherwise Riley would have lifted that too. They'd already wiped her phone clean and left it by her body, unless she had done that herself earlier. He doubted that though. It wouldn't have taken long to clear everything off it, but accessing a computer and trawling through evidence of any correspondence would have done. This person had wiped away any prints in the house. But had this same person who moved her killed her?

Dr Hobbs had put the revised time of death between nine thirty and midnight, which meant Juliette had been drugged between nine o'clock and before Riley showed up at eleven. There were no reports of anyone being seen entering the house by the front, but it was possible they could still have done under the cover of darkness, or been admitted by Juliette at the back door. Could that be Adam Croft?

Horton considered this. If not Croft, could it have been a lover, as suggested earlier? One who didn't wish to be seen because he was already married. Whoever it was had drugged her, then left the house, returned after Riley had scarpered, and had set the scene then. Or perhaps this person, on hearing Riley, had hidden in the downstairs cloakroom or upstairs.

He called Sergeant Norris on the island to see what he had for him, if anything. What he did have was negative. The post office clerk couldn't positively identify Adam Croft as the man who had collected the mail, nor could his colleague.

'They both say that Dorne looks like the man in the picture but wouldn't swear to it. I got the same from the estate agent. She only met him once. She doesn't have his address as he wasn't the client. Everything was done through Mrs Pierce, although he did telephone the agency to enquire on progress and chivvy things along from time to time. But it was a very swift, uncomplicated cash sale. The property was snapped up before it went on the market because they had a buyer specifically asking for that road.'

'No email address for him?'

'No, sir.'

Even if there had been, Dorne could have set up a false account if he had so wished.

'The sale was handled via their own conveyance specialists and everything was done online.'

'Didn't the agents think it unusual a woman of Mrs Pierce's age would have an email address and be happy conducting the transactions over the internet?'

'I asked that. They assumed Mr Dorne was assisting her. The estate agent said she spoke with Mrs Pierce on the telephone several times and she struck her as being very bright. She had no complaints. She wasn't purchasing a property, so it was straightforward.'

'The money from the sale was paid into her bank account?'

'Yes.'

Had all the money gone to Alma? Had Dorne helped her set up a new account, one he could access? Was that why he had befriended her? And he'd completely taken her in, so much so that she allowed him to use her dead child's name. Had Alma become confused enough to believe that Dorne really was her son? All the reports he'd had of her said not. But fraudsters were very clever and could play on emotions to the full.

Norris said, 'I've instigated enquiries at the hospital for their maternity records on a Juliette Croft or Inglis being admitted between August 1969 and February 1970, but they didn't sound very optimistic about retrieving them.'

'Just let me know if you pick anything up.'

Horton had just replaced his phone when it rang. It was Rosemary Chaplin, the manager of the Fareham nursing home. 'You wanted to know when Mr Croft returned to visit Geraldine. He's just arrived.'

'I'll be there in half an hour. Make sure he doesn't leave. And don't tell him I'm coming.'

CHAPTER TWENTY-TWO

'That's him, sitting with the frail lady in the orange cardigan. Do you want me to ask him over? Only it might be better for Geraldine if I do. Not that she would be fully aware of what's going on, but it might be alarming for her as you're a stranger.'

'If you could just say I'd like a word with Mr Croft, no need to mention I'm a police officer.'

'You don't look like one either.'

He watched from the doorway as she approached the couple, convinced the man he was looking at was Yellow Shirt.

Croft glanced in his direction. Horton registered puzzlement before he smiled at Geraldine, said something to her and then made for Horton. Rosemary took the seat he'd vacated and talked to the elderly lady.

'Can I help you?' Croft waved a hand to Geraldine. She didn't acknowledge it.

'I'm Detective Inspector Andy Horton.' He showed his ID. 'I'd like to talk to you about your stepmother, Juliette.'

'Ah. Shall we talk in the garden.'

It was spoken as a statement, not a question. Horton got the impression of a commanding man. That, and his bearing, confirmed what Lindley and Alice Rails had said about him.

To Horton's mind this was definitely Yellow Shirt. He could also be Dorne.

For now Horton would go along with Croft's wishes. He had no evidence that this man had drugged Juliette and therefore no grounds to caution and arrest him. Nothing was said until they were seated at a small iron table in the blustery but pleasantly warm day. Horton took out his notebook. Croft looked slightly amused at this. 'Forgive me, but my tale of woe will hardly make interesting reading, although it might incriminate me, if you believe Juliette was murdered.'

'Do you?'

'It wouldn't surprise me, but I can assure you, Inspector, I am not a killer. Not in that sense.'

Maybe he *should* caution him. But Croft's air wasn't cocky or cynically amused; there was an element of bitterness tinged with sadness about him. Horton judged him to be an intelligent man.

'I'm referring to my time in the army. Not that I directly killed anyone, but my work did. I'm an engineer. I served in the army for twenty-two years. Never married, although I've had some near misses. Now I act as an engineering consultant to anyone who wishes to pay handsomely for my services. How did you find me?'

'You were seen at two funerals where Juliette was the celebrant.' No, he quickly mentally amended, three — he was at Cranley's, and that was the niggle that had bugged him earlier. How had Croft known about that particular funeral? 'Three funerals,' he corrected. 'You stood out because of your choice of shirt — deliberately chosen, I assume, to attract Juliette's attention.'

'It worked. She saw me right enough but she didn't turn a hair. I should have known that, given my experience of her. It was stupid and childish of me to think she would. But we all do irrational things from time to time.'

'So you went round to see her?'

'Only to the outside of her house. I followed her. She went to the shopping centre after the first funeral, so I drew

203

a blank there. I struck lucky on the second one. She was delayed chatting with one of the mourners, a small, very thin man with a weathered face. Instead of him smiling and shaking her hand and thanking her he looked hard at her, said something that I took to be sharpish and turned away. It didn't seem to bother her. She went directly home. I made certain it was her home after the third funeral, and I also came to my senses. I wanted to see where and how she was living. Not quite in the lap of luxury she was accustomed to. I didn't accost or approach her. There was no point. She was never going to change, people don't. I'd wasted enough time and emotion thinking about her since my encounter with her here. It's where I first came across her after thirty years. She was singing. But then you know that. I assume you discovered it from one of Roy Whiteman's colleagues.'

'He overheard you talking.'

'I see. Well, at least I got the satisfaction of seeing her driving an inexpensive second-hand car and living in a small semi-detached house in the middle of Portsmouth. Not her usual style. I was curious to know how she had ended up working as a celebrant and singer when she had avoided work for most of her life. But no doubt she was on the prowl for her next gullible victim.'

Croft was echoing what Sperryman had said.

'All that oozing fake sympathy at that first funeral. That was enough for me. The second and third I stayed outside until they'd finished. She was adept at making people like her. She looked good, sounded good and acted well. Underneath though, she was ruthless and scheming. And, yes, if you believe she was killed then I'm putting myself right in the frame for it, but I wouldn't risk going to prison for the likes of her.'

'How did you find out about the second funeral? You learned of Georgina Barlow's and Roy Whiteman's from Rosemary, but not Norman Cranley's. He wasn't a resident or visitor here.'

'When I came out of the first one I overheard the pall-bearers talking about a big funeral the following week that Juliette was scheduled to deliver. One of them said it would make interesting listening as the deceased had died in prison and had been inside most of his life. I returned to the crematorium at the beginning of that week and looked at the list of funerals on the noticeboard outside the waiting room. There was only one listed for Lindleys: Norman Cranley's.'

Feasible, Horton thought. 'How old were you when she married your father?'

'Twelve. I was taken out of my day school, away from my friends, and packed off to boarding school.' Horton heard the man's bitterness, but his eyes held sorrow. 'I was desperately missing my mother, who had died eighteen months before my father married Juliette. I thought him cruel and uncaring. I felt as though I was being punished for my mother's death, and rejected by my father because of it.'

His words resonated with Horton. From his daughter's manner, he didn't think she felt abandoned by her mother because she was marrying Jarvis. Emma seemed happy at being separated from them. But had she sensed she wasn't wanted? Was it a relief for her to be away from them? She had told him on a couple of occasions that she was fed up with staying with Grandma and Grandad so often because they kept telling her to be careful and quiet. And she'd said she was bored with Mummy and Jarvis on his luxury superyacht. Well, he certainly wouldn't reject Emma. He'd make damn sure he phoned and messaged her often. He'd visit her at the school and she would stay with him in the holidays.

He brought his attention back to Croft. 'The school was a good one and it became my home. And that lovely lady in there, Geraldine, became my surrogate mother. She was the matron and she could see how wretched I was. I ended up spending the school holidays with her and her sister in Cumbria. Her sister is long gone. I rarely saw my father and never Juliette. After A levels I went straight into the army. They then became my family. I don't know if you understand that.'

Horton did, all too well. His Geraldine had been Eileen and Bernard Litchfield, his last and loving foster parents who had help him channel his anger into sailing and football, and by loving him unconditionally. Bernard, a police officer, had influenced his decision to join the police force. That in turn had become his family until he'd had one of his own — Catherine and Emma. Then that had been taken from him. Perhaps Croft saw his thoughts in his face, though he was trying to keep his expression neutral. He nodded and continued.

'Juliette was a gold-digger. I knew that even at the tender age of twelve, but not the extent of it until after my father's death. By then she had taken almost every penny he had, save the house, which was worth a great deal, some stocks and shares and half his pension, which was a generous one, and which she got on his death. She'd made him change his will to cut me out, no doubt promising him she would see I was all right. By the time of my father's death I was in the army. I was left with nothing except his watch, which I nearly threw back in her face after the funeral.' He shook his head, his expression distant and sorrowful at the memory. Then drawing himself up, he gazed directly at Horton.

'But I had a career to forge and was posted overseas. I put it, and her, behind me. I felt some satisfaction in seeing how narrow her life had become, while I have a nice house in Lymington, a boat in the marina, a good army pension, a fulfilling job and a good circle of friends.'

Horton registered the fact that Croft had a boat. He could easily have sailed over to Yarmouth from Lymington to collect those letters from the post office.

'I think you'll find, Inspector, that she became a celebrant to identify her next victim, a vulnerable widower.'

Sperryman's thoughts. And maybe they were correct, except that Horton believed Juliette thought she had found a different source of wealth — her son.

'Do you know a lady called Alma Pierce?'

He shook his head.

'Or a man called Rodney Pierce?'

'No. Hold on, though, isn't he the tech entrepreneur who's just died? I read about it in the city press. I have some stocks and shares and take an interest in company and financial news.'

'He was.'

'I don't know him. How is he connected to Juliette?'

Horton wasn't about to answer that. 'Where were you the Tuesday before last, the twelfth of September between nine and midnight?'

'Is that when she died? I suppose I need an alibi. I was in Lymington Sailing Club from seven until eleven. I'm on the committee. We had a meeting, followed by drinks and food. I was at home for the rest of the night. Alone. I didn't drive to Portsmouth, and I didn't see her again after that third funeral. You can check with the sailing club. The steward and the commodore will verify I was there, but no one can vouch for me after eleven o'clock, unless my neighbours care to tell you they saw my car parked outside my house all night.'

Horton jotted this down. It seemed that Croft had a cast-iron alibi. Even if he had driven from Lymington to Portsmouth directly after the meeting he couldn't have got there until midnight, and by then Juliette was dead. He could have set the suicide scene, but why should he if he hadn't drugged her? And an engineer, who paid attention to detail, wouldn't have done it so clumsily. But he asked Croft where he was between five and seven that evening.

'On my yacht in Lymington Marina from four until the time I went to the club. The marina staff can confirm that.'

Horton would get Lymington Police to check on all this, but he didn't think Croft was his man.

'Did Juliette talk about her family or her past?'

'No — as I said, I never saw her. She might have done to my father, but he never relayed anything to me.'

'Any hint of her ever having taken drugs?'

Croft's eyebrows rose. 'None that I picked up on, but she was a young woman of the sixties, albeit at the fag end of the decade, and if we're given to believe everything we've read and heard everyone was at it back then. Is that how she died, drug overdose?'

'If you could give me your contact details, Mr Croft.'

'Not saying, eh? Fair enough, but I'd be astonished if she took an overdose. Yes, she was getting older, but she was still attractive, and, as I witnessed, could charm her way into people's hearts. She'd have found someone to keep her in a life of luxury, you can be sure of that.'

The man she had chosen though, Roy Whiteman, had been married and, sadly, unexpectedly died. The other, her son, hadn't played ball. He was tough, shrewd and heartless. But even if he hadn't been, why should he financially look after the woman who had given him away? OK, so she might have had no choice. And as he'd previously considered, Rodney could have been the result of a rape. Even so, he didn't have Rodney Pierce marked as the charitable, forgiving, understanding type. Pierce's encounter with Alma, as told by Joyce Snow, and Horton's own meeting with the man, demonstrated that.

Horton asked Croft to go to Lymington station to make a statement. 'I'll let them know you'll be going in. They'll also be checking out your movements, Mr Croft — just routine.'

Again, Croft smiled knowingly.

* * *

Horton headed back to the station along the top of Portsdown Hill, where he stopped off at the burger van. He took his burger, chips and Coke to a wooden picnic bench away from the car park and a group of walkers and considered Juliette's tactics. She had located her son and approached him — how? Could she have got the address somehow and shown up at Chidham Creek House? Hallet hadn't said. Perhaps he hadn't been there at the time, or hadn't noted her. But just to be sure, Horton reached for his mobile and rang him. He got his voicemail. Horton left a message asking him to call without saying why.

He took another bite of his burger. Had Juliette called the company and asked to speak to him? She would have been put through to his PA, Miranda. He needed to check that out with her. Juliette would have said it was a personal call, but that was no guarantee Rodney would take it or return it. In fact, Horton was certain he wouldn't have done. And this would have taken place before Alma's heart attack, because Rodney's visit there was as a result of something Juliette had told him.

Horton ate some chips. The wind had whipped up and there was rain in the air, but he ignored it. Perhaps she had written him a letter marked 'private and confidential' that Miranda had passed to her boss, another thing to check. Pierce would have had no option then but to contact her. They arranged to meet somewhere privately, and what he learned caused fury. Perhaps he didn't know he was adopted because as far as he was concerned he had a valid birth certificate. He discovered that Alma was not his mother and that she and Juliette had arranged it. Yes, that would certainly have sent him into a rage. But was there more?

Maybe Juliette had told him who his father was. And Alma confirmed it. If there had been something wrong with his biological father, some medical problem, then Rodney would have seen that as a flaw. What would Rodney despise the most? A weak man? A sick man? A man with a mental illness who had been committed? Had Rodney discovered he might have inherited a dreadful fatal disease? Alzheimer's, hereditary cancer, motor neurone disease? Would he have had a genetic test to see if he carried the defective gene? Another thing that Horton thought he should check. Perhaps he'd had the devastating results the day of his death. He went for a walk down to the shore. Perhaps Dr Hobbs would find evidence of a drug, self-administered. Pierce despised weakness and ill health. Teesdale might find evidence of all this on the hard drive, along with emails from Juliette to Rodney and vice versa.

Would this have been enough to have led him to kill Juliette? The answer was yes. Rodney had the lorazepam and agreed to meet her early evening, before returning home and then going to Goodwood airfield at seven and returning just before midnight to give himself an alibi. He must have parked his car some distance away, and made sure, or hoped, he wasn't seen entering her house. He had a drink with her, slipped her the drug, then left her long before Riley Ballantine arrived. But, according to Ballantine, there had been nothing on the coffee table, and Juliette had been on the floor. Had Pierce paid Hallet to return to the house, where Hallet deliberately cocked it up so as to lead them to the truth about his soon-to-be former boss? Somewhere along the line Hallet developed a grudge against Pierce. If that was so, they needed to find the reason. And Hallet could still be in the frame for drugging Pierce. After all, he was the only one there.

Horton polished off his lunch and returned to his office, keen to follow up his ideas.

CHAPTER TWENTY-THREE

First he telephoned Miranda, explained who he was and said she was at liberty to check and call him back, but she was happy to speak.

'Yes, a woman called for Rodney three times saying it was personal. We get those type of calls often. It's usually a journalist, or someone trying to convince Rodney they have a new development he must have. She wouldn't give her name, so I didn't put her through.'

'When was this?' He felt a stab of triumph. He'd been right.

'December. I remember it was close to Christmas.'

The timing also fitted. 'Would she have emailed him?'

'She might have done, but he never mentioned it and I never give out his email address, although it's not difficult to guess it as others are mentioned on our website. But he did get two letters marked "private and confidential", one just before Christmas, the other after the New Year when I was back in the London office. I remember them because it's rare to get correspondence like that these days. You used to get junk mail marked with it in a brown envelope trying to look official, but that stopped years ago. This was in a plain white envelope and it was handwritten. I thought it was probably some crank, or anonymous letter, and I offered to open it and screen it for Rodney but he said leave it. He came out of his office in a foul mood and wanted to know if a woman had been trying to contact him. I said she had but that I hadn't wished to bother him with it because she wouldn't state her business or her name. He then gave me the third degree. What had she sounded like? Old? Young? Did she have an accent? I said I couldn't really say. That's all I can tell you, Inspector. Have you any more news on his death?'

'Not yet. Did he mention to you at any time feeling unwell, or being worried about his health?'

'Never.'

He rang off and called Giles Weatherby in Harley Street. After introducing himself to Weatherby's secretary, he requested that the doctor return his call that day if possible, and said it concerned Rodney Pierce. 'Did you know Mr Pierce?' he asked her.

'Not really. I only saw him a handful of times. He'd come for his yearly check-up and wasn't the talkative type. I'll get Mr Weatherby to call you.'

Horton informed Lymington Police to expect a visit from Adam Croft, who would make a statement, and to send it over to him as soon as that was done. Also to check out his alibi.

Walters returned and briefed Horton on the operation organized for the betting shops in Albert Road on Saturday night.

'There are five along that stretch, guv, and we don't know which one is likely to be raided. I've been down there to scout around and I've picked out the most likely. It has vacant premises either side and directly opposite. Sergeant Stride and I have arranged for them all to be watched from nine onwards, but I, and a couple of officers, will be inside that one. I've forewarned the manager. They close at ten, which is when there'll be money on the premises, and, if this fits the pattern of the others, Damien Cranley and his mate will storm in just before then.'

212

Weatherby returned Horton's call and, after some token protest about patient confidentiality and grumbling that he'd already spoken to DS Curran, he said that Rodney had not asked him for a genetic test, nor had he requested details of a reputable genetic testing organization. That didn't mean he hadn't approached one. He could have researched and contacted them independently.

Horton had just hung up when he saw that the test results on Alma had been sent over. He read them eagerly, and then reread them more slowly. A substance had been found in her system identified as the drug zopiclone. As far as Horton was aware, that hadn't been prescribed for her. He didn't know the drug, even though he had spent some time on the drug squad. He could ask Hobbs. Instead he called Olewbo. 'Are you around?'

'Yeah, just grabbing something to eat in the canteen.'

'I'll buy you a coffee.'

Horton made for the muscular, fit man in the far corner, casually and expensively dressed in designer clothes with a leather jacket draped over the seat Horton took.

'You look expensive.' Horton placed a coffee in front of Olewbo.

'Suppliers are always well kitted out.'

'Anything much going down?'

'A few things. We're getting closer to that gang from Manchester and have found a Pompey connection.'

'What do you know about zopiclone?'

Olewbo didn't even need to think about it. 'It's one of the "Z-drugs". It has pharmacological similarities with benzodiazepines used for sleep disorders and insomnia.'

Maybe Rodney had had some then, thought Horton, recalling what Hallet had told him about Rodney not sleeping much. Rodney had given it to Alma. 'How does it react?'

'It has a calming effect on the brain. It's a prescription-only drug and NHS approved. But not free from risk. Its hypnotic effect means some people experience difficulty recalling events. In extreme cases this can leave them very vulnerable.' Olewbo pushed away his empty plate.

'As in date rape?' asked Horton.

'Yes, and it's very risky if taken with alcohol or other depressants, such as the opioids. It can put extreme pressure on the heart and liver.'

Horton picked up on that. 'If someone already has a heart condition and is given a large dose . . .'

'He or she might never wake up.'

'She didn't.'

Olewbo's eyebrows shot up.

'How long would it take to have an effect?'

'Usually about an hour, although you'd feel drowsy before that.'

'Thanks, Hans.'

'Any time.'

Horton stepped outside and called the medical surgery. He asked to speak to Dr Goodson, giving his rank and saying it was concerning Alma Pierce. Some minutes later he came off the phone. Cantelli pulled into the car park. He'd been reviewing a case with the Crown Prosecution team due to be heard in two weeks' time. Horton waited for him to join him.

'Zopiclone.'

'Is that a new swear word?'

'No, it's a drug found in Alma's system. It certainly wasn't prescribed to her and, if taken by someone suffering from pulmonary arterial hypertension, as Alma was, it is highly dangerous. According to Dr Goodson, a large dose would certainly have killed her.'

Cantelli looked troubled. 'Taken deliberately herself or given to her without her knowledge?'

'Both Dr Goodson and Olewbo say the drug takes about an hour to work before the person falls asleep. It's often prescribed for insomnia and you could feel drowsy a while before dropping off. One of the carers saw Alma at eight thirty that night and she was fine, although tired, and Dr Goodson said rigor was well established when she examined Alma at eight fifteen the next morning. She believed her to have died in the early hours of the morning, three or four o'clock. That means no one slipped her the drug, she took it voluntarily.'

'Why would she do that? And how did she get hold of this zopiclone if the doctor didn't prescribe it? Could she have been prescribed it in hospital and kept a supply back?'

'Too dangerous for someone with her condition, and Dr Goodson says it's not on her medication record.'

'So who gave it to her? Pierce? Dorne?'

'Dorne is not Adam Croft. I've had a long talk with Croft; he has a rock-solid alibi if Lymington Police confirm it, which I believe they will. He hated Juliette but he didn't kill her, or move her body, and he doesn't know Alma or Rodney Pierce.'

As they walked to CID, Horton told him of his interview with Adam Croft and Riley's arrest and how he had found Juliette already dead. Outside the office, Horton halted. 'I wonder if Teesdale and his colleagues will find evidence of Rodney having obtained zopiclone and lorazepam on his hard drive.' Then he added, 'But Pierce would know that even if he deleted the files they could still be recovered. He wouldn't be daft enough to leave a trail. And why would Dorne get the zopiclone for Alma?'

'Because she asked him to, which means he has access to drugs, or got them off the internet, or had been prescribed them and kept hold of them for Alma. They've both been planning this for some time. Planning what though?' Cantelli added, somewhat exasperated.

'The murders of Juliette Croft and Rodney Pierce.'

Walters looked up from his computer. 'The coroner's report on Joseph Pierce's suicide has come through, guv. His body was found in his car with a hosepipe attached to the exhaust. A rambler discovered it in a copse not far from Carisbrooke. There was a suicide note. It said . . .' Walters read from the screen: '*My darling Alma, we made a mistake, and we've paid for it. I can no longer live with it. Sorry, my darling, to leave you. Not your fault. I let you down.*'

215

'What did the coroner make of that?'

'He thought Joseph alluded to their marriage and that his mind was unbalanced, full of regret for not providing for her in a way she had expected.'

'And what did she say?'

'She agreed. She said her husband felt a failure because he hadn't achieved what he wanted. His expectations had been too high for both himself and her. Whereas we know the real reason: they made a mistake agreeing to the illegal adoption of Rodney.'

'Was he questioned?'

'Not according to this.'

'And he wasn't living with them then. He'd already left for London.'

Cantelli pulled off his suit jacket and draped it on the back of his chair. 'I wonder if Pierce returned for Joseph's funeral.'

Horton answered. 'I doubt it, especially if he already knew about the adoption. I think he did, which was why he left home. Alma and Joseph told him, and Joseph took his own life after Rodney said some extremely hurtful, deeply wounding things.'

'But if he knew back then, he took a long time to confront Alma in January.'

'Which means there was something more that Juliette told him.' Horton relayed his theories. 'It could have taken him from January until now to find out if what Juliette told him was true and to plan her murder. But that doesn't explain why Alma moved close to him, who Dorne is and why she took her own life, holding that photograph. Come Monday, we'll have something from Hobbs on Pierce's autopsy. And you, Walters, might have Damien Cranley in custody for the betting shop robberies. That will at least be one case cleared up to please Superintendent Reine.'

Walters said, 'Nice of Damien to arrange it for when I'm duty CID.'

216

'He might not yet spoil your weekend. And I'm not going to let him spoil mine.' Or thoughts of the case. Horton wanted to clear his mind of it and come back fresh on Monday. By then something new might have struck him. 'I'm going sailing.'

'Lucky you,' Walters muttered.

CHAPTER TWENTY-FOUR

Monday

'I hear congratulations are in order.' Horton took a seat beside Walters in CID. He hadn't succeeded in clearing his mind of the case but he had enjoyed some sailing. He'd also spoken to Emma and listened to her excited chatter about ballet classes and her friend, Sophie, which had reassured him. He'd telephoned Catherine to say that Emma would spend at least one week of her half term holiday in October with him. She'd muttered something about not having finalized arrangements. 'I have,' he'd answered. 'It's agreed between me and my daughter. And you wouldn't want to disappoint her. Besides, you'll be busy clearing out the house now that you're selling it. And I'm sure you and Jarvis will have lots of things to do, what with work, the wedding and honeymoon plans.' He didn't think he had sounded bitter. She'd said she'd be in touch and had abruptly terminated the conversation.

Walters opened a packet of biscuits. 'Yeah, we caught young Cranley in the act, but he's admitting nothing until his solicitor arrives.'

'He has one?'

'Says Granny will get him one.'

'Good old Granny. Nice to know Cranley's following the family tradition. Did you get his accomplice?'

'Yes, Ishan Kumar. He looked as though he'd lost his cat when we nabbed him. I thought he was going to cry. He doesn't have a solicitor, only a very irate, hardworking father who swore in Hindi when he came in. At least, I think he was swearing. I wouldn't like to be in Ishan's shoes when we release him. Damien hasn't been the best influence on the lad. No previous. Just gone off the rails with his help . Ishan's only too eager to spill everything, unlike Damien, who's all bullshit and bravado.'

Horton again congratulated him, took a couple of biscuits and entered his office. He pulled back his blinds and saw Uckfield's and Trueman's cars in the car park. He'd become more convinced over the weekend that Pierce had learned some new devastating fact about his birth that he was loath to believe. This had caused him to rush over to the island to establish from Alma whether or not it were true. This meant she knew who his father was, and that secret had been kept until January, when Juliette had revealed it. Maybe she thought it was her trump card, and Rodney would pay up to guarantee her silence, and perhaps he had for a while. Could his father have been Joseph Pierce? Had Joseph had an affair with Juliette? But if so, why would that so infuriate Pierce? Horton felt he was on the edge of discovering what this secret was. He was convinced that there was a point he had alluded to early on in the investigation that meant something, but it was proving irritably elusive.

He checked his messages and emails. There was one from Dr Pooley, who said he had found a faint trace of a print on the tablet bottle and at the bottom of the champagne bottle. No match on the database.

There was still nothing from the Lisbon police. Horton politely chased them, requesting any information, no matter how sparse, about Juliette Croft.

They had cleared up the case of Yellow Shirt, but that seemed to be about it. Maybe if they could identify the source of the lorazepam and zopiclone that would give them a lead. And had Matthew Teesdale found anything on Pierce's hard drive or laptop to show he had obtained it, and that he had corresponded with Juliette after receiving those letters?

Horton took Teesdale's card from his wallet and rang the mobile number on it. There was no signal. Perhaps he was in a reception black spot or had forgotten to charge his phone. Horton called the management consultancy and asked to speak to him. Half an hour later he came off the line deeply troubled.

'The shit has hit the fan,' he said glumly to Walters and Cantelli. 'And it's about to get a great deal thicker and dirtier. Teesdale is not who he claimed to be.' He sank heavily on to the chair beside them. 'Simon Jepson, Aldsworth Consultancy's managing director, has never heard of Teesdale, and Jepson didn't ask for Rodney's hard drives to be taken.'

'Blimey!' Walters exclaimed.

'Not good,' was Cantelli's verdict.

'Jepson used a number of descriptions of the police, and me in particular, that almost rivalled Sheila Cranley's.' Again something nagged at the back of Horton's mind but there was no time to consider what it was.

'But you didn't authorize it,' Cantelli said.

'I didn't check his ID though. Nor did Kingston, who arrived at the same time as me. Hallet might have done. I'll call him in a moment.' Hallet hadn't returned his call yesterday. 'Teesdale only offered his card.' Horton put it on the desk. 'Send it over to the fingerprint bureau to see if they can get any prints off it that aren't mine. Jepson is going to make an official complaint about our incompetence.'

Cantelli said, 'That will include the chief constable then because, if I remember correctly, Teesdale telephoned him direct and the order was passed down for you to go there to oversee the removal of the hard drives.'

'Yes, but the hierarchy have a knack of passing the buck, and I know where it will stop. Teesdale has in his possession not only the hard drives associated with Rodney's work but also his laptop, which could contain personal information. Jepson's frantically telephoning Bridget, Kingston, Rodney's PA, and his lawyers and accountants to put a stop on all bank accounts.'

'Bit late for that,' Walters said. 'He could have cleaned them out by now if that was his intention. And if he has the passwords.'

'I think for a man like Teesdale getting them will probably be child's play.'

'So who is he?' Walters asked. 'I mean, why would he want this information aside from the obvious of getting his paws on all their money? I'd have thought a good hacker would have been able to do that remotely.'

'According to Jepson, Teesdale could be a competitor, a journalist, a seller of highly sensitive and lucrative information, a con man, a Russian spy, a Chinese agent, an insider trader and probably Jack the Ripper. That's my addition. I said that as yet nothing has been leaked to the press, but Jepson scoffed at that. If Teesdale is a competitor, or working for one, then they wouldn't be so crass as to leak anything. Over time, similarities to Pierce's company products would emerge and be launched onto the market ahead of them, with enough differences to avoid accusations of theft of intellectual property. I don't think Teesdale is any of those though, I think the hard drives were taken to hide his real interest, and that was to make sure that nothing points at his involvement in the deaths of Juliette, Alma and Rodney.'

'He's Dorne,' Cantelli said.

'The description and age — mid-to late fifties — fits, and I saw him!' Horton groaned. 'Another black mark against me. I didn't even get his vehicle licence number. It was a dark blue Ford Focus estate. Not a new one by what I can vaguely remember, about five or six years old. I'll phone Hallet.'

'I'll check Teesdale out on our records.' Cantelli turned to his computer. Horton returned to his office, knowing Cantelli would get nothing.

'Ed's just been on the phone.' Hallet answered Horton's call immediately. 'If I hadn't been leaving I'd have got the sack. I didn't remind him that he was here too.'

'Did you ask for Teesdale's ID?'

'Didn't have to. He showed me his security pass for Aldsworth. It all looked legit to me. He was wearing it on a lanyard.'

Horton had missed that. What was wrong with him? His powers of observation and thought seemed to have deserted him. 'But you didn't scrutinize it.'

'No, because I was told by the police to expect him,' Hallet stressed.

Exactly. And Horton too had fallen into the trap. Silently, he cursed his idiocy. Clever Teesdale had gone right to the top, and no one could or would have believed he, or his request, was anything but legitimate.

'And before you ask, I haven't any CCTV images of him,' Hallet continued. 'Because I don't keep them. I saw him drive up the private road and I was out front to meet him when he pulled up in a dark blue Ford Focus estate. I glanced at the registration number but by then Teesdale had got out and the licence plate was muddy like the wheels. I only remember it had the number sixty-five in it. I wasn't expecting the man to be a phoney. And Ed Kingston didn't get the number either. Did you?'

'No. What did you and he talk about before I showed up?'

'He said he hadn't been there before, which I can bear out, unless he came on my days off. But then someone else would have taken over from me. Ed's going to check with my replacements. He asked me if there was news on how Rodney had died. I said if there was I wasn't party to it. He hazarded a guess that it was a heart attack, pressure of work, et cetera. He said it seemed a waste for Rodney to live there when he wasn't a sailor. I muttered something about it not being easy to get a boat this far up the creek.'

'How did he know he wasn't a sailor?' Horton picked up.

'No idea. I assumed Rodney must have mentioned it to him. I didn't know at the time he was a fraud. He wasn't here long before you and Ed arrived. He was a very smooth operator, but then con men usually are. If they're not, they get banged up.'

Not always. 'Why didn't you return my call yesterday?'

'Sorry, I forgot.'

Maybe. 'Have you ever seen a woman visit the house — slender, short white-grey hair, early seventies?'

'No.'

'Did Pierce ever mention taking zopiclone, or have you seen it in the house?'

'No.'

Horton rang off. He relayed the latest to Cantelli, who confirmed that they had nothing on a Matthew Teesdale. 'I'll see if I can pick up anything from the DVLA.'

'And I'd better break the bad news to Reine. He might ask me to clear my desk.'

Horton was sure Reine would have done if he and the chief constable hadn't likewise been taken in by Teesdale's duplicity. Reine curtly reminded him that the police were meant to investigate and prevent fraud, not be a party to it.

'Don't you have any idea who he is?' he demanded.

'Only that he's connected with Alma Pierce and Juliette Croft, as was Rodney Pierce. And as all three are dead, that doesn't take us much further forward. Except it does point at those deaths being suspicious.'

Reine snorted. 'Two suicides and one natural death.'

'We haven't the results of the latter yet and the first is dubious.'

'I want more than dubious, Inspector, and so will the chief. It's clear to me this Teesdale read about Rodney Pierce's death and took advantage of it to steal highly valuable information. Both you and the security man . . . underperformed.'

Horton knew he had intended to say 'acted incompetently', only he'd remembered in time that Teesdale had duped the chief constable too. That would be Horton's saving grace. He'd been acting on the chief's command.

'I will inform the chief constable and see what action he wants to take. Meanwhile, I suggest you get your finger out and find this Teesdale.'

'Yes, sir.'

'Do you need a cardboard box, guv?' Walters greeted him.

'Not yet, my desk and its contents are safe for now. Where's Cantelli?'

'Got called out. There's been another spate of keyless car thefts.'

'I thought the thieves had moved on.'

'So did Inspector Tadley. I'm just going to interview Damien. His solicitor has arrived. The sarge said there are a couple of Matthew Teesdales on the DVLA database but they don't fit the age profile. One is ninety, lives in Sunderland, and the other, seventy-eight, lives in Hereford.'

'It's a fake name anyway, just like Dorne, and this blighter's damn clever at forgeries. Bring me back some good news from your interview with Damien.'

'I'll do my best, guv. Let's hope Granny's spent all her money on hubby's funeral and Damien doesn't get bail.'

'Granny didn't pay for it, Norman's old cell mate Jackie Alfleet did, according to Jago, and Alfleet might cough up bail for her grandson.'

'Hope not.'

Horton did too. His conversation with Walters, though, had triggered a chain of thoughts, connected not with Dorne but with Juliette. Before he could follow it through, Danby rang him.

'I hear things are bad.'

'You could say that.'

'Kingston is torn between disbelief and anger. It doesn't look good on him or his company if it comes out.'

'It doesn't reflect well on the police either, or me in particular,' Horton said with slight bitterness. He was truly annoyed with himself.

'There's always that job with me if they kick you out.'

'So you keep saying.'

'And I'll continue to. One day you might say yes.'

'You make it sound like a marriage proposal.'

Danby laughed. 'I didn't ring you for that reason. I've looked deeper into Hallet; as you know, I've offered him a job. He's accepted it. I can't find any link between him and Rodney Pierce. He wasn't born or raised on the Isle of Wight or in Portsmouth. He's not related to Bob Spiley, so no axe to grind for the poor man dying before he could benefit from the sale of his and Pierce's gaming company. He's never worked directly for Pierce or a competitor, and isn't related to Juliette Croft or Alma Pierce, as far as I can tell. He's clean, Andy.'

'I thought he might be.'

'Any idea who this man Teesdale is?'

'None whatsoever.'

Danby scoffed. 'Not saying, eh? Good luck.'

'I need it.'

He rang off and picked up the threads of his earlier thoughts. He recalled what Jago had told him about Jackie Alfleet paying for Cranley's funeral and how he had lived abroad, in Spain or Portugal: *He's been spending a lot of time with a certain widow.* Then there was what Adam Croft had said about the man at Cranley's funeral talking to Juliette after it: *a small, very thin man with a weathered face* who had looked hard at her and it hadn't bothered her. No, because she'd found someone else to squeeze. Walters' words also resounded in his head when they had first been discussing those funerals: *I'd have thought the Co-op would have been her first choice.* Yes, why did Sheila Cranley pick Lindleys, the other side of the city? And why choose Juliette as the celebrant? Sheila wouldn't have known her, but he was betting Alfleet did, and intimately. Horton made for Sheila's flat.

CHAPTER TWENTY-FIVE

He parked the Harley in the nearest public car park close to the Hard, not wanting to risk it being vandalized or stolen outside Sheila's flat. From there he walked the short distance to the run-down tower block with a small graffiti-sprayed skate park close to it. She didn't recognize him in his leathers and helmet when he asked to speak to Jackie, which was just as well, although she eyed him with deep mistrust and hostility.

'Some Hells Angel wants to speak with you, Jackie,' she shouted over her shoulder.

A bony man with a slight stoop and a cigar in his small hand appeared. His casual trousers and shirt looked expensive and there was some impressive jewellery on his fingers and wrists. 'What do you want?' he asked, aggressively cagey.

'A word.' Horton jerked his head and set off along the veranda, expecting Alfleet to follow. He did.

Turning, Horton looked to see if Sheila was watching them, but she wasn't. He showed his ID.

'Don't look much like a cop. Is it about those betting shops? You're not drug squad, are you? I told the stupid squirt I won't have anything to do with that. I've got him a brief and I've told Sheila I'll pay for it and then it's finished.

No bail, no more, no nothing. I promised Norman I'd see Sheila was all right and take care of things and I have. I've done my bit. The slate's wiped clean.'

'It doesn't concern Damien. It's Juliette Croft.'

Alfleet was momentarily stunned. Then his small eyes narrowed. 'She's dead. I read about it in the paper.'

'Where were you Tuesday before last from nine until midnight?'

'Why should I tell you?'

'You want me to take you in?'

'I was with Sheila.'

'She'd alibi the devil himself.'

'I've got no reason to kill Juliette.'

'Then perhaps Sheila did. She was jealous of Juliette's attention towards you,' Horton bluffed. He didn't believe for a moment that Sheila was the killer.

'She had no reason to be, what was between me and Juliette was over and done with. I told Juliette that.'

He'd been right. 'When?'

'After the funeral.'

'And how did she take it?'

'She didn't give a toss. She'd got what she wanted and she had bigger fish to fry.'

'She said that?'

'Well, she wasn't heartbroken, but then I wouldn't expect her to be. That woman wouldn't shed a tear for anyone, though you'd never believe it to look at her. She did a good job at Norman's funeral, but then she was clever at twisting things round so that it sounded good, or made her look like bloody sweetness and light. And she was a born liar. She said what Sheila wanted to hear. I told Juliette what was needed and I paid her handsomely to deliver it. That's one of the things I said to her after the funeral — she'd got everything she was going to get from me, including sex.'

'Was she blackmailing you?'

'Like hell she was.' Alfleet laughed. 'Nothing to black-mail me over. I've stayed clean since being released. She was like a reptile that tempts you into her lair and then begins to devour you. I'd seen her operate on Tom Wheeler.'

'Her lover in Portugal,' guessed Horton. Alfleet was backing up what Adam Croft and Dennis Sperryman had told him.

'You know about him?'

'We've been in touch with the Lisbon police.' The truth, although they hadn't responded yet.

'Not much point in me playing dumb then.'

'No.'

A woman with a shopping trolley interrupted them. Horton waited until she had hobbled along the veranda.

'I had a villa in Cascais just outside Lisbon on the coast. Juliette and Tom were neighbours. Being fellow expats, we got together for drinks and meals. Wheeler was a good bit older than her. Made his fortune in real estate and probably other dodgy deals, but unlike me he'd never been to prison. Might have got nicked a few times and got off, I don't know, and I didn't much care. He had pots of money, or so everyone thought until he died two years ago. Then Juliette found herself laden with his debts and had to sell the villa. She'd already told me she had a house here in Portsmouth, which Tom had given her the money to buy. A nest egg, she said, in case she needed it when he popped his clogs. Wheeler was probably siphoning money off from somewhere to avoid tax or being caught for money laundering.'

The shouts of a man blaspheming came from below. He sounded drunk. Horton hoped he didn't come up and disturb them. After another choice phrase, he shut up.

'Someone probably landed him one,' Alfleet said, unconcerned. 'Or gave him another bottle to swig. I sold my villa and returned to London three years ago, before Tom died. My health is none too good, as you can probably see by my skinny frame. I decided I'd rather die here than on foreign soil. I'd kept in touch with Sheila, who I'd met on visiting days, and who I'd kept an eye on from time to time after my release. I promised Norman I would. He was my minder. I'm fast on my feet and good with the punches but sometimes in the nick that's not enough. Norman was not to be messed with. He had a reputation as a hard man, and he was. We came from the same city, this one.'

But Horton knew that wasn't enough for Norman to have attached himself to Alfleet. Payment would be required on Norman's release, and Alfleet would settle the debt then, only Norman died before he could collect.

'Juliette and I had kept in touch. She told me about Wheeler's death and that she'd moved into her house here.'

Hoping to rekindle old flames. 'And Juliette thought she could pick up with you where Wheeler had left off.'

'I'm not that daft. I saw right through it. Juliette was always out to get what she could. No problem with that. I took it while it was on offer. No harm in having a bit of fun, especially at our age when it might be our last fling. And I had a lot of lost years to make up for.'

'And when you didn't propose to her, or offer to keep her in the style to which she'd become accustomed, she had to resort to singing and being a celebrant.'

'Yes. She told me that in the hope I'd be sympathetic and cough up more money, but I'm good at stalling.' He smiled. 'When Norman died, Sheila wrote to me. I said I'd take care of everything for her. I came down to Pompey. I thought Juliette could do the funeral. She thought Sheila was a scream, her words, and took the piss out of her. I joined in, behind Sheila's back, but only to keep Juliette sweet, and where I needed her.'

'Until after the funeral, when you told her it was bye-bye.'

'Yes, and she said that suited her fine. By her manner I knew she'd found some other sucker to bleed dry.'

So did Horton: Rodney Pierce. Only he wasn't having it. He was as smart as Alfleet had been.

Alfleet continued. 'She said, "I won't need you anyway when the ship comes in."'

And hers had, but not in the way she'd foreseen. Horton pressed Alfleet further but he had nothing new to add, and he'd never heard Juliette talk of an Alma or a Rodney Pierce.

229

On his return to the station, Reine summoned him to say that the theft of the hard drives had been handed over to the Met fraud squad, who would work in conjunction with the high-tech unit. 'You're to inform Dr Hobbs to send the full results of the autopsy on Rodney Pierce to Detective Superintendent Dawson, who is leading the investigation.'

'And Juliette Croft and Alma Pierce?'

'I don't see that's relevant.'

'Juliette's computer is still missing.'

'She ditched it before taking her own life, or Ballantine stole it and won't admit it. Give Dawson anything he needs, Inspector. And get on with your other duties.'

Horton relayed this to Cantelli and Walters, and his interview with Alfleet, including the fact that he wouldn't be coughing up for Damien's bail.

Walters beamed. 'Best news I've had all day. He's a cocky sod. Boasting about his dad and grandad going to prison as though it's a badge of honour. Criminal activity is a way of life for them and they don't see anything wrong with it, not until they're on the other end of it, then they're screaming for us. You all right, guv?'

'What did you just say?'

'You all right?'

'No, before that. About Damien Cranley.'

'I didn't think your memory was that bad. Maybe you should see the quack.'

'You said something about a badge of honour.'

'Yeah. Instead of being ashamed of all his relatives being banged up and him heading for a stretch, Damien's proud of it. Not an ounce of shame or guilt—'

'Shame. That could be it.'

'Could be what?' Walters was clearly puzzled. He glanced at Cantelli, whose brow knitted.

'Rodney Pierce.' Horton sat forward as thoughts raced through his head. 'You know I said that perhaps Rodney had discovered his real father might have had a hereditary illness or been mentally unbalanced and committed? Both

230

were enough to make him see red, according to what we've learned of him. But what if his birth father was a criminal? Juliette gave up the baby because the father was in the nick. How would Rodney have felt after learning that?'

'Shocked, I'd say,' Cantelli answered. 'And pretty livid at being lied to.'

'Not to mention furious when Juliette made it clear she thought her son owed her something, and if he didn't pay up she might have to sell her story to the gutter press, or anyone else prepared to pay for it. Rodney's father could have been a big-time criminal. Maybe one or two of Rodney's clients, or investors, might wonder about *his* ethics if it came out.'

'And his competitors would love it,' Walters added. 'You could be right, guv. If rumours started flying round on social media, it might be enough to make people wonder how he'd made his money in the first place. How many crooked deals had he been behind? The taxman might also have come nosing around.'

'And it's motive enough for him to silence her by agreeing to meet her and putting lorazepam in her drink — only he couldn't have done, he has an alibi, unless he did it earlier that afternoon. But I think someone else knows the truth of Rodney's parentage: Dorne. Alma told him. And Dorne could have killed Juliette to protect Alma. He could also have used the information to blackmail Pierce into coughing up for Alma's care. That doesn't explain why Alma trusted this man. We'll come back to that in due course. First, we need to find out if we're on the right track. I'd say Rodney's father is dead and he obviously knew nothing about the fake adoption, or who his son was, otherwise he'd have tried it on Pierce himself. So what do we know about this man? That he was sent to prison after Juliette became pregnant.'

'Be a neat trick getting her pregnant in the nick, would have caused quite a stir during visiting time. Stir . . . Get it?' Walters grinned. 'Please yourself.'

Cantelli picked it up. 'We're looking at a time frame then from June 1969 to early February 1970, when Rodney was born, assuming he wasn't premature. Her school friend, Sharon Rainey, didn't mention that Juliette was pregnant, or that she looked to be.'

'Re-interview her tomorrow, see what more you can get from her.'

Cantelli nodded.

'The crime could have been committed during that period, or earlier if he was out on bail. We should look from between the beginning of January 1969 to the end of January 1970.' Horton suddenly sat up as another elusive fact crystallized. 'I think you might have been right yesterday, Walters, when you said Juliette could have been talking bullshit when she met Sharon on her way to the Isle of Wight Festival. She might not have been going there at all. Crime . . . prison . . .'

'Parkhurst! Category A. Lifers,' Walters declared. 'She was visiting her lover in Parkhurst, where he was serving his sentence.'

'Yes, and we roughly know when from Sharon. Now all we need to do is examine the visitors' log for that week in August 1969.'

'I like the way you say "all". They probably haven't been digitized, but are stuck in a dusty cupboard somewhere no one can remember.'

'Get on to it tomorrow.'

Cantelli said, 'It must have been a major crime for him to end up there, and that's what really riled Pierce.'

'Anything big happen around then?'

'That didn't involve the Krays?'

'Hadn't thought of them. Sharon said Juliette left for London to become a singer, and if she sang in the nightclubs then it's possible she came across them. The Krays would be enough to cause massive media attention, which Rodney certainly wouldn't want.'

Walters was keying into his computer. 'Couldn't have been them. The time frame's wrong. Their trial, and those of their accomplices, was held in March sixty-nine and they were all convicted.'

'OK, so we rule them out, but we're still looking at murder for this man to have ended up in Parkhurst, and it's possible that because Juliette was living in London, according to Sharon, the crime was committed or tried there. Walters, if you have no joy with the Parkhurst visitors' log, check out the major trials in the London courts for that period, in particular the Old Bailey. Also try the national newspapers. Their records will be digitized and probably easy to search online.'

'Might take some time.'

'Or you might strike lucky.'

'I don't see how it will help find Dorne.'

'Why not? He could be the son of a villain who was also banged up in Parkhurst at the same time. Alma or Joseph knew Dorne's father. Could have been a relation. Alma or Joseph met Juliette on visiting day. It's either there or in St Mary's Hospital. Anything from Norris on the maternity records?'

Walters shook his head.

Horton felt sure they were now on the right track but, as Walters had said, he wasn't sure it would lead them to Dorne, even though he had said it might. It involved a lot of work and they were under-resourced. He was also under orders from Reine to drop it. There was no proof that Juliette or Alma had been murdered, and if they had been then the prime suspect, Rodney Pierce, was also dead and no one seemed to be clamouring for justice. Not unless Bridget Pierce suddenly did, which she wouldn't. He was about to make for his office when his phone rang. 'It's Dr Hobbs.' He put it on loudspeaker and informed Hobbs of that.

'Rodney Pierce died of an intracranial haemorrhage. In plain English, bleeding on the brain.'

A natural death then, thought Horton. 'What would have caused it?'

'Several things, most of which I've ruled out, given my examination and his medical history. He didn't smoke and as far as I'm aware wasn't a cocaine taker. There's no evidence of a trauma to the brain, no tumour or rupture, or malformation. It could have been as a result of an infection, although

I can't find any signs of that. His medical records show no evidence of vasculitis, inflammation of the blood vessels, or coagulopathy, a bleeding disorder where the blood's ability to coagulate is affected — you've probably heard of haemophilia and Von Willebrand disease, clotting factor deficiencies. Deep venous thrombosis is another coagulation disorder. But as I said, he didn't have any of these, because if he did they'd have shown up on his medical records, and he'd have been on an anticoagulant like warfarin.'

'Alma Pierce was on warfarin.'

'Yes, and the zopiclone she took reacted with that to her detriment, causing heart failure, not an intracranial haemorrhage.'

'Could he have taken, or been given, a massive dose of warfarin?' asked Horton. Had Dorne acquired warfarin from Alma, enough to kill Pierce?

'In a healthy patient such as Pierce, a single dose of warfarin wouldn't be a problem, but if combined with other drugs such as aspirin, supplements and certain drinks — and if he didn't get medical help quickly, which he didn't — it is just possible.'

And Horton had learned that Pierce took vitamins and aspirin.

Hobbs said, 'We need to wait for the test results. They should be through within a couple of days.'

'How quickly would the haemorrhage have occurred? Would he have had any symptoms beforehand?'

'It can be very rapid. The most common sign is a sudden and severe headache, although this may not always occur, particularly among older people. Although he wasn't that old. Other intracranial haemorrhage signs could be tingling, weakness or paralysis on one side of the body, difficulty speaking, disorientation and confusion, loss of, or change, in vision, difficulty swallowing and a change in his level of alertness.'

'So that could have happened during the evening.' Horton glanced at Cantelli. 'He stumbled out into the dark. Being confused, he left his mobile and torch behind and ended up above the shore before suffering this massive haemorrhage.'

'Possibly. Or, as I said, it might have come on so rapidly that he'd already got to the shore when he fell ill and there was no one around to help him. Even if there had been, he wouldn't have survived. That's all I can tell you at present, Inspector.'

Horton asked him to send a copy of his report to Detective Superintendent Dawson as well as to him, and gave him Dawson's contact details.

Cantelli said, 'Sounds as though his death was sadly just one of those things.'

'I'm still not convinced. I'll call Hallet.' Horton did so, again leaving it on loudspeaker, while Walters went to fetch some drinks. Without giving Hallet the details, he asked if Pierce had exhibited fatigue, confusion or any symptoms of that kind before his death.

'If he did, he didn't show it or let on to me. Like I told you, after Sunday he shut himself away in his office complex and I only saw him briefly, once. He was very terse but that wasn't unusual, and he looked paler, but that probably came from working too hard and marital problems.'

'Is Bridget on any medication?'

'I don't know.'

'Are you?'

'No.'

Horton rang off and said to Cantelli, 'I'll call Bridget. She needs to be informed of the results of the autopsy. I'm not sure if she'll answer my call though, given what's happened to her husband's computers.'

She did though, and promptly. That was explained by her first question.

'You have the results of the post-mortem?'

'Yes, although there are still the results of the blood and tissue samples to come. Your husband died of an intracranial haemorrhage.' There was silence while she digested this.

He'd love to have seen her expression. Perhaps he should have suggested a video call. He continued. 'We're trying to determine the cause, hence the sample analyses. I know this is a difficult time for you, Mrs Pierce, and I don't wish to delay or upset you, but are you on any tranquilizers such as lorazepam or zopiclone or an anticoagulant like warfarin?'

'Me? What's that got to do with it?'

'There's the possibility that Mr Pierce might have taken one of those by mistake.'

'Well, he didn't get them from me. I'm drug free.'

'Did he complain of a headache when he returned on Sunday?'

'If he did, I didn't hear him. You'll let me know if you have any further news?'

'Of course. And I'll be liaising with Detective Superintendent Dawson, who is investigating the theft of your husband's hard drives and laptop.'

'So he said.'

'She doesn't sound too upset,' was Walters' verdict as he put their drinks in front of them.

'Or impressed with Dawson,' Cantelli added.

'It might just be her way of coping. She must be under a lot of stress. And I won't be a hundred per cent satisfied he died a natural death until we get those results. Teesdale, aka Dorne, is top of my list of suspects if the results come back positive. He's clever, he knows about drugs and their effects.'

'That can all be researched,' Walters dismissed.

'He has access to drugs, which could be from a pharmacy, or from the internet. He evidently knows a lot about computers and hard drives.'

'Anyone can unscrew a computer and remove the hard drive.'

'But he knew it could still contain valuable information even if the files had been deleted, and not everyone knows that. He was someone Alma trusted, who must have had a strong enough grudge against Juliette and Rodney to have killed them, because he surely wouldn't have done so on the whim of an old lady he liked.' Horton sat back thoughtfully. 'Or he owes Alma or Joseph a debt. Or he's out for revenge. Juliette's old flame and Rodney's father, who might have been in prison with Dorne's father, did something to cause that.'

Cantelli said, 'Fitted him up? Beat him up? Killed him? Or it could be connected to whatever charge Juliette's lover, if she had one, was sentenced for. And Dorne recently discovered that fact via either Alma or Juliette, because Rodney only knew of it in January and shortly afterwards Alma sold up and moved to the mainland.'

'Yes, and that indicates she confided in Dorne while in hospital. It could be a hospital visitor, a chaplain, padre, doctor, male nurse, rehabilitation officer, member of the admin staff—'

'Who happens to be a whiz on computers,' said Walters.

Horton looked hopeful. 'And who recognized Alma or knew her of old, and suddenly she was telling him all about Rodney. He must have known Rodney as a child. Look at their ages, they're similar, possibly even the same.'

'We might get something from his school records,' Cantelli said dubiously. Horton knew why. It meant checking which of his school chums were still around and interviewing each one of them. It would take for ever and they could be scattered to the four winds. Reine wouldn't sanction putting out a press statement asking for assistance, and Pierce's management and PR companies certainly wouldn't approve it, especially on the basis of Hobbs's autopsy findings.

He said, 'Our best bet is to find out which ward Alma was on and ask the ward sister. That still might throw up a lot of people, but it could be worth a try. It's probable that this person sat with Alma several times. It could have been under the guise of health reasons, but perhaps someone on that ward remembers any regular visitors.' He stretched his aching limbs. 'I'll go over to the island tomorrow and follow up that line of enquiry. I'll also re-interview Joyce Snow. I didn't ask if she visited Alma in hospital and I'm sure she must have done. Cantelli, you take Sharon Rainey, and Walters, see what you can find on any court cases about that time that might be relevant. If we draw a blank, that will be it. We'll spend no more time on it, unless Pierce's blood and tissue results come back with something patently suspicious.' Even then it would be handed over to Dawson. 'Having got this far, let's give it one more shot.'

CHAPTER TWENTY-SIX

Tuesday

Horton was on the ferry the next morning when Cantelli phoned. 'Sharon said that Juliette looked similar to when they had been at school together, which was just over a year before. She hadn't put on weight, not so she noticed. She was wearing a long printed dress that flowed from under her boobs. Sharon noted it because she was envious. Juliette looked very cool in it, a hippy with a band tied round her forehead and her long fair hair.'

'Fair?'

'Yes. I've got a photo of her taken at school. I'll send it over. It's Juliette. She obviously a changed her hair colour when she changed her career to the cruise ships. Probably because it was fashionable in the seventies to be dark-haired. Just guessing. We know that Juliette was pregnant when Sharon saw her, but not massively, so the style of the dress could have hidden it. And she didn't mention it to her old school friend. But there was one interesting thing Sharon remembered. I'd sparked her memory.'

As Horton knew could happen. He hoped it might with Joyce Snow.

'Juliette was wearing a ring on the third finger of her left hand. Not a traditional wedding or engagement ring. It was a modern one with a kind of emblem on it, like a signet ring but not gold. She didn't know what it was made of and she didn't have the chance to ask Juliette if she was engaged or married, but Sharon was of the opinion that, knowing Juliette, she'd probably broken the conventional rules of the era and was living with someone. But what if she was married in 1969 and Rodney *wasn't* illegitimate? We didn't check. We assumed her first marriage was to Howard Gleeson because the marriage certificate gives her maiden name, Inglis. But we know that Juliette was involved in perjury concerning her baby's birth—'

'So she could have lied to Gleeson and the authorities. She committed bigamy.'

'She didn't,' Cantelli firmly replied. 'But she did give false information by using her maiden name when she married Gleeson.'

Horton could hear the excitement in Cantelli's voice. 'You've tracked the first husband down?'

'Yes, and it's given us a short cut in trawling through those court cases and prison visitor records. You were right about Pierce's father being a criminal. The Register of Births, Deaths and Marriages shows Juliet Inglis married Roddy Sumners in 1969. And Sumners died in 1971, the year Juliette went to work on the cruise ships, and two years before she wed Gleeson. Sumners' death certificate says he died in Dartmoor prison, suicide.'

Horton gave a low whistle while his brain grappled with this new information. 'Not Parkhurst. She wasn't visiting him.'

'No. Walters looked up his prison record, thankfully digitized. No next of kin was named. Sumners was convicted of murder on 22 December 1969. We've applied for the case record and trial notes, and there will be stuff online from the press reports.'

'Keep me posted.' Another piece of the puzzle of Juliette's life slotted in, but he still didn't see how Dorne was involved.

As he disembarked the ferry and made for Carisbrooke, he thought how his view of Juliette Croft had changed over the last two weeks since first seeing her body on that sofa. Then he had been looking at a respectable seventy-year-old woman, living alone and possibly lonely, who had sadly taken her own life because of personal, financial or health problems. Now he saw her as a compulsive liar, someone who had no qualms about committing perjury and fraud, a woman who had exploited and manipulated men for her own financial gain until she met one who would not cave in — her son. By all accounts, Rodney had been brutal, obsessive and competitive to extremes. Everything Horton had learned about him hinted at a sociopath. Had his father been like that too? Had Rodney always been that way, even as a child? Horton suspected it.

He turned in to the leafy lane close to Carisbrooke Castle and pulled up outside the Snows' bungalow. An estate car was on the driveway and several builders' vans littered the road, their music booming out. Horton knocked, setting off the dogs who continued barking as the door was opened by an amiable, fit-looking, suntanned man in his early seventies.

'You must be the detective my wife told me about,' he said smiling, eyeing Horton's motorbike leathers. 'I'm Wilf Snow. Come in.' He led Horton through to the same room as on the previous occasion and let the dogs out. 'A bit of barking won't be noticed among all that racket.' He waved Horton into a comfy chair while Joyce Snow made him a coffee even though he had refused one.

'I hear you've been asking about Alma. The missus told me she'd passed away. Sad. After that last heart attack it was touch and go. I never thought she'd come out of it. To be honest, I don't think it did her much good moving away like that from here to the mainland. It was all very sudden. I think she was pushed into it. She probably didn't expect to get a buyer that quickly. I know the housing market has its ups and downs and this is a popular area, but if you ask me that chap had someone already lined up for next door and did a deal on it.'

'You mean the estate agent?'

'No, but I bet this man who helped her was in league with them. I asked her who he was. She said he was a dear friend, but we never saw him visit her in all the years we'd been neighbours — did we?' He addressed his wife as she returned and put a mug of black coffee on a coaster of Carisbrooke Castle on the little table beside Horton.

'Who?'

'That tall man I told you about, about fifty-five, with a nice suit, grey hair.'

'You mean the welfare worker.'

'No, I don't. He was younger, about thirty, and came once when she first came out of hospital. Then this older man came. I suppose he could have been from social care, he wore one of those things round his neck.'

Could this be Dorne? The description fitted. 'You mean he was wearing a lanyard.'

'That's it. Like they do in schools and in local government. It was tucked inside his suit jacket when he left next door. I was cutting the grass. It being so mild, it was growing and I was taking the top off it like they do the greens on the golf course, never does them any harm even in January, or all winter come to that, and we don't get harsh ones here.'

And it was a good way of being nosy without appearing to be. But Horton welcomed that.

'I stopped and asked him if Alma was all right. He said she's very well thank you. Then he got in his car and drove off.'

'Did he try to hide the lanyard?'

'No.'

'I don't suppose you saw what it said?'

'No, sorry.'

'Can you remember the make of car?'

'Yes, a blue Ford Focus.'

Horton hid his excitement. He had hoped for a break but had never really expected one. It was the same make as Teesdale had driven. But then he told himself there were a lot of blue Ford Focus cars about. 'Do you remember the number?' he asked hopefully.

'I know it was sixty-five because I thought it an old car for an estate agent to drive, they're often in new ones. There was also a J and an S, them being Joyce's initials, but that's about it.'

Was this enough to run through the DVLA database? It was still vague. Maybe Walters could check out some permutations.

'Did you ask Alma for his name?'

'No.'

'And you didn't see him, Mrs Snow?'

She looked thoughtful. 'Not then, but now you come to mention him I might have done. They wear those lanyard things in hospitals, don't they?'

Horton nodded and sipped his coffee, his pulse in overdrive.

'That's where I saw him then. He fits Wilf's description.'

'But he could have been anyone,' her husband interjected. 'Lots of men fit that description.'

She tossed him a withering look before bestowing a more kindly one on Horton. 'He was at the nurses' station when I visited Alma. I thought he must be a doctor or welfare worker.'

Her husband cut in. 'How do you know he had anything to do with Alma? You never said this when I told you about him visiting her here.'

'That's because you didn't describe him,' she quipped. 'I was walking the dogs. Someone has to.'

'They're your dogs.'

'Yes, and I get more sense out of them than I do you,' she quipped. 'You just said a man called. For all I knew he could have been short, fat, forty and spotty.'

'Are you sure you're not making it up about seeing him in the hospital?'

A point Horton was considering.

She looked affronted. 'Of course I'm not. Are you accusing me of lying? And in front of the police! Why, I—'

'Mrs Snow, why did you think he was a doctor or welfare worker?' Horton quickly interceded to prevent a bickering match.

'He was the other side of the desk, talking to the sister, and they were looking at a computer. They were discussing something to do with systems. I thought he might be looking up a record or something. They were very polite and the sister asked if she could help. I enquired where Alma Pierce was and she told me. I had a nice chat with Alma. She was a bit down and I tried to cheer her up. I didn't stay long because she was tired. But when I got to the lifts I realized I'd left my gloves behind. I went back and that man was at Alma's bedside. They were talking quite close together and she looked more cheerful. I asked the sister if she would fetch my gloves as I didn't wish to intrude with the doctor there. She said he wasn't a doctor but one of their IT managers and a friend of Alma's. She was sure neither Alma nor Mr Tavistock would mind, but I—'

'She gave you his name?' Horton almost shouted. He could hardly believe his luck. His blood was pumping fast with excitement.

'Yes.' Joyce looked dazed by his reaction. 'I remember it because of the place. But I still didn't like to burst in on them as they looked to be so close. And *he* was waiting outside in the car park.' She jerked her head at her husband. 'And you know how impatient men are, and how expensive hospital car parks are. The sister was lovely, she went across and fetched the gloves and slipped them to me without them noticing.'

Horton could have kissed her. Horton could get Tavistock's details from the hospital trust, but the DVLA might be quicker. He thanked them warmly and rode to Newport where the hospital was, but instead pulled up at the quay and silenced the Harley. Walking down to the River Medina, where a handful of boats were moored, he saw he'd missed a call from Cantelli. Eagerly he returned it while sitting on a bench.

244

'It's been pretty straightforward getting information on Sumners. The case notes haven't been digitized, so I haven't been able to access them, but the trial transcripts have. I've only just started reading them, and very interesting reading they make too. Sumners was convicted of the murder of a girl at the Isle of Wight Festival in 1969.'

'The one Sharon saw Juliette heading to?'

'Yes. Gillian Preston was a vocalist like Juliette. She was found dead in their caravan. Sumners was seen leaving it. Gillian Preston was pregnant.'

'His child?'

'Don't know. No DNA testing then. Sumners was one of the road crew. I wonder if any of them are still around.'

'Well, it can't be Teesdale aka Dorne who is really Tavistock, too young for that.'

'You've located him?' Cantelli cried excitedly.

'I'm about to. Joyce Snow saw him with Alma on the ward, and her husband saw him visiting Alma only once, after she was discharged. The description and make of car fit to a T. He's involved in hospital computer systems.'

He heard Cantelli call to Walters to check out Tavistock on the DVLA database. 'Blue Ford Focus.'

'I've also got the numbers sixty-five and the letters J and S.'

Cantelli relayed this.

Horton said, 'Given his age, and now we know his background in computers, I'd say that he knew Rodney Pierce when they were younger because he knows Alma.'

'He might be Roddy Sumners' son by another woman.'

'He'd have been putting it about a bit.'

'Free love and all that.'

'Yes, but I can't see how that would involve him being so close to Alma and killing Juliette and Rodney Pierce.'

'If he did.'

'What else have you got?'

'The gist of the prosecution's case is that Roddy Sumners arranged to meet Gillian in the band's caravan while they

245

were on stage checking over their gear. He was seen going into the caravan and was heard to be having an almighty argument with her. Gillian was pregnant by him, he wanted her to have an abortion and she refused. Another witness saw him leaving after ten minutes.'

'How did she die?'

'Massive overdose of heroin. The post-mortem found bruises on Gillian's body where she was held down while being injected with a lethal dose. It also revealed she was not a drug user. The syringe and heroin were found in Sumners' van. Medical evidence confirmed he was not a heroin addict. The defence state that when Gillian didn't show on stage Sumners was sent to fetch her. He found her dead and the police were called. He denied killing her but admitted to going to the caravan to have it out with her about the baby. He claimed it wasn't his child.'

'It's a bit circumstantial.'

'That's what I thought. But there's a lot I haven't read and the case notes will tell us more when we get them. They should be with us in a couple of days.'

'Where was the trial held?'

'The Old Bailey.'

'And he was convicted just before Christmas?'

'Yes. On 22 December.'

'Is Juliette mentioned as a witness?'

'That's another interesting thing. I skimmed some of the trial notes to see if she was called. She was. Under her maiden name Inglis. No mention of their marriage. The indictment says he was Rodney Charles Sumners, single, aged twenty-seven from Brixton, London. Maybe he didn't say he was married to Juliette and she kept silent because it would have given him an even stronger motive for murder, especially with her being heavily pregnant by the time of the trial. When called she promptly fainted, after being sworn in under her maiden name. Perjury again. She was excused and provided another written statement swearing under oath that she was on the stage at the time, and this was backed up by the band and crew. Perhaps she believed he'd get off and when he was convicted there was no way back on that. And no one thought to check her marriage certificate. Just as we didn't check earlier on.'

'Or she didn't say because she was furious with him after learning about his infidelity.'

'That would have given her a motive to get back at him by revealing the marriage. But she didn't.'

'Perhaps by then she was already tired of him, or didn't see the rosy future she had imagined.' Horton stared across the river, recalling what Juliette had told Dennis Sperryman, that she had been in the wrong place at the wrong time. Had she been referring to the murder?

Cantelli said, 'Or perhaps Sumners wasn't the father, or she didn't know for sure who was. This was the tail end of the sixties — hippies, make love not war, sex, drugs and rock 'n' roll, living in communes. They could all have been putting it about, as Walters told me.'

'I wonder then why they went through a wedding ceremony. Very conventional that.'

'They might have had the ceremony for whatever reason, but perhaps they agreed not to have a conventional marriage. Or they were semi-spaced out when they got married. According to the trial notes, Gillian, Juliette and Sumners were all living together in a commune just outside Guildford. Hang on, Walters is waving excitedly at me.' Horton could hear him say, 'Got him,' before Cantelli handed over the phone.

'Jeremy Tavistock, aged fifty-three, drives a Ford Focus, the registration number checks out and he lives on the Isle of Wight, the Pines, Wootton Creek.'

'Great. I'll pay him a visit.

'You taking backup, guv?'

'No, but I'll ask Sergeant Norris to accompany me.' He wanted this down in black and white and he wanted a car available to escort Tavistock to the station.

CHAPTER TWENTY-SEVEN

Horton left his Harley at Newport police station and travelled to Wootton Creek with Norris, briefing him on the way. Tavistock could be at work, although it was getting late. But then IT people often worked shifts. However, as they pulled into the driveway they saw the Ford parked in front of the tastefully designed bungalow surrounded by trees. Horton wondered if he kept a boat there, and if that boat had been used to reach another house at the end of another creek — Chidham.

Tavistock, who Horton had last seen masquerading as Teesdale, opened the door before they had climbed out. Just like Pierce's place, this would have the latest video cameras and discreet monitoring systems.

'Well done, Inspector, you tracked me down. Do come in. I'd very much like to know what gave me away.' He led them into an open-plan room with wide glass doors that gave on to a neatly lawned garden and the creek beyond it.

'I'd like to say good police work and persistence, and although that has played a part in finding you, Mr Tavistock, there was also a bit of luck.'

'Good in your case, not so in mine and Alma's. Shall we talk here or are you taking me to the station for questioning?'

'That depends on you.'

'And what I have to say. OK, we'll start here. Please sit down.'

'This is Detective Sergeant Norris.' Horton introduced the burly man. 'He'll take notes.'

'Of course.' Tavistock sat in a comfortable-looking modern chair.

'Are you alone in the house, sir?' Horton asked.

'Yes. There'll be no one to disturb us. I'm single. So, what piece of luck has brought you here?'

'A witness who saw you at the hospital talking to Alma after her last heart attack.'

Tavistock's face screwed up for a moment as he thought back. Then he nodded, knowingly. 'The lady who enquired where she was and who left her gloves behind.'

'Yes. And her husband spoke to you when you were leaving Alma's bungalow after she was discharged. His wife was out at the time, and it is only now that they and I have made the connection.'

'The neighbour mowing his lawn.'

'You helped Alma move to the care home on the mainland.'

'I did, and assisted her in selling her house. She was very happy to go. I didn't benefit from it in any way and you're at liberty to check.'

'We will, but financial gain wasn't the reason you did it.'

'Then tell me why.'

'Rodney Pierce.'

'I didn't kill him. He died of natural causes, intracranial haemorrhage.'

How did he know that? Dr Hobbs wouldn't have told him. But this man knew his way around computer systems and had obviously seen and read Hobbs's report when it was entered on the hospital's network. Accessing it, and Pierce's data, was child's play to him. Just as manipulating information on the system to acquire drugs would be, possibly for an existing or deceased patient, or creating a fictitious record. Faking his ID for the poste restante mail had been a simple case of getting hold of a plastic driver's licence, possibly one from the hospital's lost property office, overprinting it and sealing it after inserting the name Trevor Dorne. And Tavistock had engaged his hacking talents to obtain a false invoice from Yarmouth Harbour.

'And if you're going to accuse me of his murder, then you ought to caution me.'

Norris shifted and cleared his throat as though waiting for it, but Horton held back. He had a feeling that Tavistock would clam up if he did that, and there was a great deal more he wanted to know yet.

'Tell me about Alma.'

Tavistock studied him for a moment. 'She was a lovely, kind lady.' His expression momentarily softened before hardening. 'She didn't deserve Rodney as a son, a man with an acute personality disorder.'

As Horton had come to realize. 'He wasn't her son. His birth certificate states that, but Juliette Inglis was his mother.'

'How much do you know?'

'I know she gave him away to Alma and Joseph Pierce, who registered the birth as their own and perjured themselves. I know they must have been desperate for a child after their son was stillborn. A boy they called Trevor Dorne, the name you adopted in helping Alma to move to the mainland.'

'At her suggestion.'

'I doubt that, but we'll let that go for the moment. I'd like to know what led Alma and Joseph to break the law. And to save time, we also know who Rodney's father was — Roddy Sumners, convicted of murdering Gillian Preston at the Isle of Wight Festival in August 1969.'

'You have done well, Inspector. You've managed to get a lot further than I would have thought.'

'We've got even further. You said earlier about it being bad luck for Alma — you meant her and Joseph meeting Juliette in London that December, after Sumners' conviction, and agreeing to the illegal adoption.'

Tavistock gave him a salute. 'How did you come by that?'

'When Alma's body was found, she was clutching a photograph that no one had seen before of her and Joseph in Regent Street. Behind them were the Christmas lights. By their ages and the fashions it looked to be the late 1960s. Juliette was living in a commune just outside Guildford at that time. She would have travelled by train to and from London Waterloo for the trial of her husband, Rodney Sumners. It's incredible that in such a vast city with a teeming population they should have met, but it's not impossible, and I think that photograph represented to Alma the last happy, honest day she'd had with her beloved husband before it all began to go wrong. The lie and guilt must have eaten into them, especially when Rodney wasn't turning out how they expected.'

'You're right. I didn't know about the photograph. I take my hat off to you, Inspector. It was one of those chance meetings.'

And one that changed so many lives, thought Horton.

'Neither Alma nor Joseph had been to London before. They went to try and help them get over the tragic death of their son in November. It was 22 December, the day Roddy Sumners was found guilty. Alma and Joseph were at Waterloo station before returning to the Isle of Wight, having a cup of tea in the refreshment room. The trains were delayed. The dining room was packed, it being Christmas, but two seats had just become vacant at the table of a young, heavily pregnant woman. Juliette. They got talking. It was painful for Alma seeing Juliette pregnant, but she couldn't hide from expectant mothers for ever. Soon she was telling her how they'd recently lost their baby and that she couldn't have any more. The doctors had told her it was too dangerous. Juliette suggested they adopt.'

'But Alma and Joseph were too old.'

'Yes. Different rules back then.'

'And Alma could see that Juliette wasn't wearing a wedding ring even though she was married. Yes, we have discovered that and a lot more,' Horton said at Tavistock's startled expression. 'She'd taken it off, either because it might betray her marriage to Sumners in court, or because she was disgusted and angry with him for sleeping with Gillian. Juliette saw Alma looking.

'She said the father had chucked her when he knew she was expecting. And times were different then. There might have been free love and all that but it resulted in pregnancy and illegitimacy, which was a stigma back then. Juliette was lumbered with a baby and no father to support it. It wasn't the life she thought she was going to have, and she believed she deserved better. She told Alma and Joseph she was going to give the baby up for adoption, she had no means of support and couldn't cope with a child. She said she was a singer and that she had got a contract to sing on the cruise ships but that her future employer didn't know about the baby.'

'That was another lie. She didn't start working for the cruise lines until seventy-one.'

'Juliette was an accomplished liar. She lied to get what she wanted and Rodney did the same. They didn't care how many lives they trampled on and how many people they destroyed on the way. Juliette, like her son, was predatory, scheming and selfish, although Rodney was cleverer and more ruthless. Neither of them cared about anyone except themselves. Alma and Joseph rued the day they met her.'

Norris cleared his throat. Tavistock smiled at him. 'Getting all this down, Sergeant?'

'Yes, sir.'

'Good. Would you like a drink, Inspector?'

'No thank you.'

'Sergeant?'

Norris shook his head.

'Don't mind if I do?' He crossed to a cabinet on the far side of the room. Norris threw Horton a worried look. Interpreting it, Horton thought Norris was worried Tavistock would reach for a gun, but he just extracted a glass and a bottle of whisky and poured himself one before resuming his seat. Horton could hear the safety announcement of the Wightlink ferry as it made its way out of nearby Fishbourne.

'Alma was the complete opposite of Juliette,' Tavistock resumed. 'She was a gentle, kind, compassionate woman. Joseph loved her. He would do anything to make her happy. They sat together on the train, and Juliette skilfully steered the conversation. The outcome was obvious. Alma and Joseph would take on Juliette's child, and they began to make plans. Juliette suggested they meet in Portsmouth after the baby was born. Joseph quit his job on the farm, got another with the council in Carisbrooke and took a rented house where no one knew them. If anyone asked where his wife was, he was to say she was staying with relatives until the baby came, as the move was too much for her. She stayed in a small boarding house in Sandown. He telephoned the commune and gave Juliette his new address. Juliette would write to let them know when the baby was born. This she did. Joseph then travelled to Portsmouth with Alma. Juliette handed over the baby.'

'Did she ask for a fee?'

'I see you've come to know Juliette's ways. No. They all agreed never to see, speak or correspond with one another again. Alma and Joseph settled down to life with their new baby. Juliette went off to do whatever it was she wanted.'

'And Roddy Sumners committed suicide in prison. Was he guilty of that murder?'

Tavistock shrugged. 'How should I know?'

But Horton thought he might well have found out. How? From Juliette perhaps? If so, that meant she had known a great deal more about the murder of Gillian Preston than she had admitted, but then that was par for the course with her.

Tavistock was saying, 'They were very happy at first. They loved that child but sadly he didn't love them back, not in the same way, and they couldn't understand that. He was cruel even as a child, not in a physical way, but he was distant, unloving, scathing of them and their lack of intelligence. He despised their ordinary, uninspiring lives.'

'Did Alma tell you all this?'

'She didn't need to. I had first-hand experience. I was his best friend. They did everything they could to make Rodney happy, which meant they ended up spoiling him and making him worse. The guilt ate away at them. Guilt over the fact they had perjured themselves, because they were decent, law-abiding people. Guilt that they couldn't love this boy, and the realization that, no matter how hard they tried, they couldn't stop comparing him with the son they might have had if he had lived.'

'Yet you put up with him?'

Tavistock gave a bitter smile. 'He couldn't be like that with me because he needed me more than I needed him. Even so, I didn't come to realize that until it was too late, nor did I understand how he had manipulated me to his ends. I had a lot to apologize to Alma for. I'll explain.' He drained his glass and crossed to pour another. Horton could see that he had waited a long time to tell all this to someone. It began to explain his actions following Alma's heart attack.

He returned to his seat and resumed. 'Rodney and I were at school together. I was very bright, in fact cleverer than him. He saw this even as a child, and yet we were both doomed to a mediocre comprehensive that didn't challenge us at all. We could have turned to crime to relieve our boredom and frustration, but instead we turned to computers and in particular the gaming world.'

Horton was beginning to see where this was leading.

'Video games had been around in the fifties and sixties but it really got its start in America in the late seventies and early eighties with the creation of arcade games like *Pong* and *Computer Space* and with the first home video game console, the Magnavox Odyssey. No need to write all this down, Sergeant. You can get a potted history, or an in-depth one, off the internet.'

Norris threw Horton a look. He nodded his agreement.

'Rodney and I were eleven coming on for twelve. We acquired our first games consoles, paid for by Alma and Joseph. They even paid for mine. We played incessantly and thought we could improve on the games. I won't bore you with all the techy stuff but the video games industry in the US went belly up in eighty-three and the Japanese took the lead. Nintendo released its Nintendo Entertainment System in the United States in eighty-five and things started to move again. The latter part of the eighties and early nineties included video games driven by the improvement and popularity of personal computers and it sparked the console war between Nintendo and Sega as they fought for market share. The first major handheld video game consoles appeared in the nineties, Nintendo's Game Boy platform.' He sipped his drink.

'By then Rodney was working in London for a video games company. I worked for a company on the mainland in Southampton that was developing computer programmes for emerging markets. But we still worked together, keen to develop our own games. The plan was to create something so spectacular and successful that we would sell it to one of the big boys and with that money set up our own company and develop more games. We kept close tracks on the development of the World Wide Web, and were using it in its infancy in late ninety-three, then more so the year after, when it began to take off. We could see the way the games industry would develop as people remote from one another could be connected and compete.'

He tossed back his drink and crossed to close the glass door that Horton hadn't registered was open.

'We worked round the clock. Rodney was highly capable of that. He needed little sleep. I thought I was the same. I came to see I wasn't. My mother died, then my father four months after. I had hardly seen them or spoken to them. I was totally focused and driven. Rodney had long since lost touch with Alma. Joseph had killed himself just after Rodney had left for London. There had been a big row. Rodney had been scathing and critical of Joseph, and of Alma. Joseph had tried to defend his wife. Rodney never returned to the island, not even for Joseph's funeral. I shut it out. All that mattered was perfecting and launching our video games. By then we had three in development and close to perfection. Then I had a breakdown. Complete and utter shutdown. Mind, body, the lot.'

Norris scratched a few notes.

Horton said, 'Rodney went ahead alone, without giving you any credit.'

'Yes.'

This was a motive for killing Rodney, but why wait this long?

'It took me four years to climb out of the pit, and another four to feel "normal" again. By then I was twenty-nine, coming on thirty. I'd obviously lost my job and I hadn't heard a word from Rodney, not since the moment I became ill. At first I steered clear of computers but I soon found refuge in them, writing programmes, looking at ways of doing things differently, reading and exchanging views with others on the internet as it became increasingly popular and user-friendly. But I never went near a game, or Rodney, as I saw how he had driven me to the mental breakdown. Oh, it wasn't all his fault. I'm not blaming him, not entirely. I should have stepped back. I should have stood up to him, said "no", but he's a hard man to argue with. My desire to keep up with him, and his constant pressure, had sent me into overload.'

As it probably had done with poor Bob Spiley. 'You came back to live on the island?'

'When I was discharged from hospital, yes. My parents had left the house to me. I sold it, picked up the pieces of my life and learned how to pace myself. I knew I had a talent in designing programmes. I'd seen enough of the health service, being on the other end of it, and got a job as a computer technician with them. I swiftly got promotion. I read about Rodney's success.'

'How did you feel when you saw he'd profited off the back of your hard work?'

'I didn't care. I was healthy, successful at my job and loved it. I was comfortable. I didn't want to know about him and he obviously didn't wish to know about me. Life moved on.'

'Did you approach him and ask for a share when he sold the company to the Americans?'

'He'd have laughed me out of court. I didn't want the hassle or the strain; that could tip me back into the darkness again. I read about his partner's death, Bob Spiley, and thought, *poor sod*. He wasn't as lucky as me.'

'What did you expect to find on Rodney's hard drive?' Horton asked.

'Not sure. But I thought it would be interesting to examine before the management consultants could say they'd been damaged or lost. There's enough on them to make the Inland Revenue and the fraud squad interested. I was always going to hand them over.'

'How do we know you haven't deleted anything?'

'Because I've nothing to hide. Besides, even if I, or Rodney, had deleted files they can still be recovered, as you're no doubt aware. It takes time, but anything can be found unless you smash the hard drive with a hammer.'

'Is there correspondence between him and Juliette?'

'He wouldn't be so stupid as to have emailed or messaged her.'

'Any record of the purchase of lorazepam?'

'No. Is that how she died?'

'Where's Juliette's computer?'

'I have no idea.'

'Why did you kill Alma?'

'I didn't.'

'But you got zopiclone for her.'

'Did I?'

'Did you arrange to meet Rodney on the Sunday with Alma?'

'No. I took Alma out for tea to the Millstream Hotel in Bosham.'

'Why?'

'Why not?'

'You hadn't seen her since she'd moved. Why did you choose then to visit her?'

'It was the earliest opportunity I had. It's been busy at work.'

Unlikely, thought Horton.

Tavistock noted Horton's dubious look. 'OK, I wanted to tell her in person that Juliette was dead.'

'You killed Juliette?'

'No. I read about her death on the internet. Juliette was no longer a threat to Alma, and the truth of what Juliette, Alma and Joseph had done would never come out.'

'You also told her that Rodney would be dead within a couple of days.' Horton recalled what Yvonne at the care home had said when Alma returned, that she was happy. Yes, because the lie was over. The poor woman.

'You met him on the shore at Chidham Creek House and injected him with a drug.'

Tavistock was shaking his head. 'I haven't got a boat and I didn't inject him. I repeat. I haven't killed anyone. I told Alma she could rest in peace. An unfortunate turn of phrase, given that she died.'

Horton was convinced Tavistock had given her the zopiclone, but perhaps it had been at her request.

'If I had wanted to kill Juliette and Rodney, I would have done so years ago. I suppose you want me to accompany you to the station and make a statement.'

'Yes.' Horton rose.

'Gladly, Inspector. Are you charging me, and if so with what?'

'Theft will do for a start,' Horton replied, wearily.

CHAPTER TWENTY-EIGHT

Wednesday

'We have no evidence that he bought those drugs or killed anyone, and we're not likely to get it,' Horton said later the next morning to Cantelli and Walters. It had been midnight when he had reached his boat and his head had ached from thinking. It hadn't improved much after six hours of tossing and turning. A hot shower, a shave and a full English breakfast in the canteen, with buckets of caffeine, had helped a little. His report to Reine had set it back. Reine didn't think Juliette, Alma or Pierce had been killed. Reine's view was that Tavistock had been out to profit from stealing Pierce's company secrets. Tavistock had willingly given over the hard drives and the laptop, but neither Bridget nor Aldsworth Management Consultancy wanted to press charges — Bridget because she couldn't care less about them and Aldsworth because it would cause too much adverse publicity. As Tavistock hadn't been detained, Sergeant Norris had gone to inform him.

'We won't find anything on Tavistock's own computer or his mobile,' Horton said. They hadn't been seized because there was no case to answer as Reine saw it. 'Tavistock's not stupid enough to leave evidence on them, or on any deleted files on the system; as he stressed to me, they can be recovered anyway. And if he had found anything on Pierce's hard drives, he'd have destroyed them, which he didn't. Someone from Aldsworth is travelling down from London to the island to collect them. Dawson's also been informed because Tavistock said there was something on the system that might interest the Inland Revenue.'

Cantelli said, 'Could we find something on the hospital computer system about him getting hold of zopiclone?'

'He's in charge of it, so he'll have made doubly, no triply, sure nothing showed up.'

Walters chipped in. 'But he would have had to pick up the pills from the pharmacy, or they could have been delivered to Alma's ward.'

Horton had already considered that, among the myriad other things on the ferry home and when sleep had evaded him. 'If so, it would show up on her medical record and it doesn't, but he could have used the name of another patient, possibly a dead one on the system, and collected them. That is, if he got them that way in the first place. I think he acquired them over the internet, of which there will be no evidence. He probably used an internet café or public computer in the library to purchase them. The same goes for warfarin *if* the results on Pierce come back with that. Even if they do, there's no proof he drugged Juliette or Pierce.' Horton rubbed his sleep-deprived eyes before continuing. 'He admits taking Alma out for tea that Sunday, which we know anyway, but whether he stayed with her the entire time is another matter. I've asked DS Curran to check with the staff at the Millstream Hotel to find out if anyone fitting Pierce's description showed up, but I can't see him sitting down to tea and cake with the woman he'd almost killed by his verbal abuse, or the man he had driven to a mental breakdown and cheated out of a fortune. Curran will also ask if they recall Alma sitting alone for some time while Tavistock went off to meet Pierce. I believe he did, but he'd given Pierce a false rendezvous location and, while he was waiting there, Tavistock got into Pierce's car.'

'How?' asked Walters.

Cantelli answered. 'Keyless car theft. It would be easy for Tavistock to get into the Jaguar.'

'He slipped warfarin into a flask of drink Pierce kept there, then simply locked up and went to meet him, gaining great pleasure from telling him that he'd expose everything unless he took financial care of Alma.'

'How would he know about the flask? *If* there was one,' Walters asked.

'Either he took a chance, or thought back to the young man he knew of old, who wouldn't go anywhere without a bottle of water or a drink of some kind. Tavistock assumed Pierce wouldn't have changed that habit. Pierce could have taken a drink, then thrown the bottle away at home. And we'll only get a warrant to look for it if the test results come back positive. Even if we have a witness to that meeting, it still doesn't prove he drugged Pierce, *if* he did. When I suggested this scenario to Tavistock at the station last night he denied it, but then he would.'

'He had a motive for killing him.' Walters scratched his nose. 'But why now?'

Cantelli broke in this time. 'Because it was only this year that Juliette told Pierce about his father and the illegal adoption.'

'Yes. We assumed Alma and Joseph told him about the adoption before he left home at seventeen, after which Joseph had taken his own life and Pierce cut off all ties with them, but Tavistock says not. You see, Tavistock became Alma's confessor. She was alone, ill, heartbroken, and then this kind man, who Rodney had treated so cruelly as a boy, whom she knew very well, appeared on the scene, a quirk of fate just like Alma and Joseph being in that railway refreshment room at the same time as Juliette. Alma poured her heart out. Until then, Tavistock had no idea that Pierce had been illegally adopted or who his father was. Alma hadn't known about

Roddy Sumners either, not until Pierce went charging over to the island to confront her about it, after Juliette had told him. This knowledge finally gave Tavistock an emotional edge over Pierce, who he knew would abhor what he'd been told and how he'd been deceived. And Tavistock genuinely felt pity for Alma, and anger at how Rodney had treated her. He began to think how he could rile Rodney and use what he knew, not for financial gain, but so he could get back at him. I think he enjoyed the planning, the scheming, the whole game.'

'A rotten game,' Cantelli grumbled.

'It turned out that way. He built a relationship with Alma, and she desperately needed someone to love and lean on. They became so close that she trusted him completely. She did everything he said. He took control. He assumed her dead son's name and used it so often that I think, when he showed up at the home to take her out, she really believed he was her dead son. She'd become convinced and groomed into believing it.'

Cantelli glowered. 'He admits to that?'

Horton shook his head. 'He said she died happy.'

Cantelli took a deep breath.

Horton resumed. 'Maybe she did.' There was a moment's silence. He could hear two officers talking as they passed the CID office. 'Tavistock said that before Pierce left for London, aged seventeen, he told Joseph and Alma just what he thought of them. Pierce was vitriolic, abusive and merciless, especially to Joseph, a gravedigger, who in his eyes was common and beneath contempt. Alma saw how it had utterly destroyed her beloved husband. She knew he'd been racked with guilt for years because the son he'd raised was evil. Pierce, as we know, had a massive superiority complex and was incapable of feeling love or affection.'

'And Joseph took his own life as a result,' Cantelli said sadly.

'Yes. After his death, Alma destroyed every picture she had of them with Rodney, keeping only her wedding picture and that one in London. It was the one thing Tavistock didn't know about, the last happy day before their lives changed.'

'Then Juliette returned and thought it was about time to see how her son was doing, and to her delight discovered he was a very successful and wealthy man.'

'Yes, she approached him just before Christmas, and finally managed to persuade him to see her in January. She told him everything and threatened to go to the media, who would pay her handsomely for the story, and he went haring off to the Isle of Wight to confront Alma. Tavistock said he was brutal and wished her dead, among other vile threats. I think Juliette told Pierce a genetic test would prove she was his real mother, and I believe he took one and found it to be true. He paid her off until he could think what to do, hence her telling Alfleet her ship had come in.' Horton paused. Where had he heard that before?

Cantelli said, 'Why did Tavistock move Alma to that care home? She could hardly have wanted to be near Pierce or Juliette.'

'By then she would do what he said. Maybe he told her he'd be living close by as soon as he could sell his house. He's not admitting to anything. He claimed it was her decision, which he would say anyway. I think one of those poste restante letters was to tell Alma that Juliette was dead, and that it was all over, the past would stay firmly in the past, dead and buried, and Rodney would be joining Juliette soon. The slate was wiped clean. Maybe she believed he had killed Juliette.'

'Did he?' asked Cantelli.

'He denies it.' Horton paused and scrambled his tired brain to recall his exact words. 'He said, if we believe she was murdered, or have evidence to prove it, then someone else killed her, it wasn't him. I suspect there are others from her past who she blackmailed or tried to, who wished her silenced.'

'If it wasn't Rodney, Tavistock or Adam Croft, who could it have been?' asked Walters.

Cantelli said, 'One of the Blue Boys? Dennis Sperryman or Greg Harrison? Perhaps she was having a fling with one of them and threatened to tell the wife.'

'Could have been Jackie Alfleet,' Walters suggested. 'He'd not turn much of a hair at murder, seeing as he did it before.'

Horton tried to think. Walters had stirred something. 'She told Alfleet at Cranley's funeral that she'd be OK without him when *the* ship comes in. Why did she say *the* ship, not *my* ship, which is what most people say when they hope they're coming into money?'

'A slip of the tongue, guv,' Walters ventured. 'Or Alfleet misheard.'

But Horton wasn't so sure. Now he remembered where he'd heard the same phrase. 'Christine Harrison said the video that was played at Whiteman's funeral was set to the music of his favourite artist, Bob Dylan, and his song "When the Ship Comes In". Which brings us back to the Isle of Wight Festival in 1969, which Whiteman attended. It's all right, I'm not going mad. I don't think for one moment Mrs Whiteman or Alice Rails killed Juliette. Remember what Alice said, Cantelli — Juliette went through all their old photo albums, which helped her mother a great deal. Tiffany told me the same, that Juliette spent hours with her grandmother and her father going over everything and looking through photos, talking about her grandfather, Gideon Nichols.'

Walters said, 'It's what celebrants do.'

'Yes, and they stand up and deliver a potted history about the deceased, or in Cranley's case a fairy tale. She would have the service on her laptop but it's missing, as are some of her photo albums from before her time on the cruise ships.'

'Could have got lost in transit, or she destroyed them.'

'Or someone took them,' added Cantelli, thoughtfully.

Horton's spark of an idea ignited into a flame, and the fatigue sloughed off him. 'Then there was the funeral that she *didn't* deliver, because she was dead. Someone made sure she wouldn't stand up in the crematorium and recount Gideon Nichols' life. Why? It has something to do with that

Bob Dylan song, and the Isle of Wight Festival. What do festivals have in common?'

Walters said, 'Drugs, bands, music . . .'

'And? What else is needed aside from seating, refreshments, toilets?' Horton answered his own question. 'Staging, sound and lighting. And who provides that?'

'Lee Nichols' company,' answered Cantelli promptly.

'Yes. And his father was a sound engineer who set up his own business in seventy-one. I read that in his eulogy, so where did he work before, and more critically with whom?'

'The band that Juliette was a vocalist for on the Isle of Wight in sixty-nine?' Cantelli had already turned to his screen. 'I didn't come across Gideon Nichols' name in the murder trial, but I didn't get the chance to go through it all yesterday. I was just looking to see if Juliette gave evidence.' His fingers froze. He looked up. 'My God, you're right. At least, I think you are. Nicholas Gideon, sound engineer for the Run Around. His name's the wrong way round but it's too much of a coincidence not to be him. Hold on.' Quickly, he looked back at the screen. 'He was on the stage at the time of Gillian Preston's death. He didn't see Sumners there. Hang about.' They remained silent as Cantelli scrolled down the statement.

A phone rang down the corridor somewhere and Horton could hear the murmur of voices in the corridor by the vending machine. A police car siren spliced the air.

Cantelli sat back, blowing out his cheeks. 'His testimony says that he went in search of Sumners and saw him walking away from Gillian's caravan, shortly after her death. He put him in the dock and helped to find him guilty.'

'Truth or lie?' asked Walters shrewdly.

'Juliette knew which,' answered Horton. 'She must have recognized Gideon Nichols when she was with the family looking at the photographs they had of him as a younger man in anticipation of putting together the eulogy. The name had changed but not the man.'

'But with Nichols dead she wouldn't have been able to benefit, unless . . .' Walters paused.

'She tried to blackmail his son. Yes. I think it's time we had a word with Lee Nichols.'

No longer tired, and with his headache miraculously cured, Horton set off with Cantelli for the company offices at North Harbour, only to be told that both Lee and Tiffany had gone to Edwina Nichols' house at Lee-on-the-Solent to arrange the scattering of Gideon's ashes.

'This is going to be awkward,' Cantelli said on their way there. 'With Mrs Nichols vulnerable, having been recently bereaved.'

Horton agreed. 'We'll see if we can get Lee away from his mother and daughter. I've only met him once, but from what I saw of him I think he might be sensitive towards his mother's feelings, especially if he's committed murder in order to protect her from knowing about her late husband's part in the murder of Gillian Preston.'

Horton recalled the worried look on Lee's gaunt, lined face and the impression of a man uncertain of himself. Perhaps that uncertainty had been anxiety that he'd be exposed as a murderer.

'Do you think Gideon killed Gillian?'

'Why change his name? Why keep it a secret if he didn't?'

'The family could know of it. They didn't expect Juliette to discover it. They couldn't have known she'd been involved back then, otherwise they wouldn't have asked her to be the celebrant.'

'I think Gideon Nichols wondered if Gillian's baby was his. He confronted her and she told him he wasn't the only one. She could have been derisive, mocked him. She wanted Sumners. Perhaps she knew he was already married to Juliette and didn't care. He didn't if he was putting it about. Or perhaps Juliette and Roddy Sumners had kept their marriage secret from everyone, including the band and crew. Nobody thought much of them sleeping together in those days.'

'They don't now,' muttered Cantelli.

'Maybe Sumners persuaded Juliette it was better they kept it quiet. And she believed him. Gideon could have killed

266

Gillian and then made sure Sumners went down for it. His suicide suggests he might have been innocent.'

Cantelli pulled up outside a substantial modern house set back from the road, close to the golf course and not far from the seafront. He silenced the engine. 'And maybe Juliette knew her husband was innocent but wanted to get even with him for betraying and deceiving her. That faint might have been a very good fake.'

Horton agreed. 'Neither Lee nor Tiffany's cars are here. We're too late, but Mrs Nichols might know where they are.'

CHAPTER TWENTY-NINE

'They're at my late husband's boat at Haslar Marina,' she said, letting them in. 'We're taking Gideon's ashes out to sea tomorrow and they're making sure everything's ready. What do you wish to see them about, Inspector?'

Does she know? wondered Horton. Had she been party to her husband's secret? Could Juliette have told her? Would she have been that callous? Yes, if she had thought she could gain financially, but Horton thought that Lee Nichols was the most likely target in that respect.

'There are just a few questions we need to ask him regarding Juliette Croft.' Horton was keen to get to that boat but first he wanted some information from Edwina Nichols. 'Did Juliette visit you the day before your late husband's funeral?'

'Yes. We went over the service. She was very sympathetic and understanding.'

'What time was that?'

'It should have been mid-afternoon but I wasn't feeling too well, so she came over at six and left about eight.'

'Was Lee with you?'

'Yes, and Tiffany.'

'Did you, at some point, go through some photographs of your late husband for the video compilation?'

'Yes. We spent a lot of time reminiscing. Juliette was very patient, and being of the same age group we had a lot in common remembering the late sixties and seventies. In those days, Gideon was a sound engineer for bands. Juliette, being a singer, remembered some of them. I didn't meet Gideon until March seventy-three. We married in the December of the same year. A whirlwind romance.' Her eyes lit up for a brief moment.

'Did Mr Nichols go to the Isle of Wight Festival in sixty-nine?'

'Juliette asked me that. She said she was there and she wondered if she had met my husband. But Gideon never mentioned it to me.'

Juliette had been just testing her out. It was clear to Horton that Mrs Gideon knew nothing of the murder of Gillian Preston. 'On the night before the funeral, when Juliette was here, what time did Lee and Tiffany leave?'

'Tiffany left just after Juliette. She was meeting her fiancé. Lee left about half an hour later.'

'I don't mean to pry, Mrs Nichols, but are you on any medication — sleeping pills, tranquilizers, that kind of thing?'

She looked puzzled by his question but answered. 'I was on lorazepam because I've had terrible trouble sleeping, but I didn't get on with it, and I didn't wish to become dependent.'

'Have you still got it?'

'I suppose so.'

'Would you check?'

'But why do you wish to know?'

'I'll explain in due course.'

She shrugged and left the room.

They listened in silence as she climbed the stairs and heard her moving about in the bathroom, opening a cupboard and rummaging around. She returned looking worried.

'I can't find it. There were two bottles. I'd only opened the one.'

As he had suspected. 'Bottles?'

'I was prescribed liquid lorazepam because I have trouble swallowing tablets. I must have poured them down the

269

sink and forgotten I'd done it. I'm not thinking straight, Inspector.'

'Did Juliette use your bathroom while she was here?'

'No, she used the downstairs cloakroom.'

He swiftly thanked her before she could ask more questions, and outside told Cantelli to hurry to Haslar with only the blue light flashing. 'No siren. I hope they're both still there.'

Their cars were in the marina car park.

'Do we need backup?' Cantelli asked as they made their way to the pontoons.

'I don't think so. And sorry, Barney, not only are you going to have to set foot on a pontoon but you'll also have to go on board a boat.'

'I'll survive.' He put a piece of gum in his mouth. 'Chewing it will help take my mind off being on the sea.'

'I think what Lee Nichols has to tell us will do that.'

The boat hatch was open and Horton could hear raised voices below. The conversation stopped instantly as the occupants felt the movement on the pontoon rocking the boat. Horton nodded at Cantelli and climbed on board. Stepping down into the cabin, he registered Lee Nichols' harrowed face. Tiffany's colour was heightened and her eyes blazed.

Evenly, Horton addressed Lee. 'Your mother told us we'd find you here. There are some questions we would like to ask you, Mr Nichols, about Juliette Croft. It might be best to do so at the station.'

'That witch!' Tiffany's spat.

'Tiffany,' her father cautioned.

'Oh, everyone thinks she was sweetness and light, but the bitch was evil.'

'She's upset about her grandpa's death. She doesn't know what she's saying.'

'Yes I do. She deserved to die.'

Had he got it wrong? Had Tiffany drugged Juliette?

'Don't say anything more, Tiff.'

'Oh, shut up.'

270

Her father winced. Cantelli stiffened slightly beside Horton.

Tiffany ploughed on. 'Someone had to teach that cow a lesson. There was no way on earth I was going to let that lying bitch stand up and deliver a eulogy that was filthy lies.' She gulped in air. There were no tears. Her anger was too great for that.

Gently, Horton said, 'Tiffany, I need to caution you—'

'To hell with all that. *She* told *him*,' she hissed at her father, who looked completely defeated, 'that Grandpa was a killer. That he'd killed a girl at the Isle of Wight Festival years ago. How could he when he wasn't even there? And you believed her,' she seethed in disgust at her father. Then to Horton, 'She wanted money to keep silent or she'd stand up and say that Grandpa wasn't the saint everyone thought he was. And he, my father, the coward, agreed to pay her. I could have stuck a knife in her then and there.'

'Tiffany, I think—' Horton interjected.

'But I didn't need to,' she continued, as though he hadn't spoken. 'I know all about lorazepam. My fiancé had some at the Southsea festival. And Grandma had some to help her sleep. I'd make it look like that bitch had overdosed and no one would know.'

No one nearly hadn't.

Nichols pleaded with her. 'Please, Tiffany, don't say another word, he hasn't cautioned you. We'll call our lawyer. Inspector, you have no—'

'Oh, shut up. I'm sick of you.' She rubbed a hand over her face. 'I killed her and I don't care who knows it.'

Lee Nichols winced. 'Inspector, this can't be used—'

'Yes it can,' Tiffany declared. 'I don't care who knows. It was lies about Grandpa, and the police will prove it. Don't you see that, Dad? They know Grandpa didn't do those things she said he did.'

'But Tiffany, you've just admitted to killing her.' He could obviously see that there was no silencing her.

271

Horton interjected. 'Let's get back to the station and do this properly, as your father says.'

With remarkable speed she turned, and suddenly in her hand was a distress flare. 'Come near me and I'll set this off.'

Her father made to spring forward but Horton swiftly stilled him with a hand. He could see the girl was beyond reason and in her highly charged state she was capable of anything, including destroying herself in the process. If that flare went off it would fill the cabin with choking, dangerously hot orange smoke. It would ignite the combustible material and the boat would burst into flames, giving them no chance to escape. Cantelli tensed beside him.

Horton had to calm her. With his pulse racing, keeping his tone even, he said, 'We won't come near you, Tiffany.'

With his eyes he silently urged Lee to keep quiet, before putting his gaze back on Tiffany's tortured face. He recalled his hostage negotiation training, not for the first time in his career, and he hoped this wouldn't be the last. Tiffany was not a terrorist; he didn't even think she was a criminal, although she had committed a crime, and one she had planned in cold blood. She had been driven by rage and passion. In deep mourning for the grandfather she had worshipped, and who had also worshipped her, Tiffany had been so deeply hurt by Juliette that her fragile, obsessive reasoning had fractured, tipping her over the edge. She was the third category of hostage-taker, the mentally disturbed. He needed to build rapport, keep an even temper, show empathy and self-assurance, enough to prevent her from taking drastic action and burning them all.

'You must have been devastated when you overheard what Juliette was saying about your grandfather to your dad. When was this?'

'After she and Grandma had gone through the photo albums. I heard Dad on the phone at work arranging to meet her on this boat and thought it strange.'

'Did you ask your father about that?'

She nodded jerkily. The flare was still poised in her slender hand. 'Dad said she wanted to get a feel for Grandpa and his passion for sailing. I knew that was rubbish. I came here just after Dad and made for the boat. They'd come on board. I moved very carefully but they were so deep in conversation they wouldn't have noticed the Olympic sailing team traipsing up and down the pontoon. The hatch was open and I could hear every word that bitch said about Grandpa being at the festival and going to that girl in the caravan. Giving her a drug overdose to kill her. She said Grandpa had lied at the trial and let another man go to prison, where he'd killed himself. She said that if Dad didn't pay up she'd deliver a very different service in three days' time. And she had photographs to prove it. Maybe she'd compile her own video.'

'Did you leave rather than confront her and your father?'

'At first I couldn't move. It was like someone had tasered me. Then as her whining voice echoed in my head I felt physically sick. Dad said he'd pay up. It bought me some time. I crept away, then ran as far as I could until it was safe for me to throw up. I came back here after they'd gone and sat for a long time, her hateful words echoing in my head. I wanted to blot them out. She'd spoiled this boat. The thing he loved with a passion, where we had spent so many lovely times together. I sat here and thought of her. Then I scrubbed this boat down from top to bottom to get rid of her.'

That explained the raw hands and bitten-down fingernails he'd noticed on their first meeting.

Her hands wavered for a moment as though she was going to put them to her ears.

'You then took refuge in planning what to do,' Horton said gently.

'Yes.' She looked a little dazed that he understood. 'I couldn't talk to you,' she tossed at her father. 'You didn't understand.'

'I—'

Horton gave a slight shake of his head. Nichols snapped his mouth shut.

'There was no one you could talk to, Tiffany,' Horton said. 'Because the one man who understood you was dead.'

'Yes. I thought poison was suitable to shut her poisonous mouth. I could get hold of some drugs, I know people who can get them for me.'

Including her fiancé, thought Horton. Olewbo would be interested in that if they got out of this alive. Nichols' eyes widened but he had the sense to keep silent.

'Then I thought of Grandma's medicine. She's had terrible trouble sleeping, more so than usual, and she always has difficulty swallowing tablets, so the doctor had prescribed her liquid lorazepam.'

Dr Hobbs had told them liquid lorazepam was colourless but had a somewhat bitter taste. It always acted quicker than in tablet form.

'After she'd left Grandma's that night I followed her back to her house, parked round the corner and after a while walked there and knocked on her door.'

And no one had seen or heard her.

'She was surprised to see me but she let me in when I said that I had something to tell her about my grandfather. I had Grandma's medication in my bag. I started crying and she said she'd make us tea. I told her that Dad had told me that Grandpa had been at that Isle of Wight Festival and had killed a girl. I didn't let on that I'd overheard her tell Dad this. I said I didn't believe he was ever there and wouldn't until someone showed me proof. The bitch said she had proof.'

From what he'd learned about Juliette, he believed Tiffany. Juliette had indeed been callous and totally self-centred. She had thought nothing of destroying a family and their memories, just as she had thought nothing of betraying Roddy Sumners, which had led to his suicide, or shattering Alma and Joseph's lives with her skilful manipulation so that they perjured themselves and raised her child.

Tiffany took a deep breath. Horton felt deeply for her. Her eyes were full of pain. The flare was steady in her hands. Gently he said, 'She went upstairs to fetch her albums.'

'Yes. I emptied some of her tea in the kitchen sink and poured lorazepam in it and stirred it round before hurrying back into the lounge. She came back with the pictures. I could barely look at them, I felt so sick. Grandpa had never looked like that. It wasn't him.'

Horton was certain it was. 'Didn't she notice the tea tasted different?'

'She pulled a face but drank. Then I asked for another. She said she'd have another too. She returned and I could see she looked a bit woozy. I sipped my tea and said I couldn't let any of Grandpa's past come out and I'd talk to my father to make sure she was paid to keep silent. I said it had been a shock and pretended to be ill. I asked for a glass of water. While she fetched it I poured more lorazepam into her tea. I drank my water, waffling on about God knows what. I drank, she drank. I got her talking about the festival and her time as a young singer. She drank more without even realizing it. She started to sway. I said, "You're unwell. I'll get you some water." She got up, tried to focus on me. I said, "Now you won't be able to say anything about Grandpa," and she collapsed on the floor.'

Lee Nichols looked like an old man.

'How long did you sit there, Tiffany?' Horton asked softly.

'I'm not sure. I washed up the cup and my glass and stared at her, wondering how long it would take for her to die. Grandpa's funeral was the next day. She had to die before then. Then I heard a noise out the back. I grabbed her computer and the photo albums and hid upstairs. I heard someone moving about and when I looked out of the back window I saw a figure leaving.'

Riley Ballantine.

'My phone went, startling me. It was Dad. He wondered where I was. I told him that he didn't have to worry anymore about Grandpa or what Juliette would say. I'd dealt with it. He asked me what I meant. I said come and see.'

Nichols ran a hand across his perspiring forehead.

Horton said, 'Then what happened?'

Nichols' hand groped behind him and, when he came into contact with the table, he slumped heavily on the bench seat to the left of it.

275

'I told Dad to park in a side street and I'd open the back door for him. There's an alleyway there. Dad felt for a pulse. There wasn't one.'

Was that true? Horton wondered. Or had Nichols lied so as not to call the emergency services? 'Then you made it look like suicide.'

'Yes,' she said triumphantly.

The flare was still in her hand but she was relaxing her grip. 'I'd planned this. In my bag I also had an empty bottle of champagne, a glass and an empty bottle of tablets, you can buy them on the internet.'

Neither Tiffany nor her father had known that Juliette didn't drink.

'I also had some disposable gloves and a cloth. I told Dad what to do. I made Dad put on the gloves and we wiped everything down where he and I had been. You'd either think she'd swallowed all the tablets and died from an overdosed, or died from an adverse reaction after mixing tablets with alcohol. We took the photo albums and her laptop. I couldn't find her mobile, that worried me a lot but it couldn't be helped.'

'Whose idea was it to move the body?' Cantelli asked conversationally. She swivelled her gaze to him with a startled expression as though she had only just noticed him. As she did, Horton shifted just perceptibly.

'Dad's. We carried her to the sofa but she was incredibly heavy and we dropped her against the edge of the coffee table. Eventually we got her on to the sofa and I arranged her to look as though she'd killed herself.' She spoke almost proudly. 'We left by the back door, leaving it unlocked, and drove home. It was sad for Grandma to have the upset of that bitch not showing up at the funeral, but better that than her standing up and telling all those lies. It's fine now.'

'Yes, it's all over now, Tiffany. All over.'

She blinked as though confused.

Cantelli said, 'Give me the flare, Tiffany.' He stepped forward while Horton eased to the right.

'I protected Grandpa. He'd have been proud of me. We had so many laughs together on here. I loved him.' Suddenly her face crumpled and her body slumped. Swiftly, Horton disarmed her as Cantelli reached out to support her. Burying her head into his shoulders, she sobbed uncontrollably as though her heart was breaking, and it was.

Cantelli gently put his arm round her and said quietly, 'It's all over, Tiffany. It's over now.' Yet he and Horton knew it was far from that. Cantelli gently eased Tiffany towards her father. Horton wondered if she would reject him but she didn't. He took her in his arms and stroked her head as she sobbed. Tears ran down Lee Nichols' ravaged face. His eyes beseeched Horton.

'I'm sorry,' Horton said quietly. He and Cantelli stepped out into the cockpit.

'Such a waste,' Cantelli said. 'How she loved him.'

'Yes. She killed out of love, not hate.'

Cantelli reached for his mobile and called up a unit.

Horton took a deep breath. A grandfather's sins, and his granddaughter was paying for it. Just as his own grandfather, Viscount William Ames, had committed a murder, that of Horton's mother, Jennifer. His sons had covered it up. But William's granddaughter, Harriet, would never do so. Nor would she kill to keep it from being exposed. She hadn't known or loved her grandfather as Tiffany had done hers. Even if she had done, Horton could never see Harriet doing such a thing. Should he tell her the truth then? As Juliette had told Lee and Tiffany, if that had been the truth. Harriet's reaction would be different, but what would it be? Would she despise him for revealing it? Would she declare he was fabricating it? Would she tell her mother and brothers? Did they already know the truth? No, he could never speak of it because it would change his relationship with Harriet. He didn't want her to despise him. It was over. It was the past. He heard the siren, and walked down the pontoon to meet the police car.

CHAPTER THIRTY

Two days later the results of Rodney Pierce's tests came through. They had found nothing untoward in his system to have caused the haemorrhage. Natural causes then. Horton arranged to meet Bridget Pierce at Chidham Creek House, where he broke the news to her about her husband's test results. She wasn't the slightest bit interested. A large removal van was parked outside and she'd greeted Horton with the news that she was having some of the valuable paintings and other items put in storage and the house was being put on the market, ready for sale as soon as probate was granted. They were in the large airy kitchen at the rear. She hadn't offered him a drink, but sat nursing a coffee herself.

'All that health kick stuff, popping vitamin pills like Smarties, drinking that vile spinach juice and stuffing himself with it like Popeye the Sailor, turning his nose up at my eating habits — it didn't do him much good.'

'You can still bring charges against Tavistock for stealing your husband's computers.'

'He's welcome to them, and everything on them. As far as I'm concerned it's over. We have interest in the company from a number of sources and I've instructed the lawyers, accountants and management consultants to negotiate the best deal. Good riddance to it all.'

Horton wondered if she had also wished to add, *Good riddance to my husband too.*

'I shall stay in London until I decide what to do. I might go abroad for a while and keep the apartment in town. I might buy another now that I'll have money to spend without having to ask him and have him examining and questioning every penny.' She beamed.

Horton wondered if Ed Kingston would continue to feature in Bridget's life. He somehow doubted it. Kingston had been a relief from her boredom and frustration. Now free of Rodney, she'd find others who could provide excitement and gratification.

Horton returned to his boat. He was still surprised that Pierce's death had been a natural one. The timing seemed to be perfect for some people. But then maybe that was one of life's quirks of fate. There had been a few in this investigation. And nobody seemed to mourn Rodney Pierce. There were no grieving relatives, friends or even employees pressing and clambering for action and results. From what Detective Superintendent Dawson had told him, Pierce's staff had seemed to breathe a huge sigh of relief that the boss had gone, even if it meant losing their jobs. Horton didn't think that would be for long. The new company might keep them on, or they'd be snapped up by the competition. He thought it a sad epitaph for Pierce, but one he had created for himself. And there was no one to mourn for Juliette either. He didn't think either of them would be bothered if they knew.

As he swung into the marina car park he thought of Tiffany Nichols and her father. Lee had been charged with being an accessory to murder and bailed. Tiffany faced a murder charge and had been remanded in custody. They both had a good solicitor and Lee said he would make sure they engaged a highly competent barrister. Tiffany's charge might get changed to manslaughter on account of the fact that Juliette had been attempting to blackmail them.

Horton switched off the engine and alighted. So deep in thought was he that he didn't see Gaye or her car.

'Hello, when did you get back?'

'About two hours ago. Simon's been telling me how you've kept him busy with some puzzling autopsies, and I'm dying to know how you're getting on with the investigations. I'm also hungry.'

'I can cook or we can eat in the marina restaurant.'

'Depends if you've got any food in.'

'I haven't had much time for shopping.'

Gaye rolled her eyes. 'Then the restaurant it is.'

'I'll freshen up first.'

'Isn't that meant to be my line?' Gaye said, as they walked down to the pontoon.

'You don't need it. You look as fresh as the dawn.'

'Charmer.'

'And tanned from all that Malaysian sea air. How did it go?'

'Fabulous. Great to blow away the smell of work.' They climbed on board. 'I'll make you a coffee while you make yourself look pretty.'

'It'll take longer than a kettle boiling for that.' He entered his cabin and put his helmet on the floor and his jacket on the bunk, glancing as always at the picture of Emma. Would she be as good a sailor as Gaye and Harriet? Or Tiffany, he thought, with sadness. In the adjoining heads he splashed his face and squinted in the mirror as he dried it. He was convinced the bags under his eyes had begun to look like Cheddar Gorge.

'I'm glad to have you back. Dr Hobbs did a good job, but it's not the same as bouncing ideas off you.'

'So bounce away.' She smiled and put his mug of coffee in front of him. 'Any biscuits?'

He shook his head. Sitting, he sipped his coffee and winced. It was hot.

'You look too tired to eat out,' she said, concerned. 'I'll order a takeaway.' She reached for her phone. 'What do you fancy? Chinese, Indian, Turkish?'

'Fish and chips.'

'You've got no sense of adventure,' she teased, and quickly ordered their meal while Horton blew on his coffee.

'OK, so tell me about the Juliette Croft investigation.'

'We've made two arrests,' he began, and he told her about Tiffany and Lee Nichols, and Juliette's life.

'What will happen about the Gillian Preston murder and Roddy Sumners' conviction?'

'There are no relatives or friends left pressing for justice, or a pardon, but the Met has reopened the case. There must be some band members still around. But memories after all this time will be very vague, and the major players in the case are no longer with us. Going on Juliette Croft's record of perjury, withholding evidence and scheming as a way of life, and looking out for number one, I'd say that Roddy Sumners was probably innocent, although I'm not sure Gideon Nichols killed Gillian either.'

'You think Juliette did it?'

'It fits with what we know about her. She didn't want Gillian as a rival from a singing point of view, and certainly not as her husband's lover. Or perhaps just the latter. She'd have been furious with her, and with Sumners, and intent on getting her own back. She got the heroin, injected Gillian, then framed Sumners for her murder. Juliette wanted money, and when she saw the pictures of Gideon in Mrs Nichols' photo albums, and learned he'd changed his name, she thought she'd struck gold. It was clear that Mrs Nichols knew nothing about her husband's past in respect of that festival. Only this time, Juliette's sordid scheme didn't work. I believe Gideon changed his name to start a new life and distance himself from what had happened. I'm not saying he was pure as the driven, because he testified against Sumners. Although again that could have been the truth. He didn't see Sumners on the stage or around it because Sumners had gone after Juliette.'

Gaye sipped her coffee. 'Then Sumners was protecting Juliette.'

'Possibly. He didn't think he'd get convicted for murder. He probably thought he'd get off completely. But Juliette fainted, very conveniently, and being heavily pregnant was let off the hook. He held his silence until the Court of Appeal and when that failed, and he realized Juliette would never tell the truth, he hanged himself in his cell using two tea towels tied together and fixed to a railing. It wasn't a nice way to go. It took him a long time to die and they almost saved him.'

Gaye shook her head sorrowfully. 'You'll present this to the Crown Prosecutor?'

'Yes. It will gain Lee and Tiffany some sympathy from the jury. Not that I'm condoning what they did, but it needs to be put into context with what happened because of Juliette's lies. By the time it comes to court, the Met might also have some fresh evidence on the Gillian Preston murder.'

'It's sad about Alma. Was it her wish?'

'I think so. Tavistock got the zopiclone for her, although we can't prove that. She took it of her own volition. And Tavistock didn't kill Pierce — no one did, it seems, the test results don't show up any poisons. His brain haemorrhage was just one of those things. It's a cruel irony for a man who was so obsessed with his health. I've just come from informing Bridget Pierce. No tears there. She said her husband popped vitamin pills like they were going out of fashion. I remember his security man, Hallet, saying the same. I suppose it can happen to any of us. You look pensive.'

'I was just thinking about vitamins. What kind did he take?'

'The whole alphabet, according to his wife, from A to Z if you include zinc.'

'Then it is possible . . .'

'What is?'

'He overdosed on vitamins.'

'Can you?' Horton asked, amazed.

'Most definitely. Vitamin K and vitamin E being two of them. The first acts as a blood clotter. The second can cause excessive bleeding.'

'As in intracranial haemorrhage, Rodney Pierce's cause of death?'

'Yes. I won't bamboozle you with all the medical jargon but, briefly, vitamin E was discovered in the 1920s and is a major lipid-soluble antioxidant, which you get exclusively from the diet — for example, in avocado, seeds, vegetable oil, almonds, spinach—'

'According to Bridget he ate tons of that and drank it as a juice.'

'Then he wouldn't have needed extra vitamin E, but some people think that taking vitamin supplements on top of a healthy balanced diet will make them fitter and more resistant to illness, when it doesn't. And some vitamins taken to excess can cause serious problems and possibly death. Vitamin E toxicity occurs because of excessive vitamin supplementation, not diet alone. And it can also interact with medications including aspirin. Was he on anticoagulants?'

'Not according to his Harley Street doctor. But he took aspirin, in the belief that it helped reduce the risk of heart attacks. Would he have shown any symptoms that he was getting to a dangerous level?'

'Stomach problems, weakness, fatigue and emotional lability — quick mood changes such as heightened irritability or temper.'

Horton shook his head in wonder. 'That's exactly what he had. Bridget or Hallet might be able to tell me about the other symptoms.'

'You'd have thought he'd consult his doctor, being a health freak.'

'He probably thought he could diagnose himself, or that seeing a doctor was tantamount to admitting he was ill.' Horton took a drink. 'He might even have increased his dosage of vitamins in the belief it would help.'

'He was an intelligent man though. Surely he'd have read up about diet and supplements.'

'He might have done but was arrogant enough to think he knew best. That much has come through during our investigations. And some people get obsessed with diets and don't listen to sense, you read about it all the time, how this latest fad can keep you slim, make you fat, fitter, better looking, grow your hair and nails, save the planet.'

Gaye smiled.

'And although intelligent in some respects, especially when it came to technology, perhaps in others he had a blind spot. Will we ever be able to prove that caused his death?'

'It's possible. He'd have high levels of alpha-tocopherol, and I shouldn't think for one minute Simon, or anyone else, looked for that. I'll get on to it tomorrow. Meanwhile —' she glanced at her phone — 'our own unhealthy food has arrived.'

'I wouldn't say that. Fish is good for the brain.'

'When it's not smothered in batter. And I'm not sure if the chips qualify as healthy eating.'

'Of course they do. It will give us stamina.'

She tossed him a sideways glance. 'For what?'

'Tell you when we've eaten.'

She laughed. 'Or a stomach-ache,' she called out after him.

As long as it's not heartache, he thought, making his way along the pontoon. It was good to have her back.

THE END

THE JOFFE BOOKS STORY

We began in 2014 when Jasper agreed to publish his mum's much-rejected romance novel and it became a bestseller.

Since then we've grown into the largest independent publisher in the UK. We're extremely proud to publish some of the very best writers in the world, including Joy Ellis, Faith Martin, Caro Ramsay, Helen Forrester, Simon Brett and Robert Goddard. Everyone at Joffe Books loves reading and we never forget that it all begins with the magic of an author telling a story.

We are proud to publish talented first-time authors, as well as established writers whose books we love introducing to a new generation of readers.

We won Trade Publisher of the Year at the Independent Publishing Awards in 2023. We have been shortlisted for Independent Publisher of the Year at the British Book Awards for the last four years, and were shortlisted for the Diversity and Inclusivity Award at the 2022 Independent Publishing Awards. In 2023 we were shortlisted for Publisher of the Year at the RNA Industry Awards.

We built this company with your help, and we love to hear from you, so please email us about absolutely anything bookish at: feedback@joffebooks.com

If you want to receive free books every Friday and hear about all our new releases, join our mailing list: www.joffebooks.com/contact

And when you tell your friends about us, just remember: it's pronounced Joffe as in coffee or toffee!

Printed in the USA
CPSIA information can be obtained
at www.ICGtesting.com
CBHW012204130924
14403CB00040B/1066

9 781835 266373